KEVIN Keller™

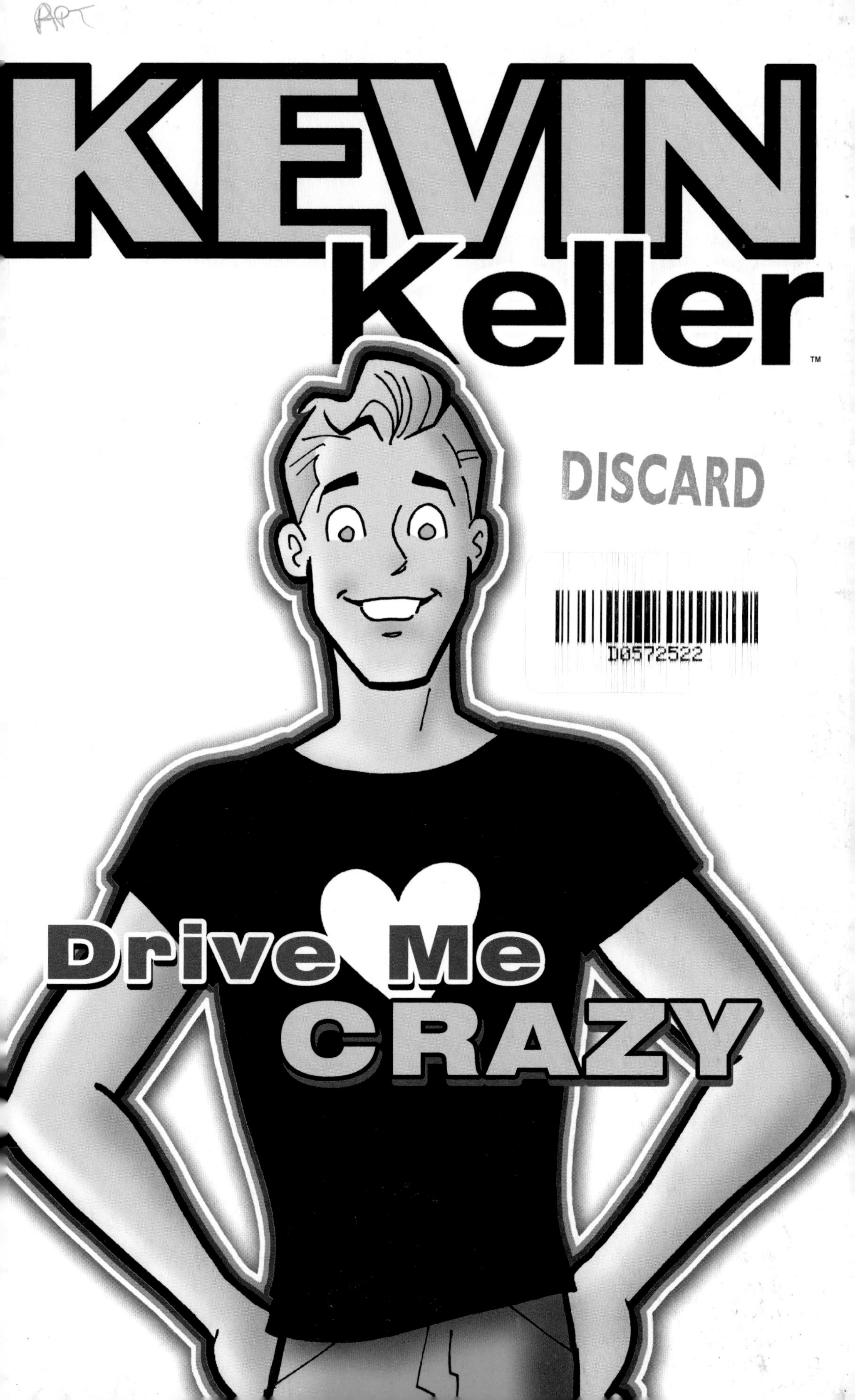

Drive Me CRAZY

Kevin Keller: Drive Me Crazy
Published by Archie Comic Publications, Inc.
325 Fayette Avenue, Mamaroneck, NY 10543-2318.

ISBN: 978-1-936975-58-7

Printed in Canada.

PUBLISHER/CO-CEO:
Jonathan Goldwater
CO-CEO: Nancy Silberkleit
PRESIDENT: Mike Pellerito
CO-PRESIDENT/EDITOR-IN-CHIEF:
Victor Gorelick
CFO: William Mooar
**SENIOR VICE PRESIDENT,
SALES & BUSINESS DEVELOPMENT:**
Jim Sokolowski
**SENIOR VICE PRESIDENT,
PUBLISHING & OPERATIONS:**
Harold Buchholz
VICE PRESIDENT, SPECIAL PROJECTS:
Steve Mooar
EXECUTIVE DIRECTOR OF EDITORIAL:
Paul Kaminski
PRODUCTION MANAGER:
Stephen Oswald
**DIRECTOR OF PUBLICITY
& MARKETING:**
Steven Scott
**COORDINATOR OF PUBLICITY
& MARKETING:**
Jamie Rotante
**PROJECT COORDINATOR/
BOOK DESIGN:**
Duncan McLachlan
**EDITORIAL ASSISTANT/
PROOFREADER:**
Carly Inglis
PRODUCTION:
Suzannah Rowntree
(original issue
cover production),
Kari Silbergleit

SCRIPTS: Dan Parent

PENCILS: Dan Parent, Bill Galvan

INKS: Rich Koslowski, Bob Smith

LETTERS: Jack Morelli

STORY COLORS: Digikore Studios

COVER COLORS: Dan Parent,
Glenn Whitmore

Introduction By

GEORGE TAKEI

As a preteen and a teenager, I read Archie Comics and really thought that Riverdale's community and Archie's circle of friends was something perfectly Americana. But I never imagined at that time that I would be a part of that Americana. I applaud a forward-thinking comic like *Kevin Keller*.

Comics play an important role in contributing to a healthy, sociable community and Kevin is a great role model for the youth of America. Riverdale reflects the diversity of America and embraces that diversity as a positive, which is why everyone wants to live there. I am honored to be a part of Archie's history and I think Dan Parent did a tremendous job—a very flattering likeness!

George Takei

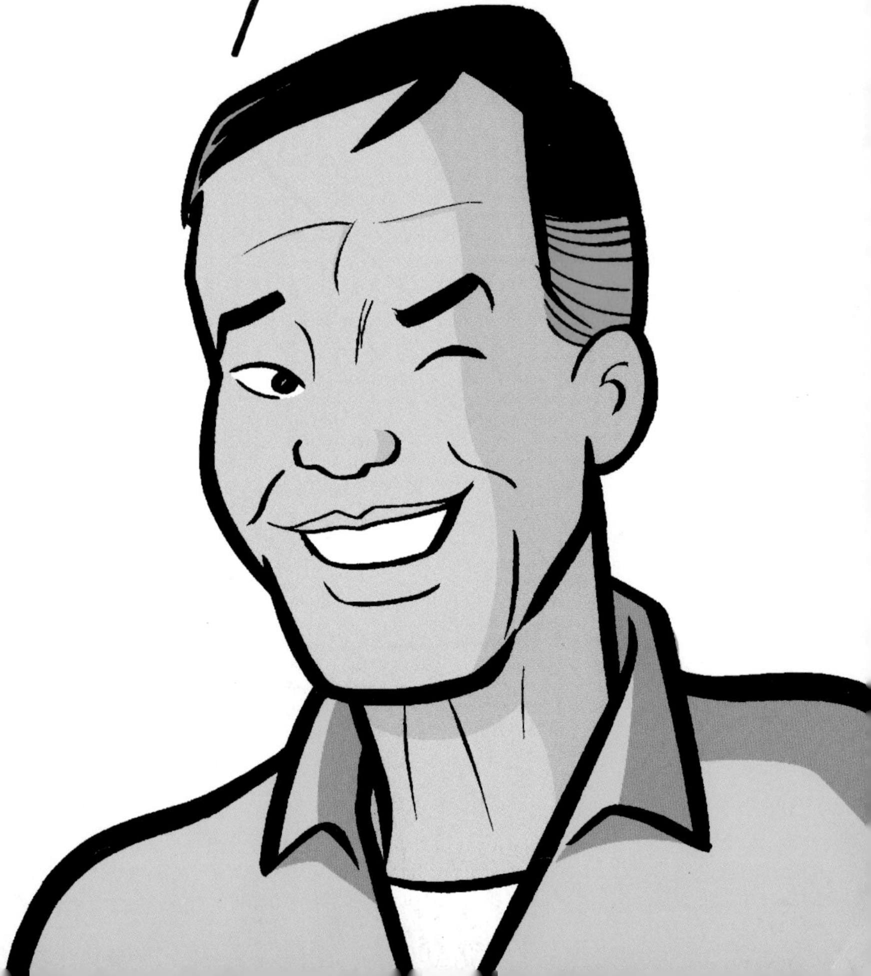

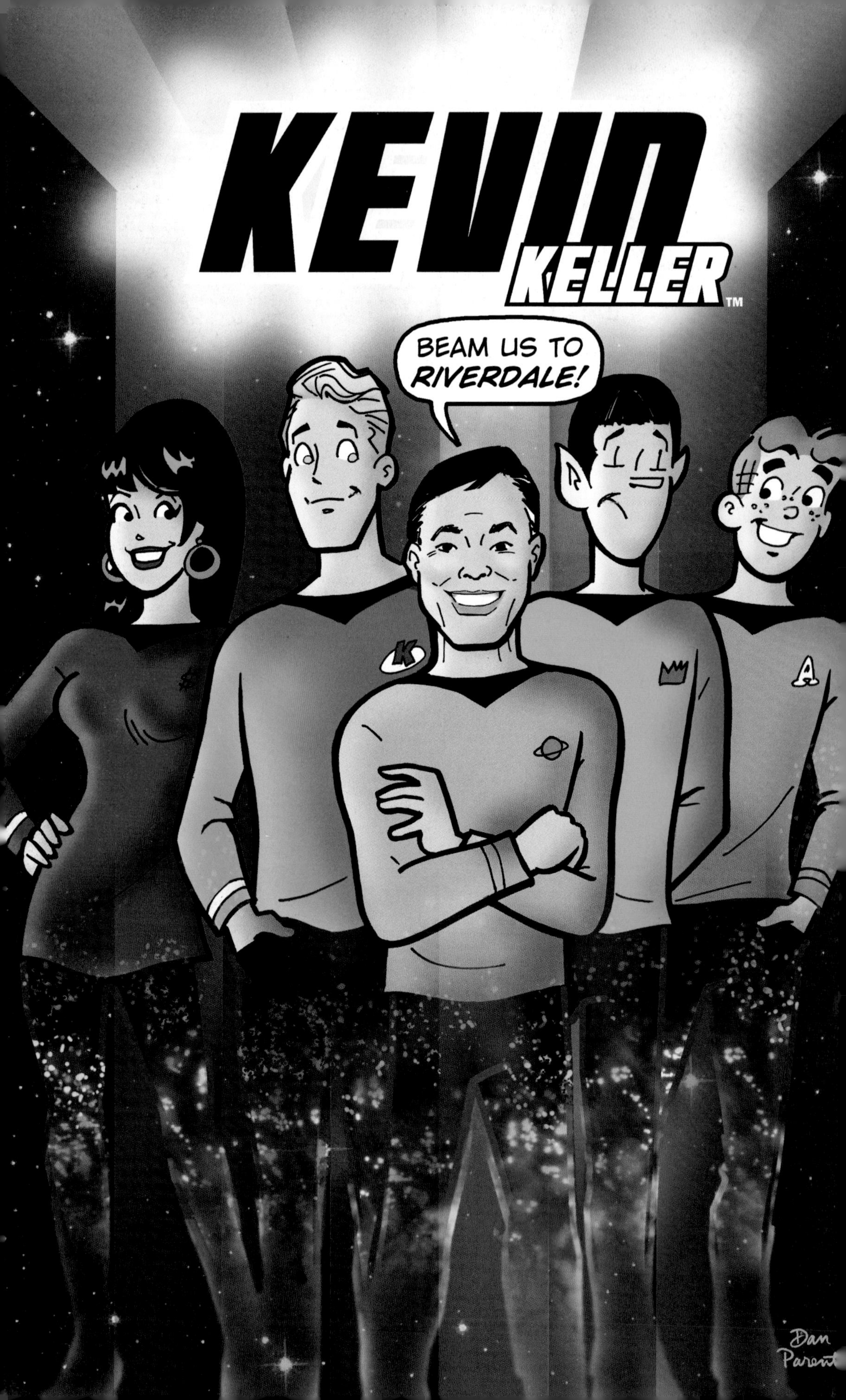
KEVIN KELLER™
BEAM US TO RIVERDALE!
Dan Parent

Chapter 1

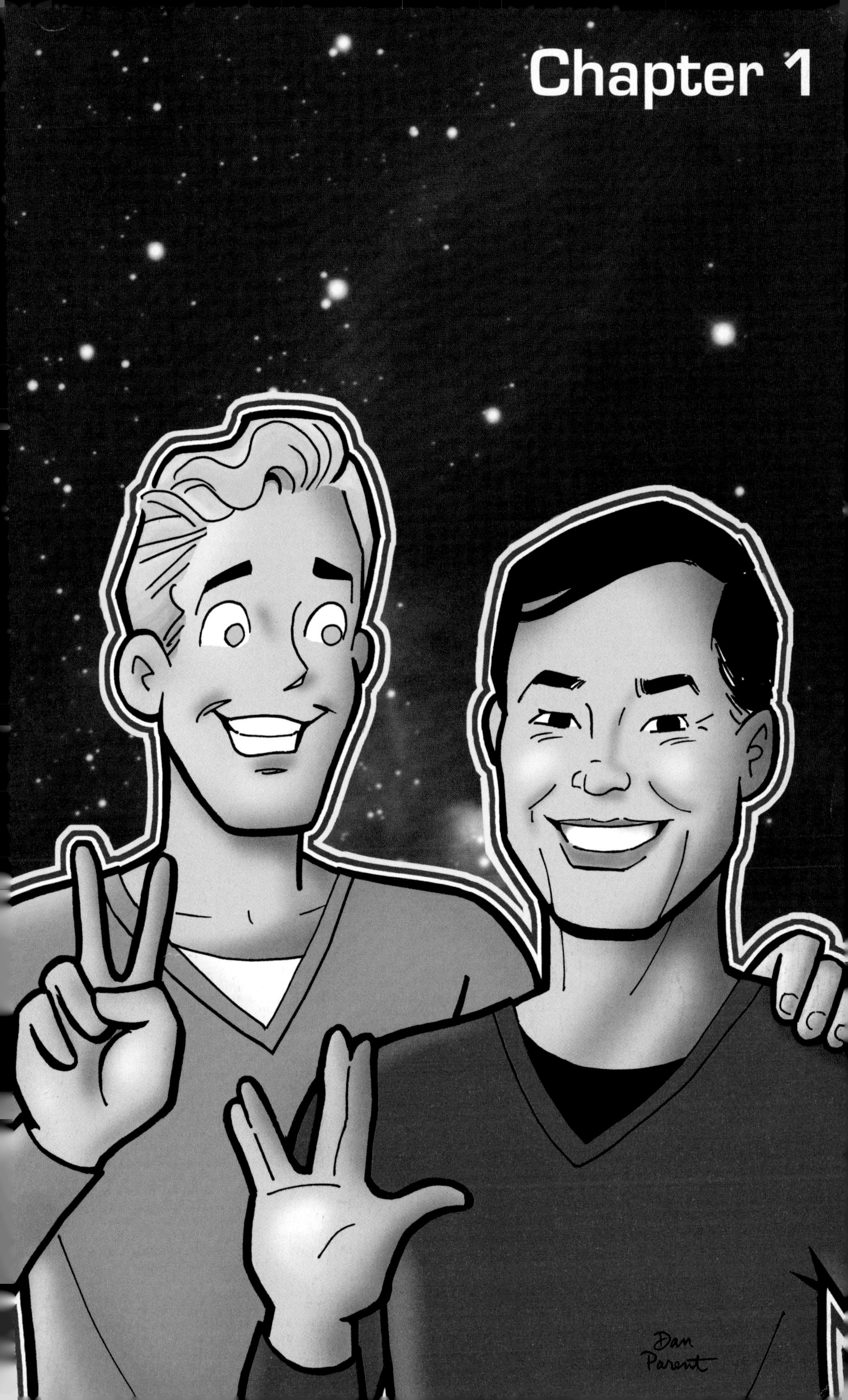

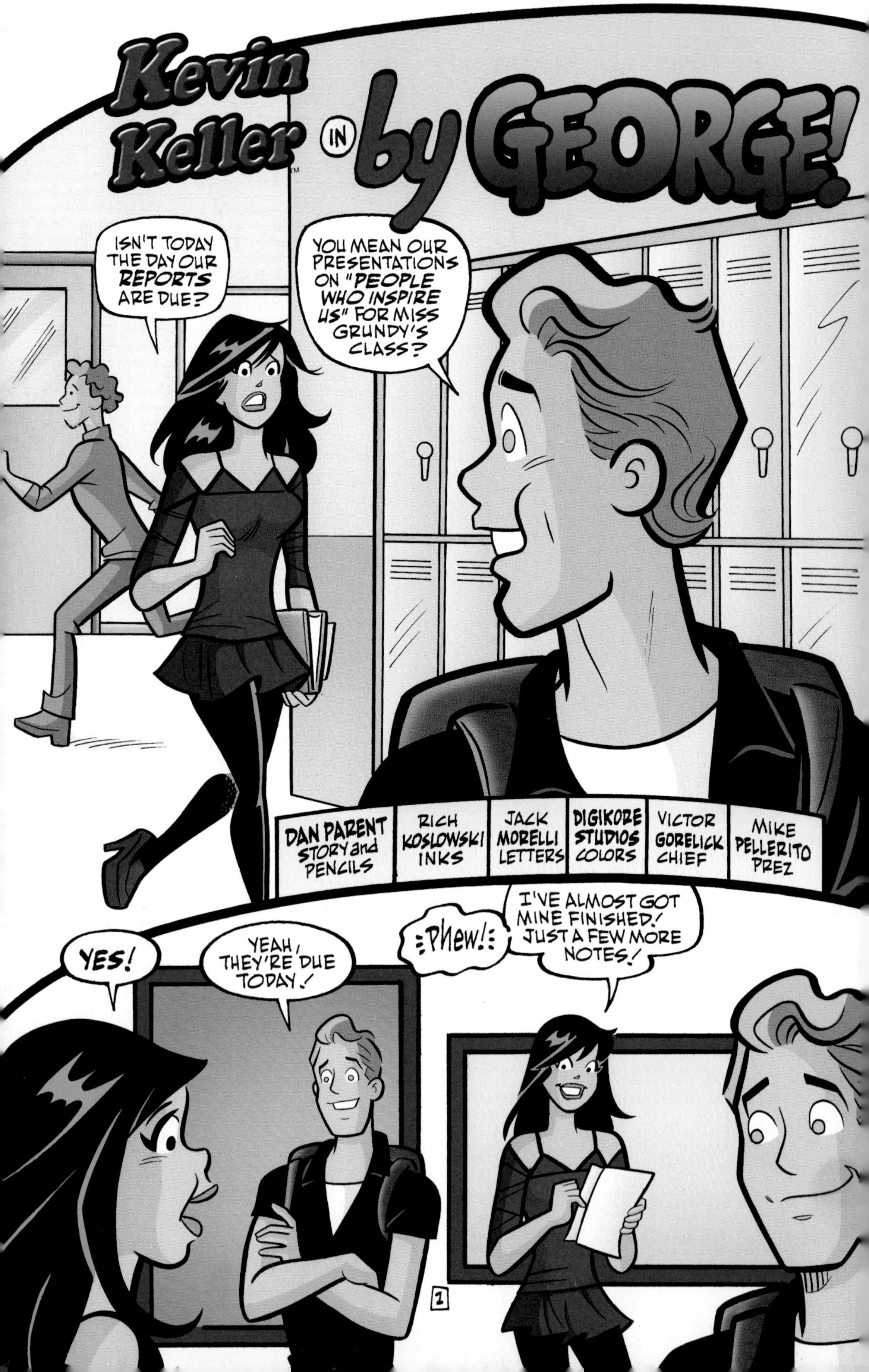
Kevin Keller™ IN by GEORGE!
ISN'T TODAY THE DAY OUR REPORTS ARE DUE?
YOU MEAN OUR PRESENTATIONS ON "PEOPLE WHO INSPIRE US" FOR MISS GRUNDY'S CLASS?
DAN PARENT STORY and PENCILS
RICH KOSLOWSKI INKS
JACK MORELLI LETTERS
DIGIKORE STUDIOS COLORS
VICTOR GORELICK CHIEF
MIKE PELLERITO PREZ
YES!
YEAH, THEY'RE DUE TODAY!
PHEW!
I'VE ALMOST GOT MINE FINISHED! JUST A FEW MORE NOTES!
1

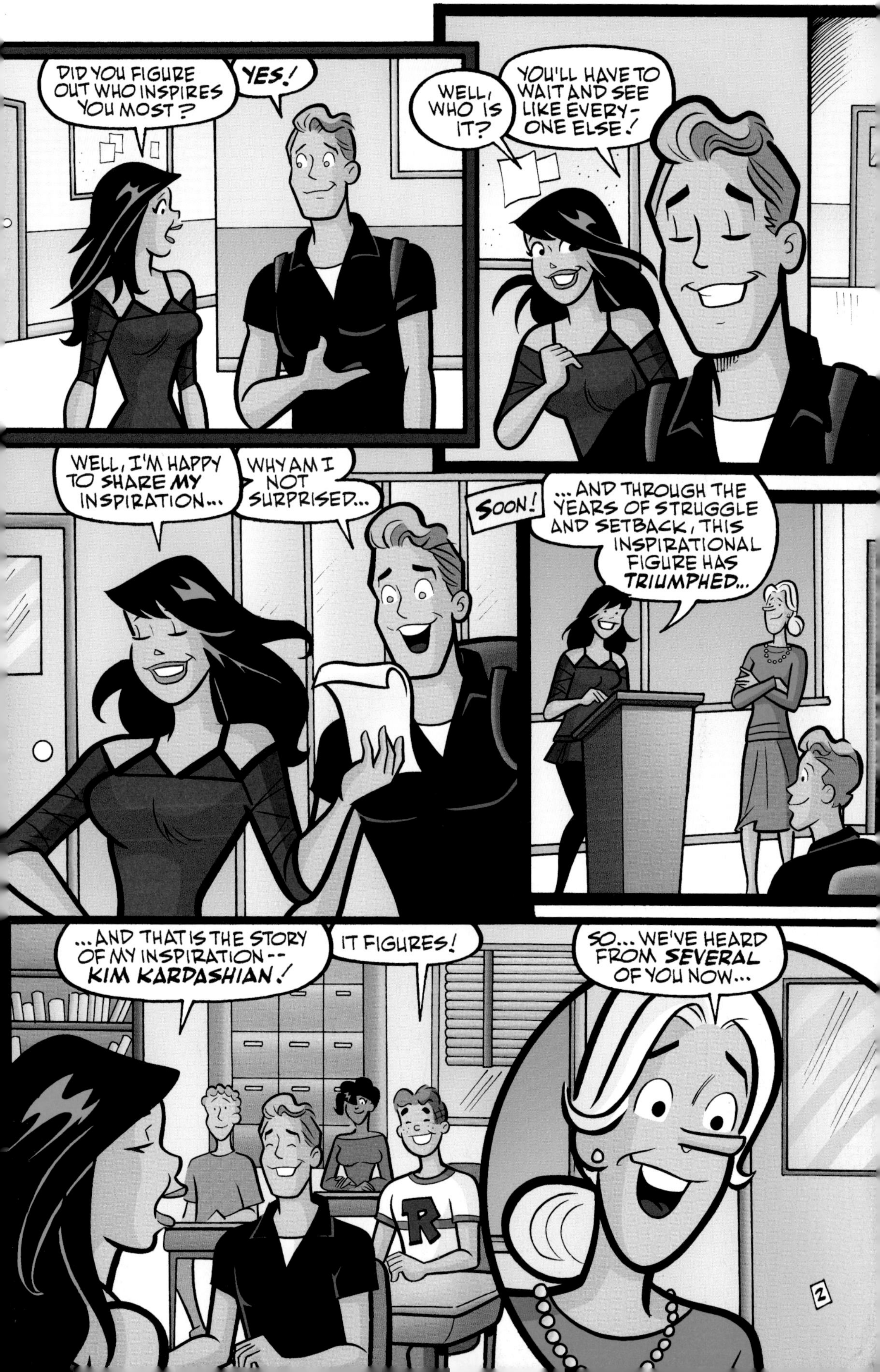
DID YOU FIGURE OUT WHO INSPIRES YOU MOST?
YES!
WELL, WHO IS IT?
YOU'LL HAVE TO WAIT AND SEE LIKE EVERY-ONE ELSE!
WELL, I'M HAPPY TO SHARE MY INSPIRATION...
WHY AM I NOT SURPRISED...
SOON!
...AND THROUGH THE YEARS OF STRUGGLE AND SETBACK, THIS INSPIRATIONAL FIGURE HAS TRIUMPHED...
...AND THAT IS THE STORY OF MY INSPIRATION -- KIM KARDASHIAN!
IT FIGURES!
SO... WE'VE HEARD FROM SEVERAL OF YOU NOW...
2

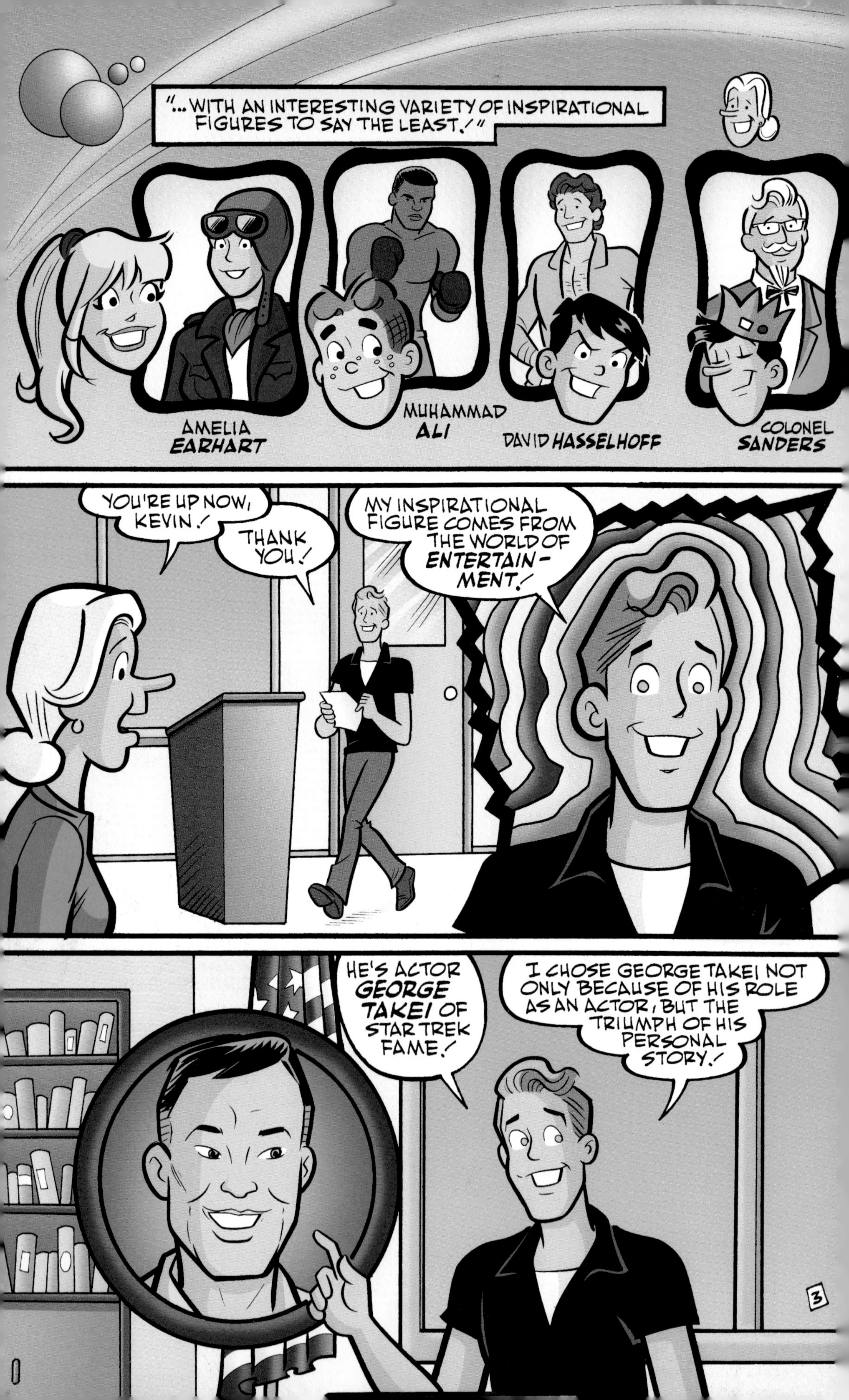
"...WITH AN INTERESTING VARIETY OF INSPIRATIONAL FIGURES TO SAY THE LEAST!"
AMELIA EARHART
MUHAMMAD ALI
DAVID HASSELHOFF
COLONEL SANDERS
YOU'RE UP NOW, KEVIN!
THANK YOU!
MY INSPIRATIONAL FIGURE COMES FROM THE WORLD OF ENTERTAIN-MENT!
HE'S ACTOR GEORGE TAKEI OF STAR TREK FAME!
I CHOSE GEORGE TAKEI NOT ONLY BECAUSE OF HIS ROLE AS AN ACTOR, BUT THE TRIUMPH OF HIS PERSONAL STORY!
3

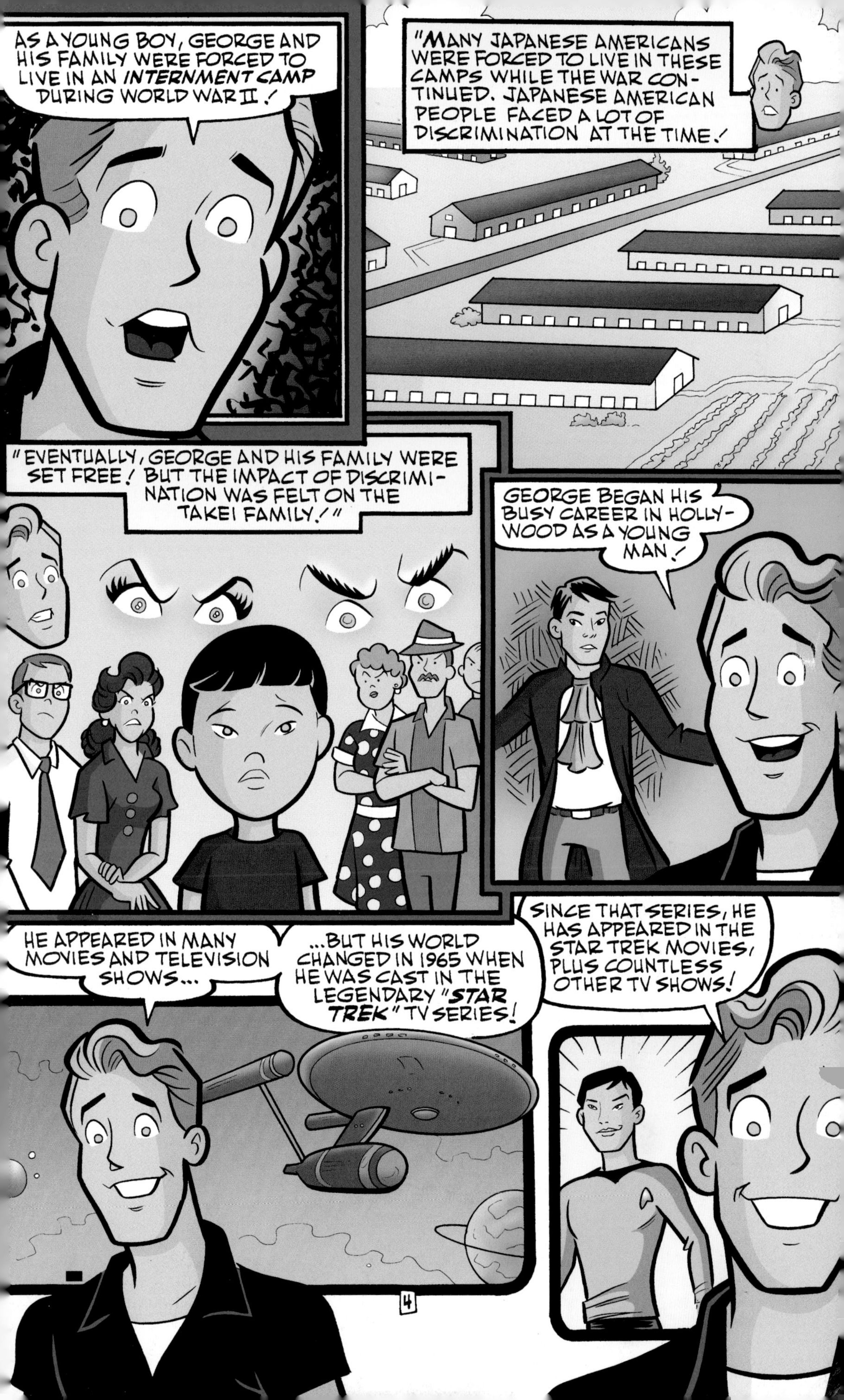
AS A YOUNG BOY, GEORGE AND HIS FAMILY WERE FORCED TO LIVE IN AN INTERNMENT CAMP DURING WORLD WAR II!
"MANY JAPANESE AMERICANS WERE FORCED TO LIVE IN THESE CAMPS WHILE THE WAR CONTINUED. JAPANESE AMERICAN PEOPLE FACED A LOT OF DISCRIMINATION AT THE TIME!
"EVENTUALLY, GEORGE AND HIS FAMILY WERE SET FREE! BUT THE IMPACT OF DISCRIMINATION WAS FELT ON THE TAKEI FAMILY!"
GEORGE BEGAN HIS BUSY CAREER IN HOLLYWOOD AS A YOUNG MAN!
HE APPEARED IN MANY MOVIES AND TELEVISION SHOWS...
...BUT HIS WORLD CHANGED IN 1965 WHEN HE WAS CAST IN THE LEGENDARY "STAR TREK" TV SERIES!
SINCE THAT SERIES, HE HAS APPEARED IN THE STAR TREK MOVIES, PLUS COUNTLESS OTHER TV SHOWS!

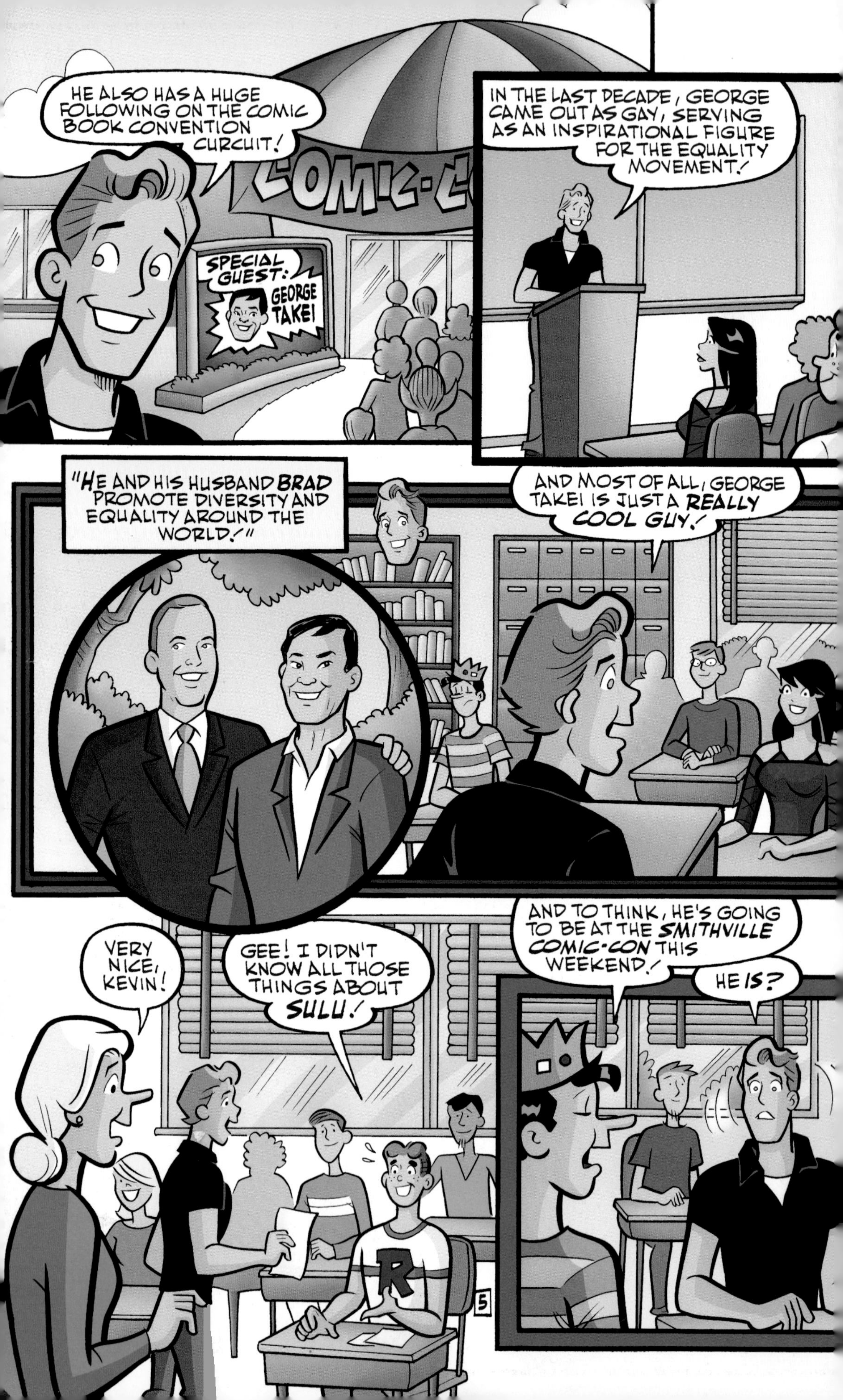
HE ALSO HAS A HUGE FOLLOWING ON THE COMIC BOOK CONVENTION CURCUIT!
COMIC-C
SPECIAL GUEST:
GEORGE TAKEI
IN THE LAST DECADE, GEORGE CAME OUT AS GAY, SERVING AS AN INSPIRATIONAL FIGURE FOR THE EQUALITY MOVEMENT!
"HE AND HIS HUSBAND BRAD PROMOTE DIVERSITY AND EQUALITY AROUND THE WORLD!"
AND MOST OF ALL, GEORGE TAKEI IS JUST A REALLY COOL GUY!
VERY NICE, KEVIN!
GEE! I DIDN'T KNOW ALL THOSE THINGS ABOUT SULU!
AND TO THINK, HE'S GOING TO BE AT THE SMITHVILLE COMIC-CON THIS WEEKEND!
HE IS?
R

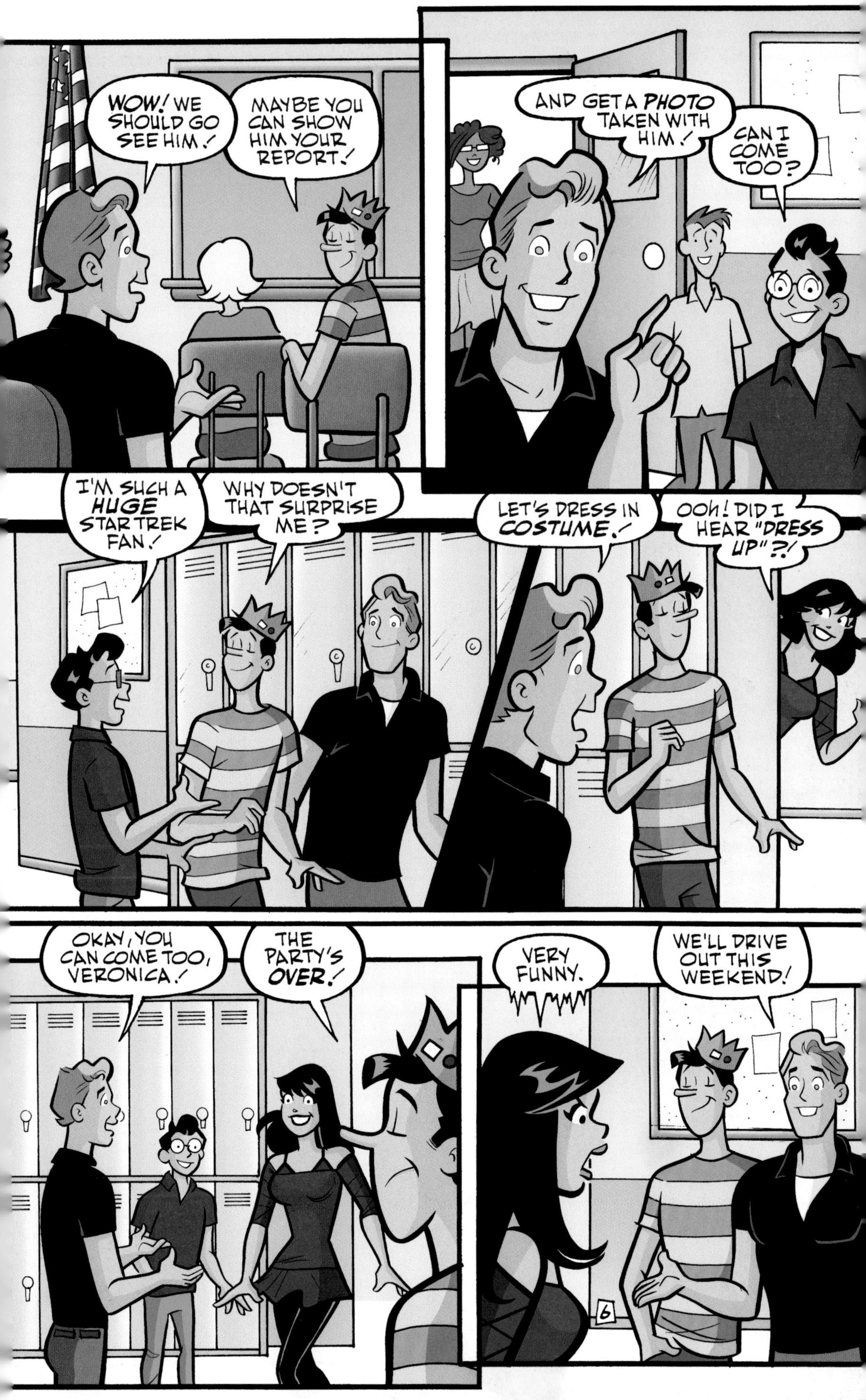
WOW! WE SHOULD GO SEE HIM!
MAYBE YOU CAN SHOW HIM YOUR REPORT!
AND GET A PHOTO TAKEN WITH HIM!
CAN I COME TOO?
I'M SUCH A HUGE STAR TREK FAN!
WHY DOESN'T THAT SURPRISE ME?
LET'S DRESS IN COSTUME!
OOH! DID I HEAR "DRESS UP"?!
OKAY, YOU CAN COME TOO, VERONICA!
THE PARTY'S OVER!
VERY FUNNY.
WE'LL DRIVE OUT THIS WEEKEND!
6

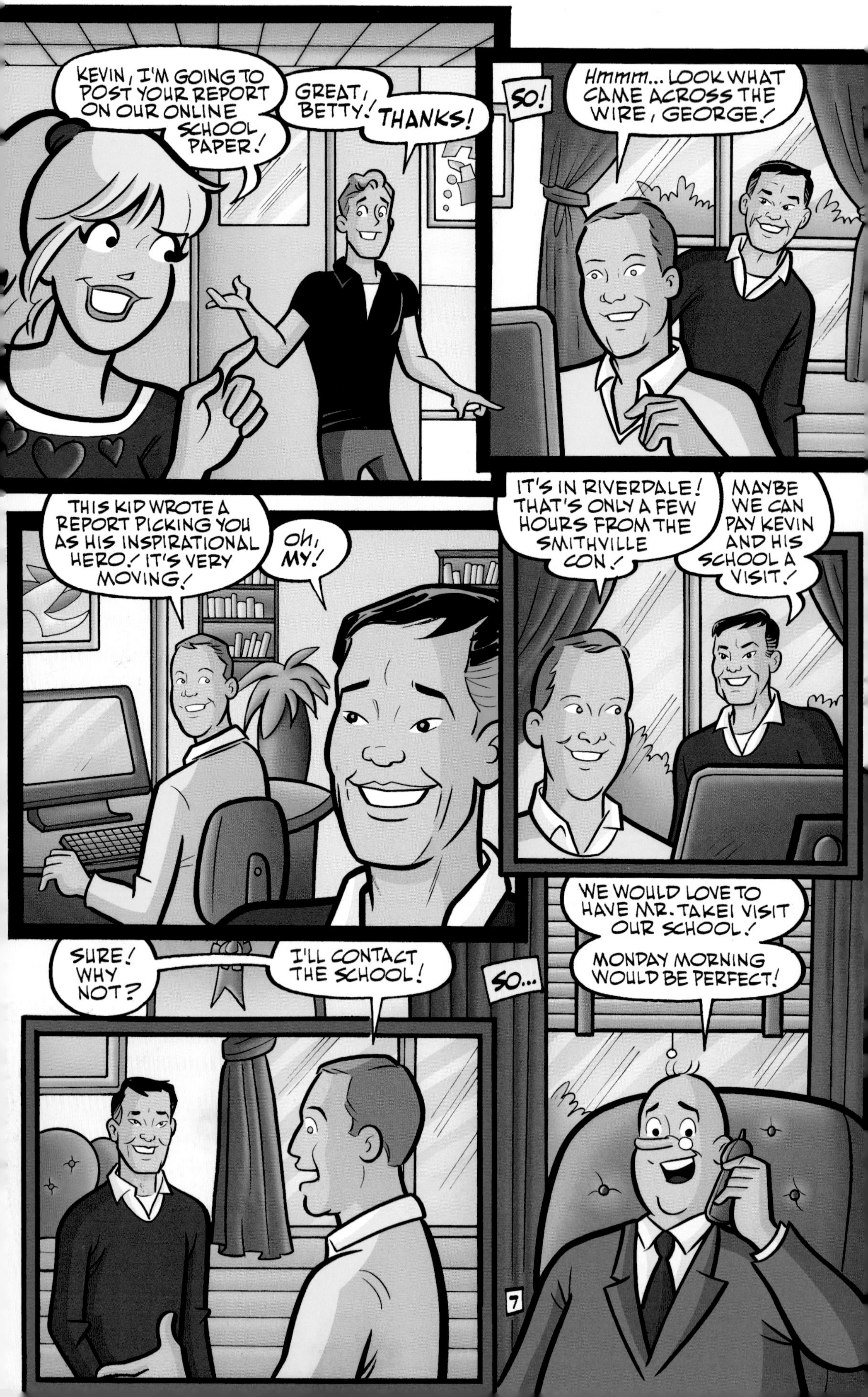

KEVIN, I'M GOING TO POST YOUR REPORT ON OUR ONLINE SCHOOL PAPER!
GREAT, BETTY!
THANKS!
SO!
Hmmm... LOOK WHAT CAME ACROSS THE WIRE, GEORGE!
THIS KID WROTE A REPORT PICKING YOU AS HIS INSPIRATIONAL HERO! IT'S VERY MOVING!
Oh, MY!
IT'S IN RIVERDALE! THAT'S ONLY A FEW HOURS FROM THE SMITHVILLE CON!
MAYBE WE CAN PAY KEVIN AND HIS SCHOOL A VISIT!
SURE! WHY NOT?
I'LL CONTACT THE SCHOOL!
SO...
WE WOULD LOVE TO HAVE MR. TAKEI VISIT OUR SCHOOL!
MONDAY MORNING WOULD BE PERFECT!

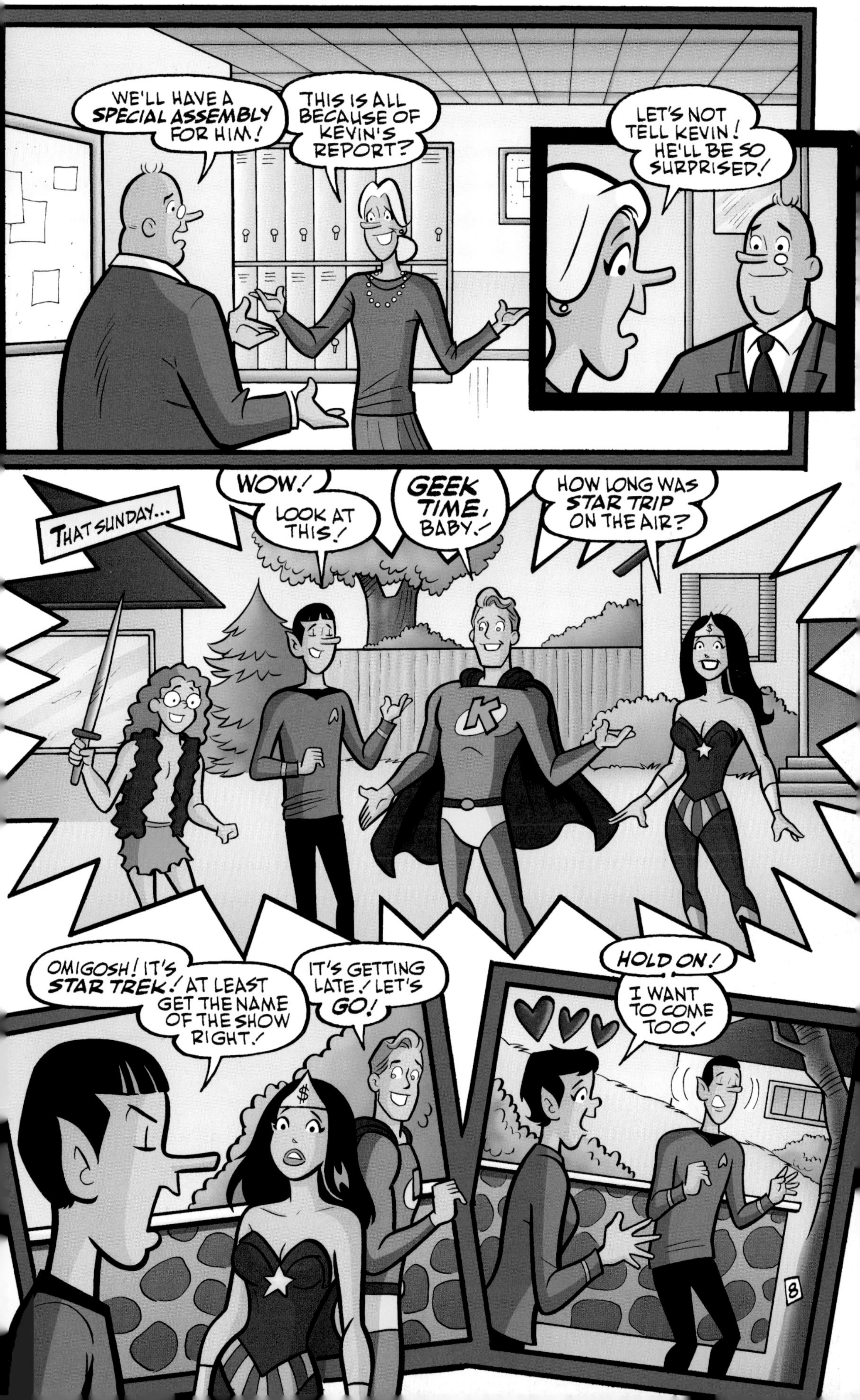
WE'LL HAVE A SPECIAL ASSEMBLY FOR HIM!
THIS IS ALL BECAUSE OF KEVIN'S REPORT?
LET'S NOT TELL KEVIN! HE'LL BE SO SURPRISED!
THAT SUNDAY...
WOW!
LOOK AT THIS!
GEEK TIME, BABY!
HOW LONG WAS STAR TRIP ON THE AIR?
OMIGOSH! IT'S STAR TREK! AT LEAST GET THE NAME OF THE SHOW RIGHT!
IT'S GETTING LATE! LET'S GO!
HOLD ON!
I WANT TO COME TOO!
8

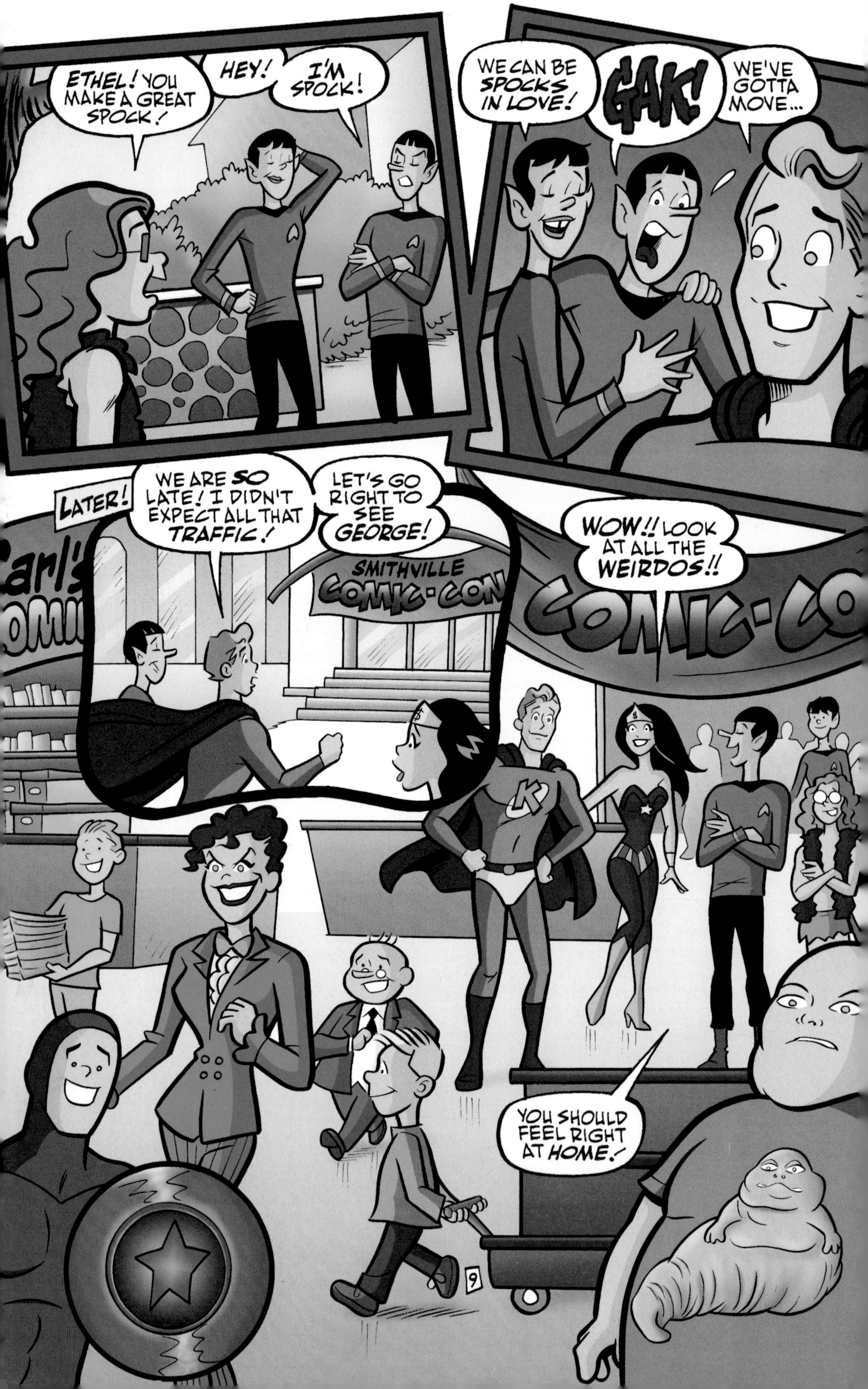
ETHEL! YOU MAKE A GREAT SPOCK!
HEY!
I'M SPOCK!
WE CAN BE SPOCKS IN LOVE!
GAK!
WE'VE GOTTA MOVE...
LATER!
WE ARE SO LATE! I DIDN'T EXPECT ALL THAT TRAFFIC!
LET'S GO RIGHT TO SEE GEORGE!
SMITHVILLE COMIC-CON
WOW!! LOOK AT ALL THE WEIRDOS!!
COMIC-CO
YOU SHOULD FEEL RIGHT AT HOME!
9

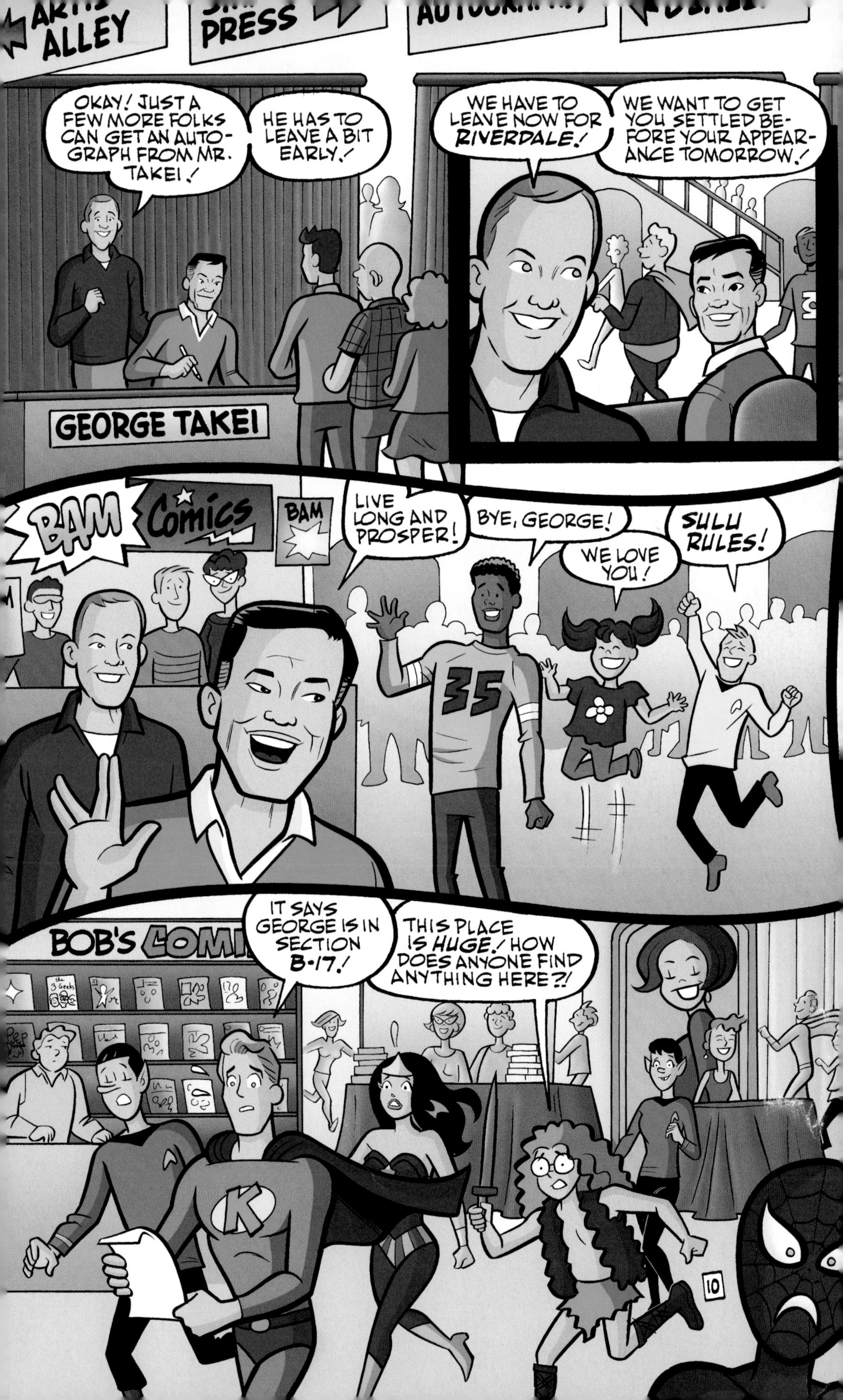
ALLEY
PRESS
GEORGE TAKEI
OKAY! JUST A FEW MORE FOLKS CAN GET AN AUTO-GRAPH FROM MR. TAKEI!
HE HAS TO LEAVE A BIT EARLY!
WE HAVE TO LEAVE NOW FOR RIVERDALE!
WE WANT TO GET YOU SETTLED BE-FORE YOUR APPEAR-ANCE TOMORROW!
BAM
Comics
BAM
LIVE LONG AND PROSPER!
BYE, GEORGE!
WE LOVE YOU!
SULU RULES!
BOB'S
IT SAYS GEORGE IS IN SECTION B-17!
THIS PLACE IS HUGE! HOW DOES ANYONE FIND ANYTHING HERE?!
10

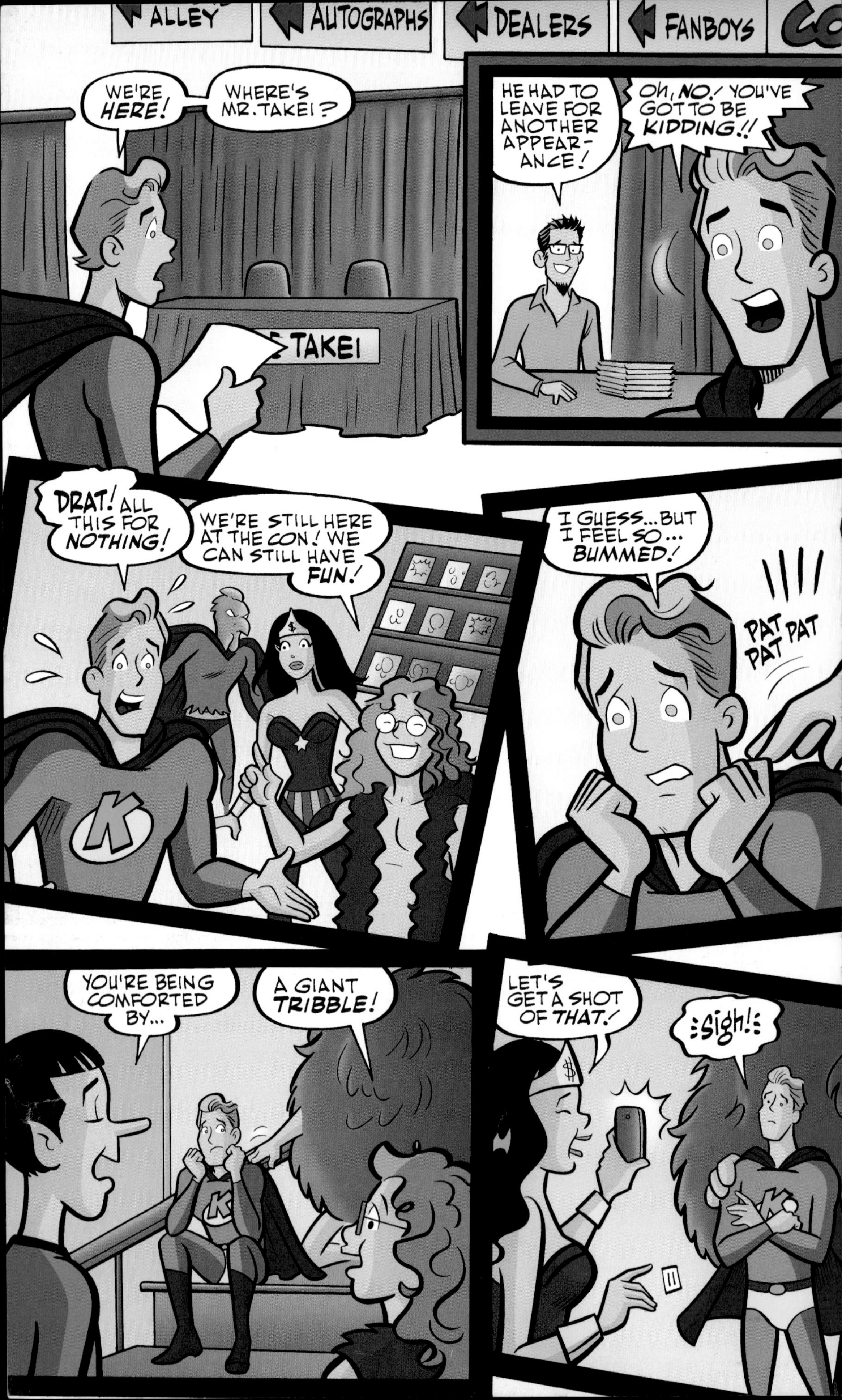
ALLEY
AUTOGRAPHS
DEALERS
FANBOYS
WE'RE HERE!
WHERE'S MR. TAKEI?
TAKEI
HE HAD TO LEAVE FOR ANOTHER APPEAR-ANCE!
OH, NO! YOU'VE GOT TO BE KIDDING!!
DRAT! ALL THIS FOR NOTHING!
WE'RE STILL HERE AT THE CON! WE CAN STILL HAVE FUN!
I GUESS...BUT I FEEL SO... BUMMED!
PAT PAT PAT
YOU'RE BEING COMFORTED BY...
A GIANT TRIBBLE!
LET'S GET A SHOT OF THAT!
sigh!
11

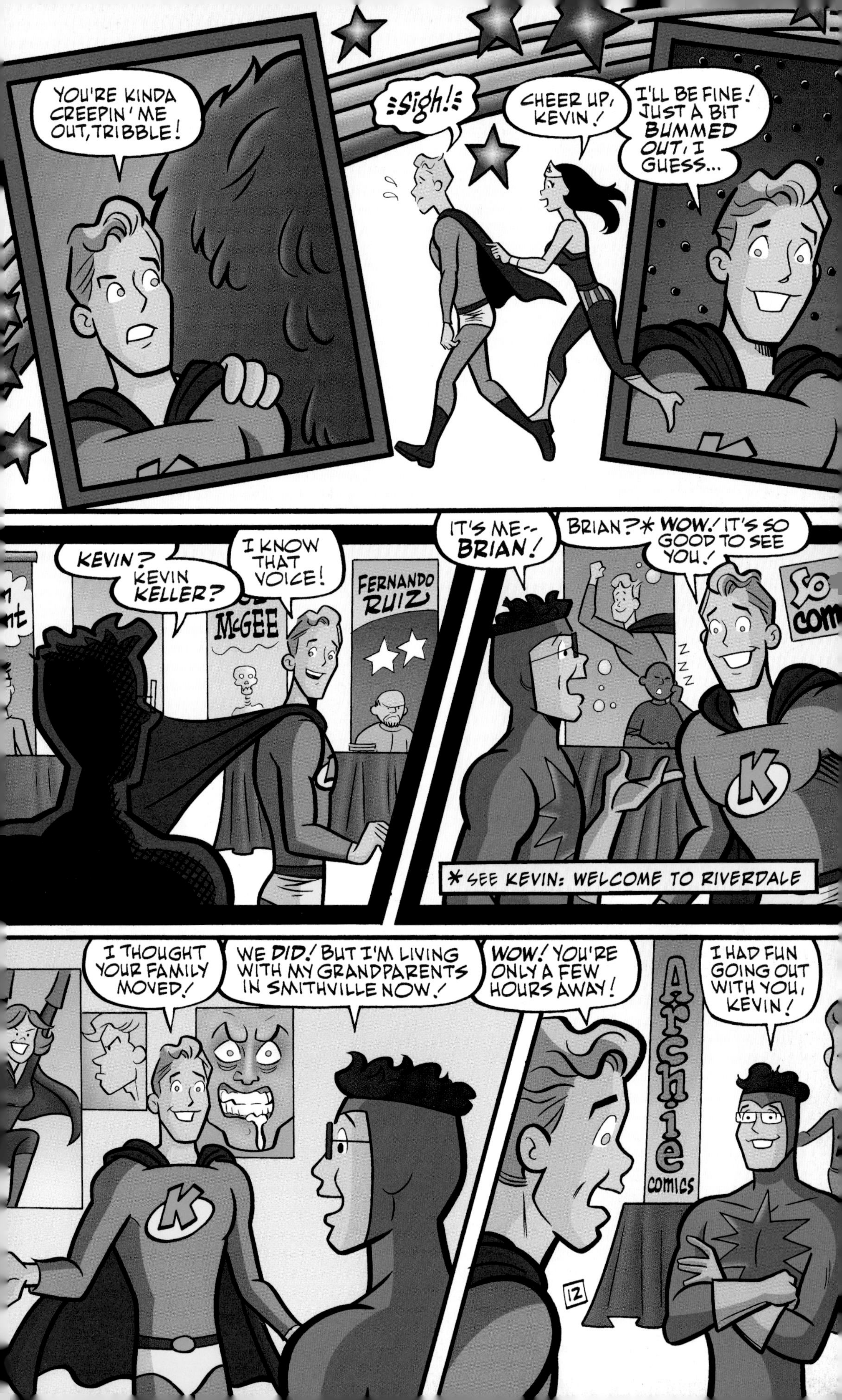

YOU'RE KINDA CREEPIN' ME OUT, TRIBBLE!
:SIGH!:
CHEER UP, KEVIN!
I'LL BE FINE! JUST A BIT BUMMED OUT, I GUESS...
KEVIN? KEVIN KELLER?
I KNOW THAT VOICE!
FERNANDO RUIZ
McGEE
IT'S ME-- BRIAN!
BRIAN?* WOW! IT'S SO GOOD TO SEE YOU!
Z Z Z
* SEE KEVIN: WELCOME TO RIVERDALE
I THOUGHT YOUR FAMILY MOVED!
WE DID! BUT I'M LIVING WITH MY GRANDPARENTS IN SMITHVILLE NOW!
WOW! YOU'RE ONLY A FEW HOURS AWAY!
Archie COMICS
I HAD FUN GOING OUT WITH YOU, KEVIN!

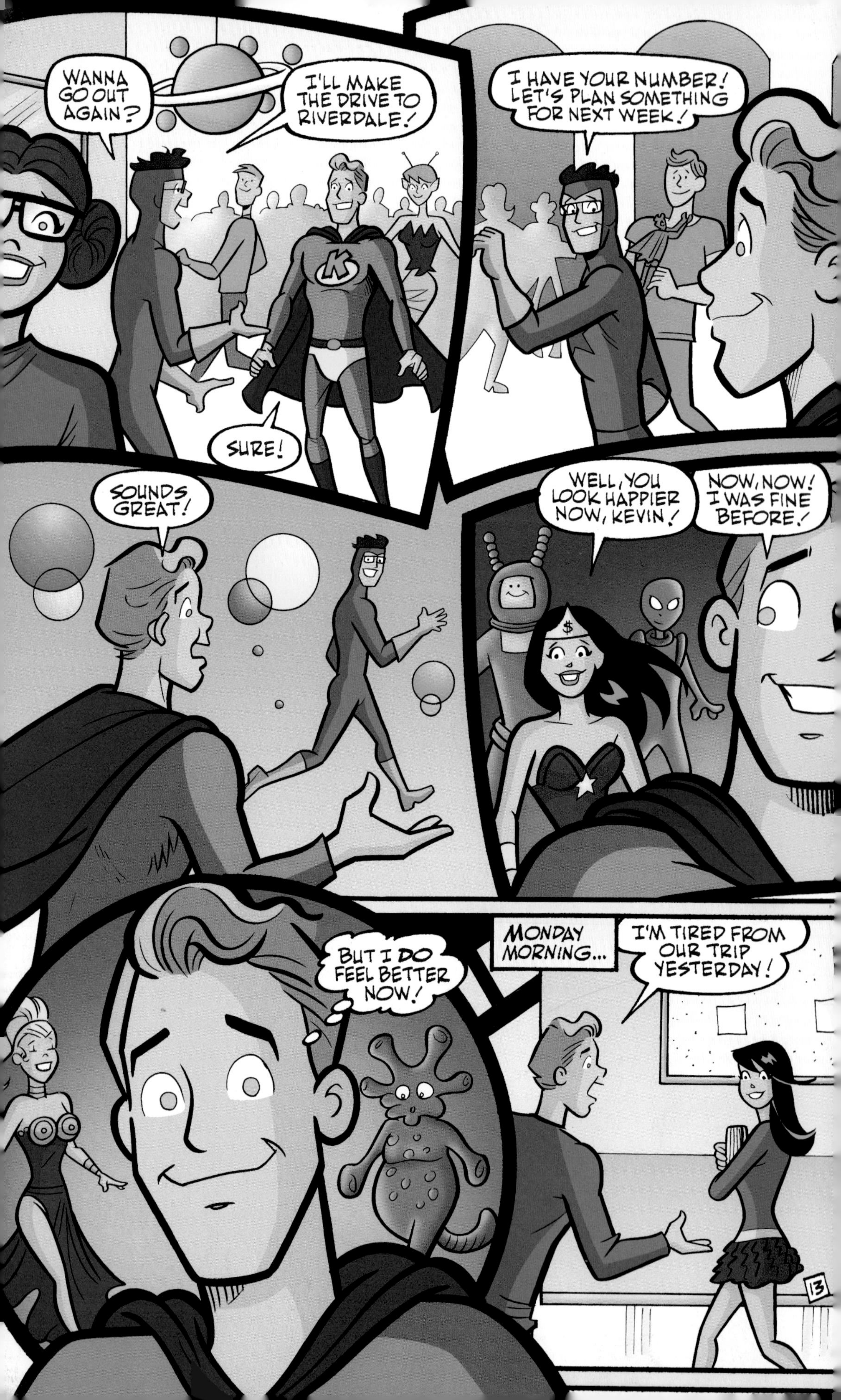
WANNA GO OUT AGAIN?
I'LL MAKE THE DRIVE TO RIVERDALE!
SURE!
I HAVE YOUR NUMBER! LET'S PLAN SOMETHING FOR NEXT WEEK!
SOUNDS GREAT!
WELL, YOU LOOK HAPPIER NOW, KEVIN!
NOW, NOW! I WAS FINE BEFORE!
BUT I DO FEEL BETTER NOW!
MONDAY MORNING...
I'M TIRED FROM OUR TRIP YESTERDAY!
13

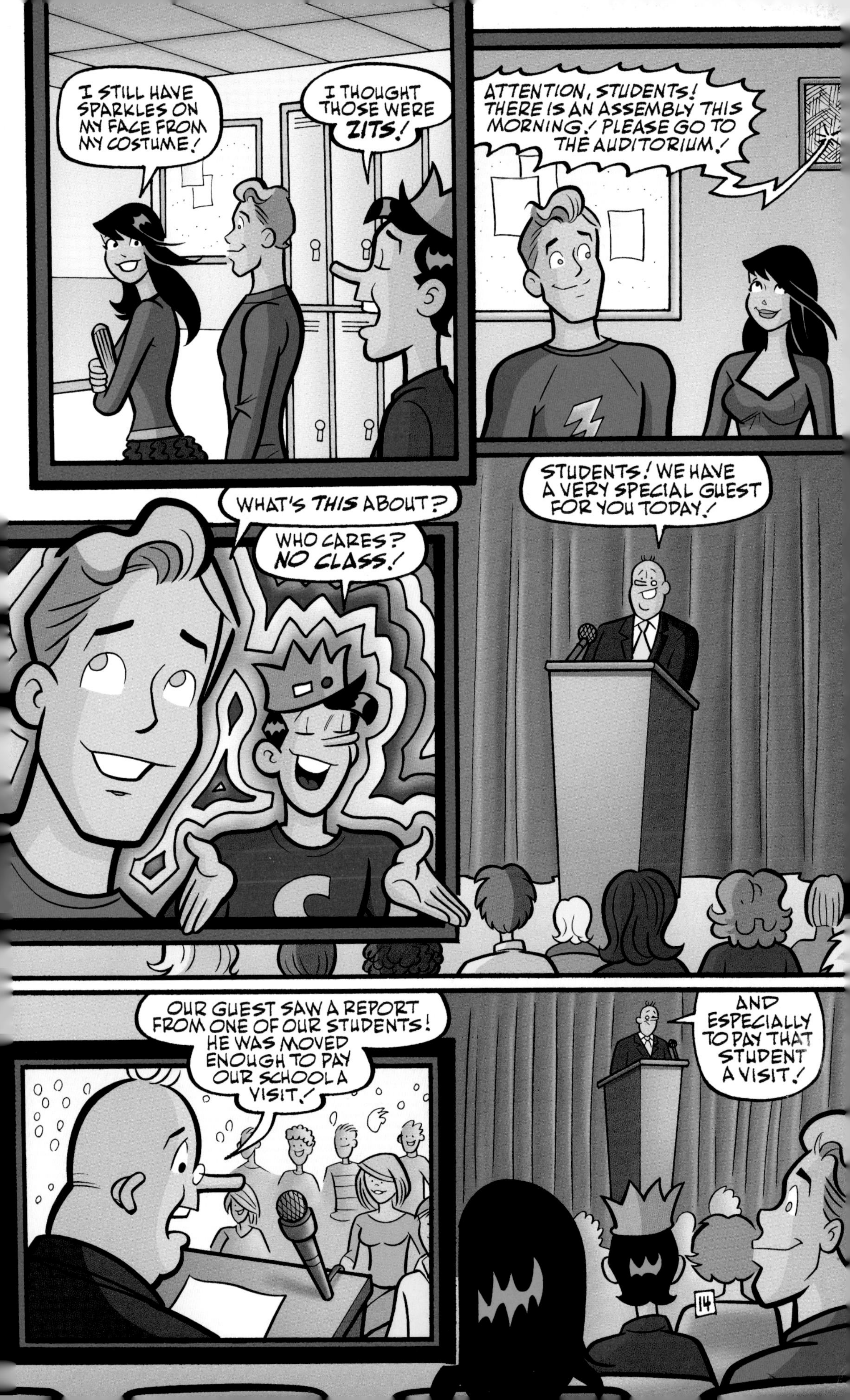
I STILL HAVE SPARKLES ON MY FACE FROM MY COSTUME!
I THOUGHT THOSE WERE ZITS!
ATTENTION, STUDENTS! THERE IS AN ASSEMBLY THIS MORNING! PLEASE GO TO THE AUDITORIUM!
WHAT'S THIS ABOUT?
WHO CARES? NO CLASS!
STUDENTS! WE HAVE A VERY SPECIAL GUEST FOR YOU TODAY!
OUR GUEST SAW A REPORT FROM ONE OF OUR STUDENTS! HE WAS MOVED ENOUGH TO PAY OUR SCHOOL A VISIT!
AND ESPECIALLY TO PAY THAT STUDENT A VISIT!
14

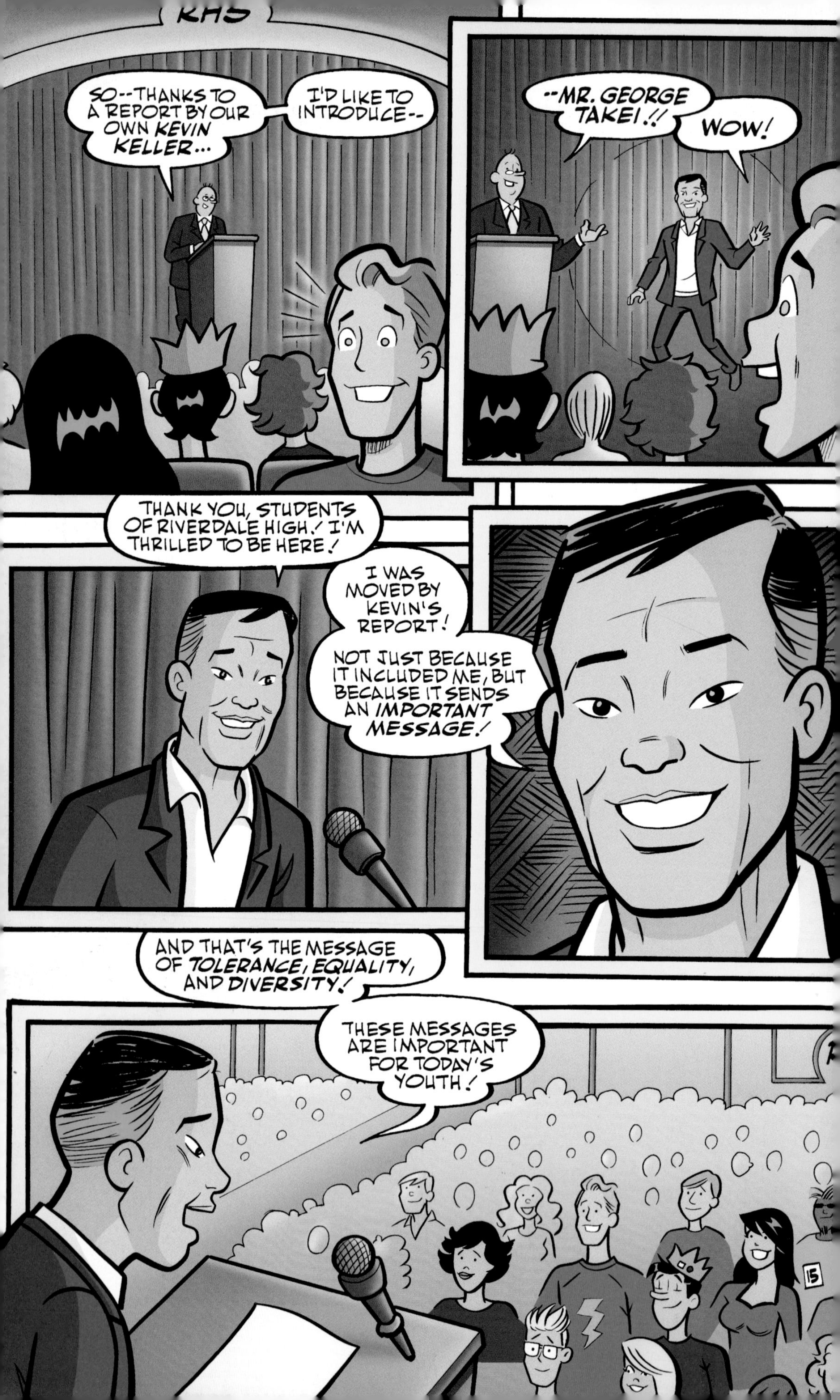
RHS
SO--THANKS TO A REPORT BY OUR OWN KEVIN KELLER...
I'D LIKE TO INTRODUCE--
--MR. GEORGE TAKEI!!
WOW!
THANK YOU, STUDENTS OF RIVERDALE HIGH! I'M THRILLED TO BE HERE!
I WAS MOVED BY KEVIN'S REPORT!
NOT JUST BECAUSE IT INCLUDED ME, BUT BECAUSE IT SENDS AN IMPORTANT MESSAGE!
AND THAT'S THE MESSAGE OF TOLERANCE, EQUALITY, AND DIVERSITY!
THESE MESSAGES ARE IMPORTANT FOR TODAY'S YOUTH!
15

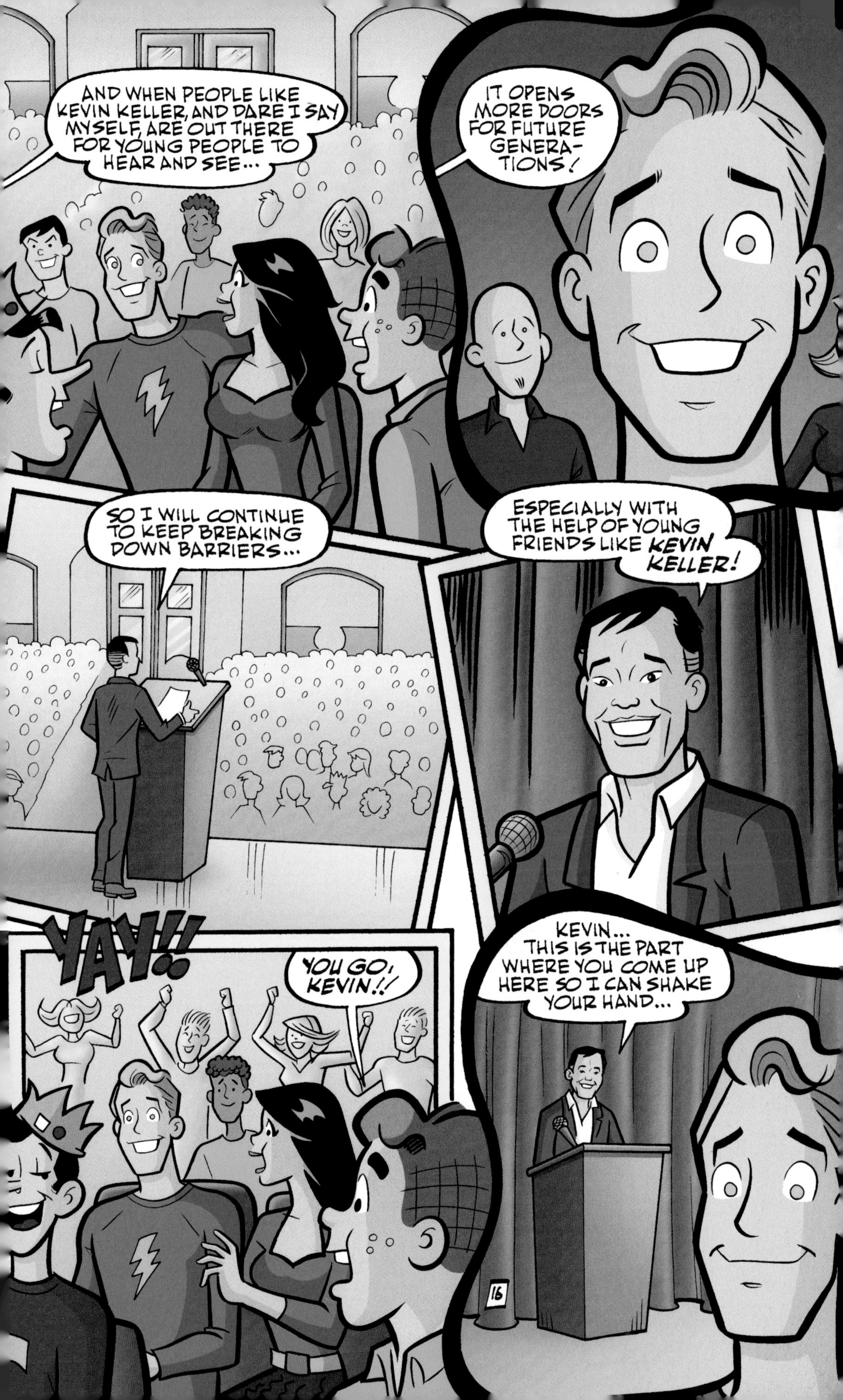
AND WHEN PEOPLE LIKE KEVIN KELLER, AND DARE I SAY MYSELF, ARE OUT THERE FOR YOUNG PEOPLE TO HEAR AND SEE...
IT OPENS MORE DOORS FOR FUTURE GENERA-TIONS!
SO I WILL CONTINUE TO KEEP BREAKING DOWN BARRIERS...
ESPECIALLY WITH THE HELP OF YOUNG FRIENDS LIKE KEVIN KELLER!
YAY!!
YOU GO, KEVIN!!
KEVIN... THIS IS THE PART WHERE YOU COME UP HERE SO I CAN SHAKE YOUR HAND...
16

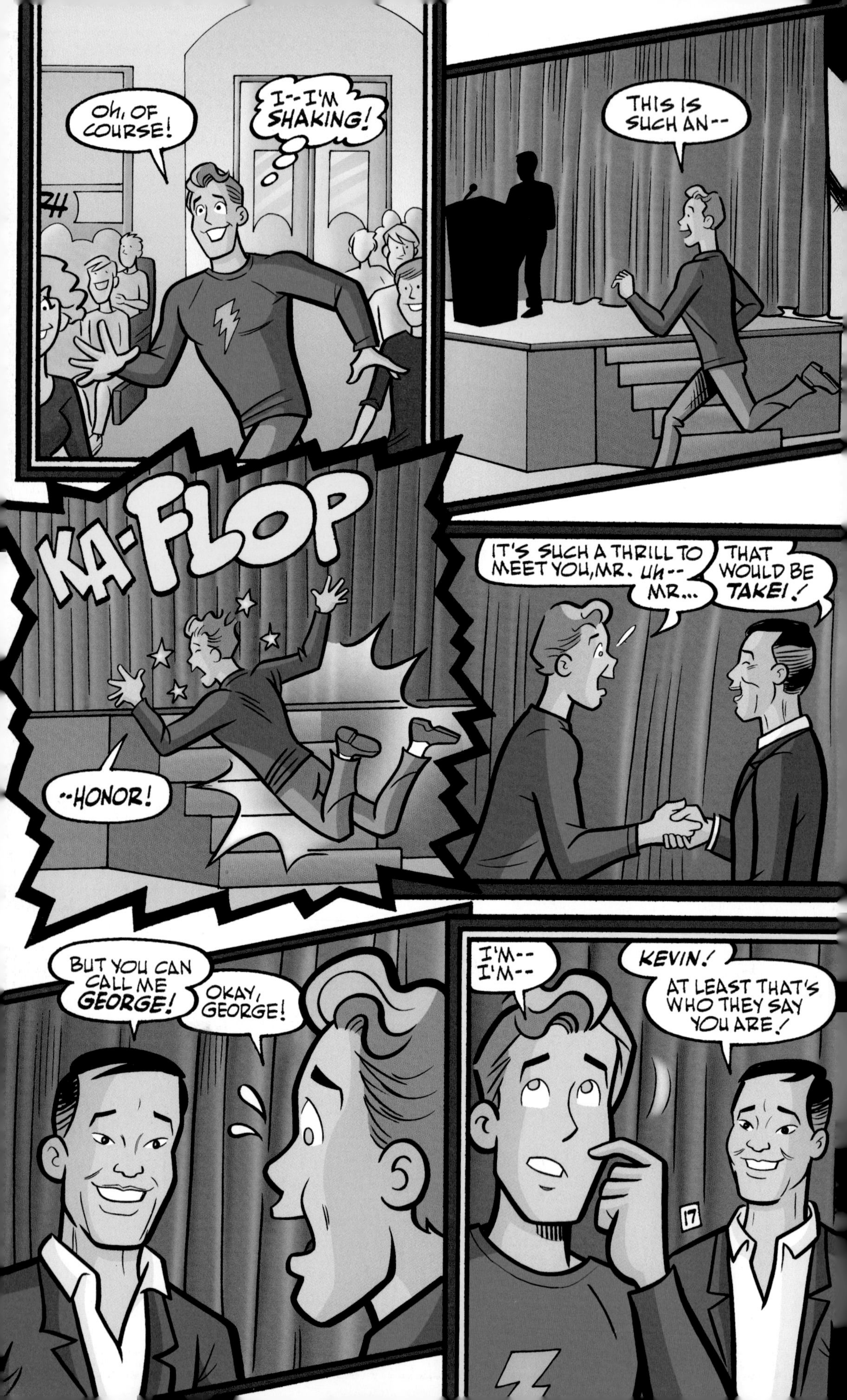
OH, OF COURSE!
I--I'M SHAKING!
THIS IS SUCH AN--
KA-FLOP
--HONOR!
IT'S SUCH A THRILL TO MEET YOU, MR. UH-- MR...
THAT WOULD BE TAKEI!
BUT YOU CAN CALL ME GEORGE!
OKAY, GEORGE!
I'M-- I'M--
KEVIN!
AT LEAST THAT'S WHO THEY SAY YOU ARE!
17

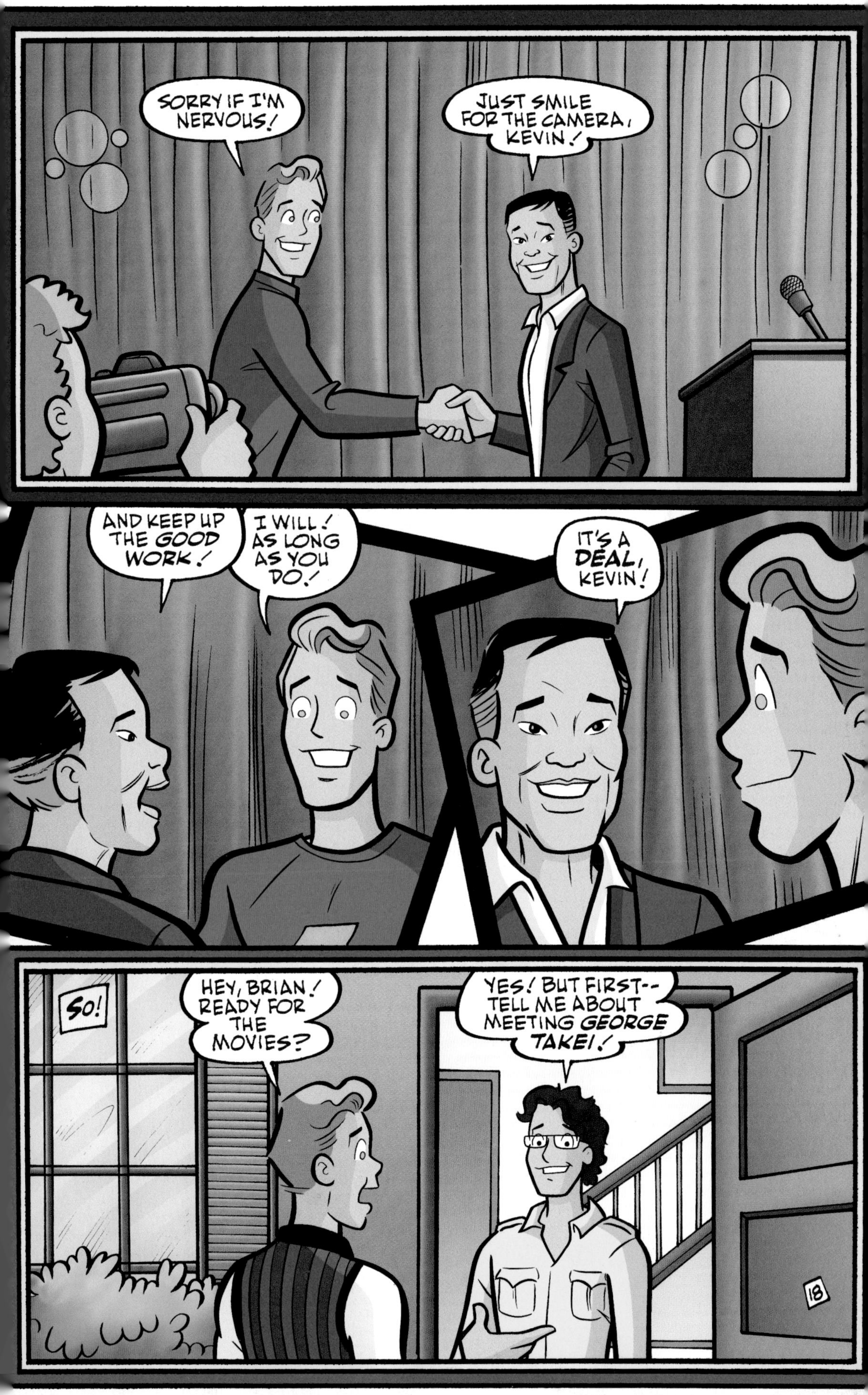
SORRY IF I'M NERVOUS!
JUST SMILE FOR THE CAMERA, KEVIN!
AND KEEP UP THE GOOD WORK!
I WILL! AS LONG AS YOU DO!
IT'S A DEAL, KEVIN!
So!
HEY, BRIAN! READY FOR THE MOVIES?
YES! BUT FIRST-- TELL ME ABOUT MEETING GEORGE TAKEI!
18

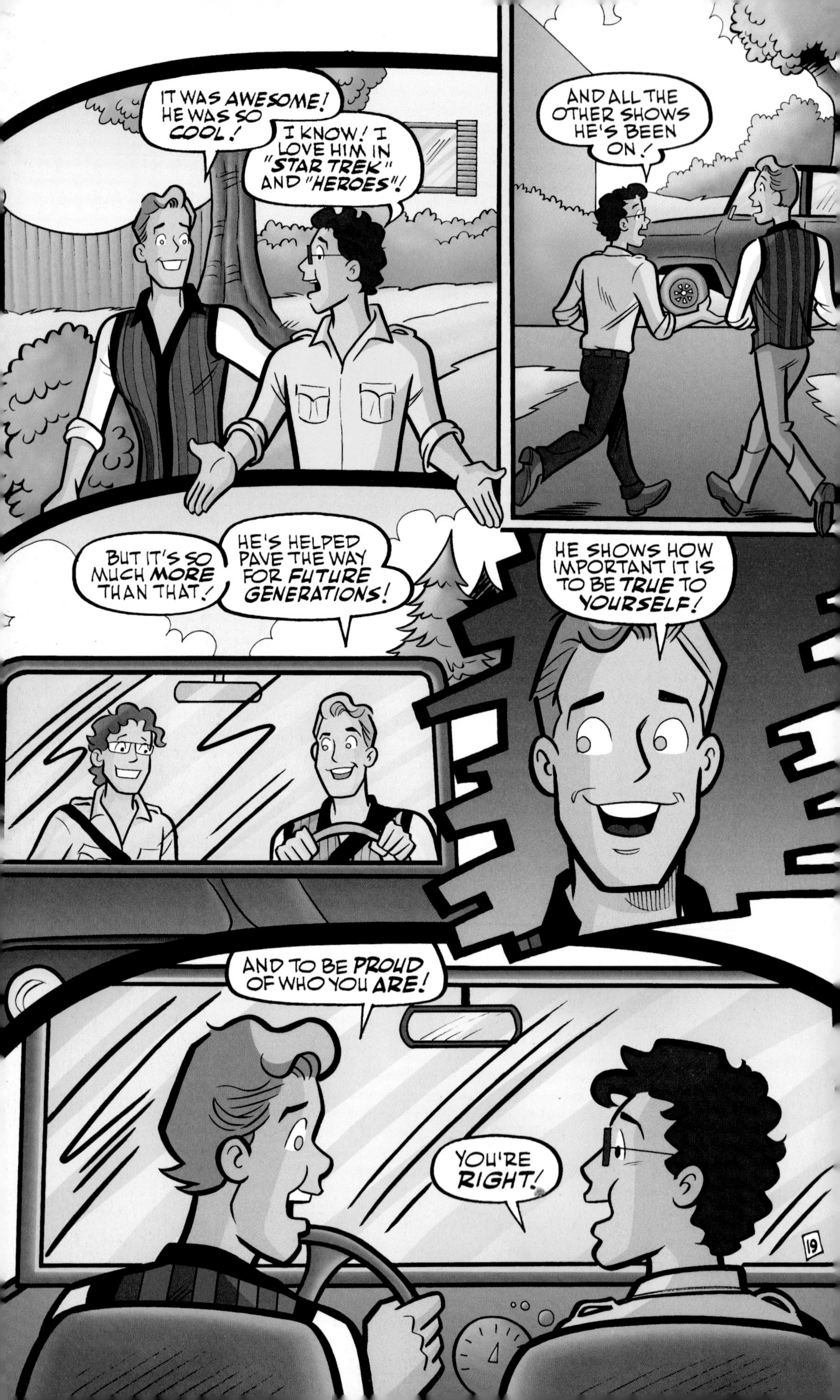

IT WAS AWESOME! HE WAS SO COOL!
I KNOW! I LOVE HIM IN "STAR TREK" AND "HEROES"!
AND ALL THE OTHER SHOWS HE'S BEEN ON!
BUT IT'S SO MUCH MORE THAN THAT!
HE'S HELPED PAVE THE WAY FOR FUTURE GENERATIONS!
HE SHOWS HOW IMPORTANT IT IS TO BE TRUE TO YOURSELF!
AND TO BE PROUD OF WHO YOU ARE!
YOU'RE RIGHT!

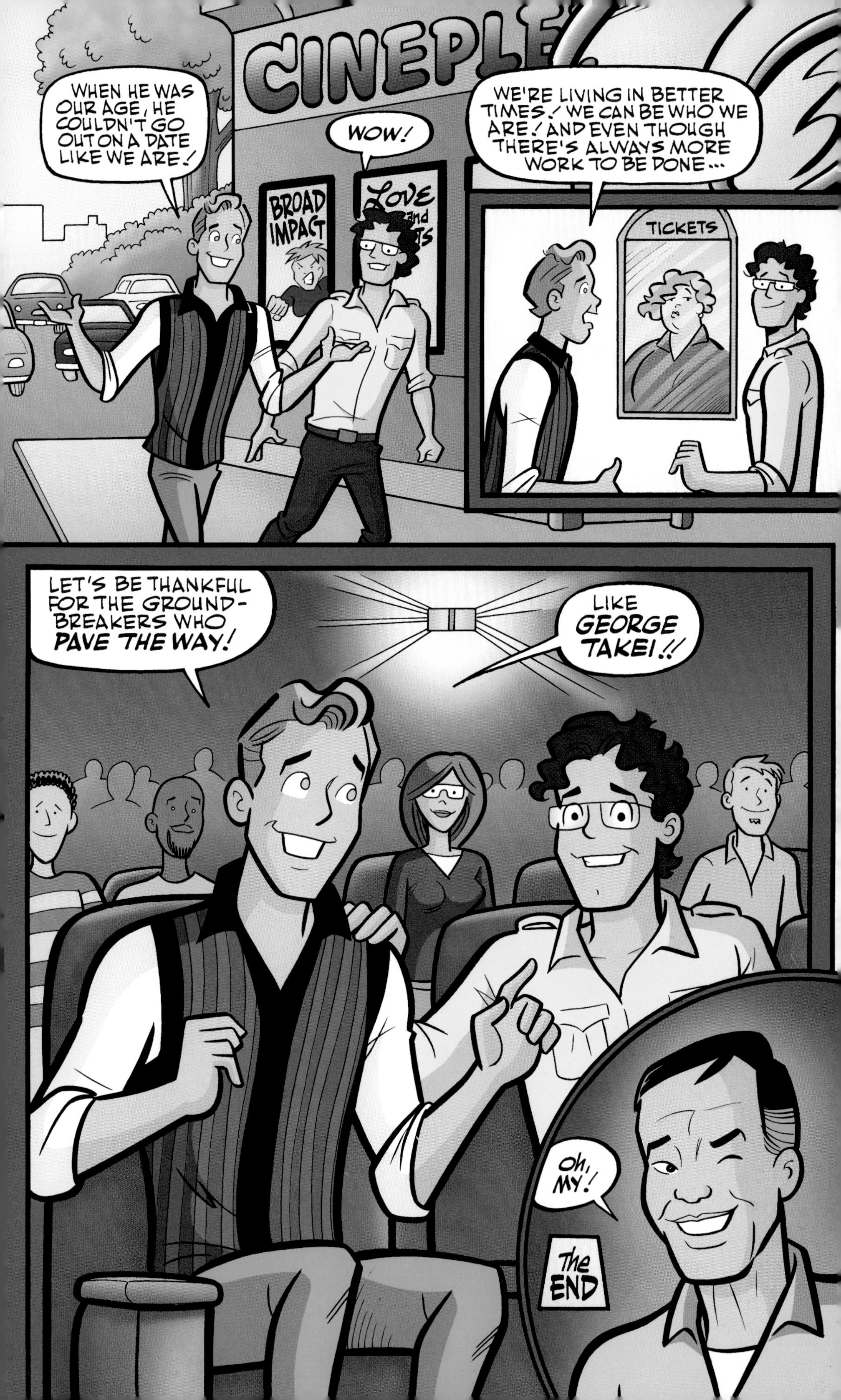
CINEPLE
WHEN HE WAS OUR AGE, HE COULDN'T GO OUT ON A DATE LIKE WE ARE!
WOW!
BROAD IMPACT
Love and
WE'RE LIVING IN BETTER TIMES! WE CAN BE WHO WE ARE! AND EVEN THOUGH THERE'S ALWAYS MORE WORK TO BE DONE...
TICKETS
LET'S BE THANKFUL FOR THE GROUND-BREAKERS WHO PAVE THE WAY!
LIKE GEORGE TAKEI!!
Oh, MY!
The END

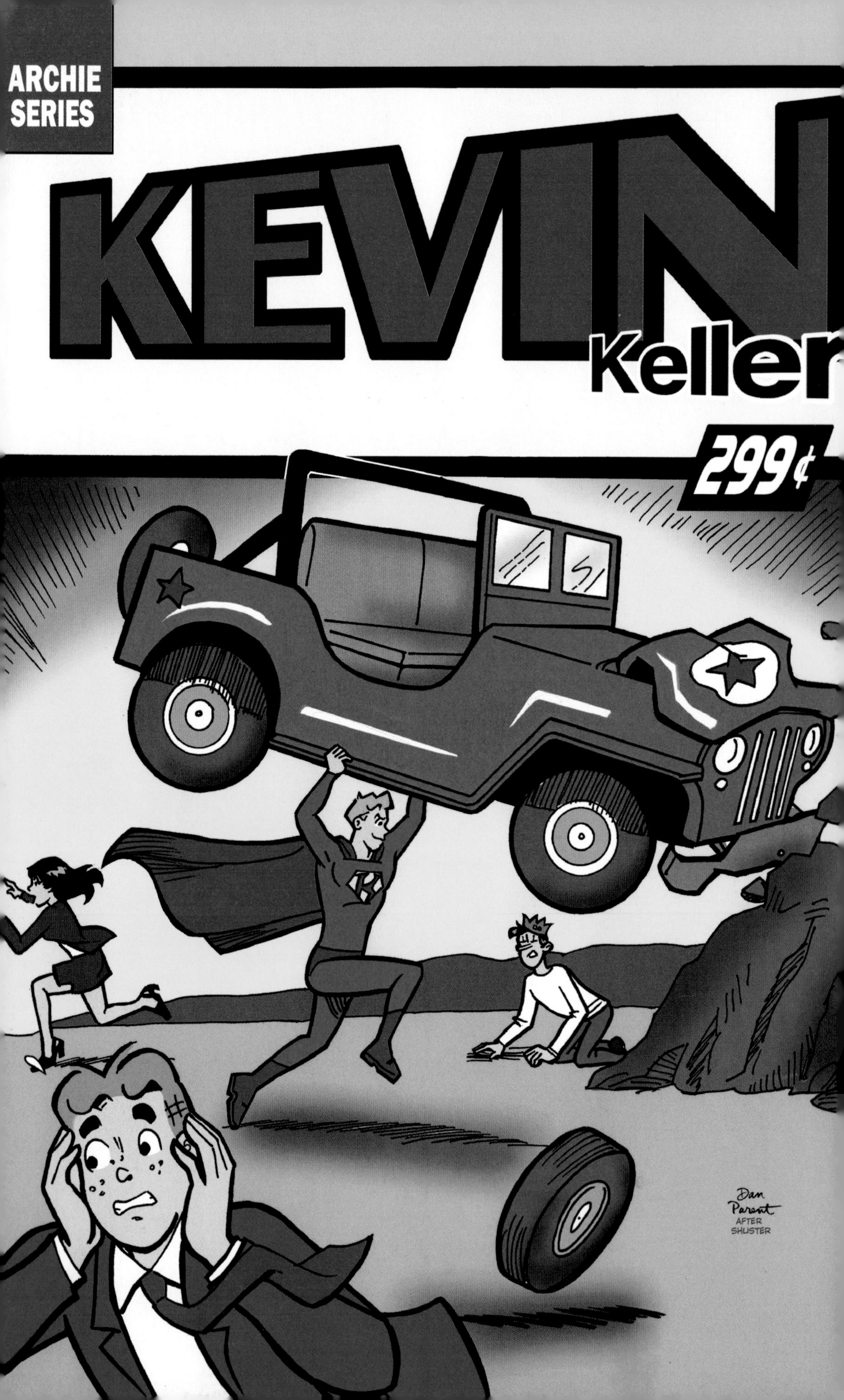
ARCHIE SERIES
KEVIN Keller
299¢
Dan Parent AFTER SHUSTER

Chapter 2

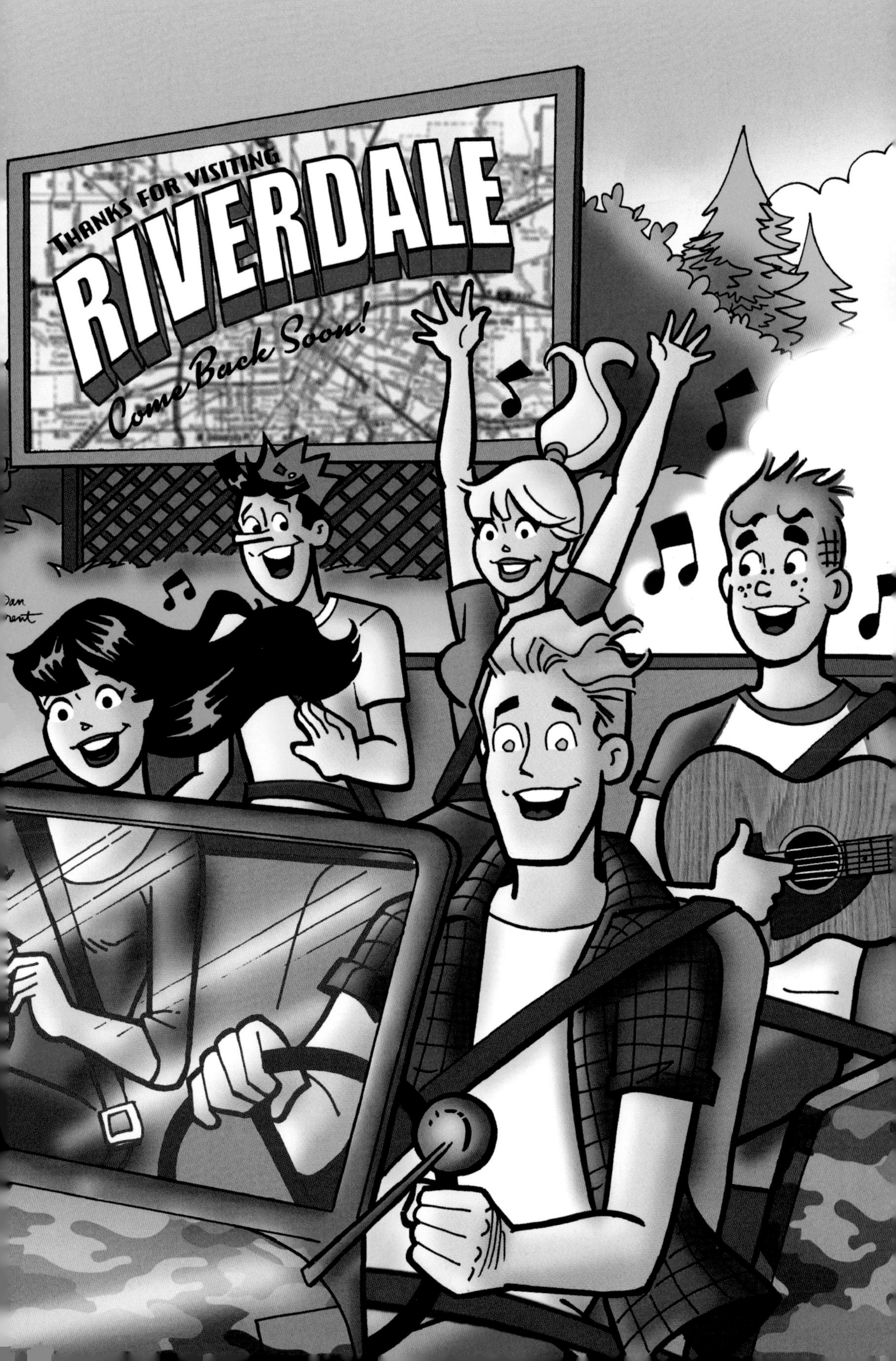

THANKS FOR VISITING
RIVERDALE
Come Back Soon!

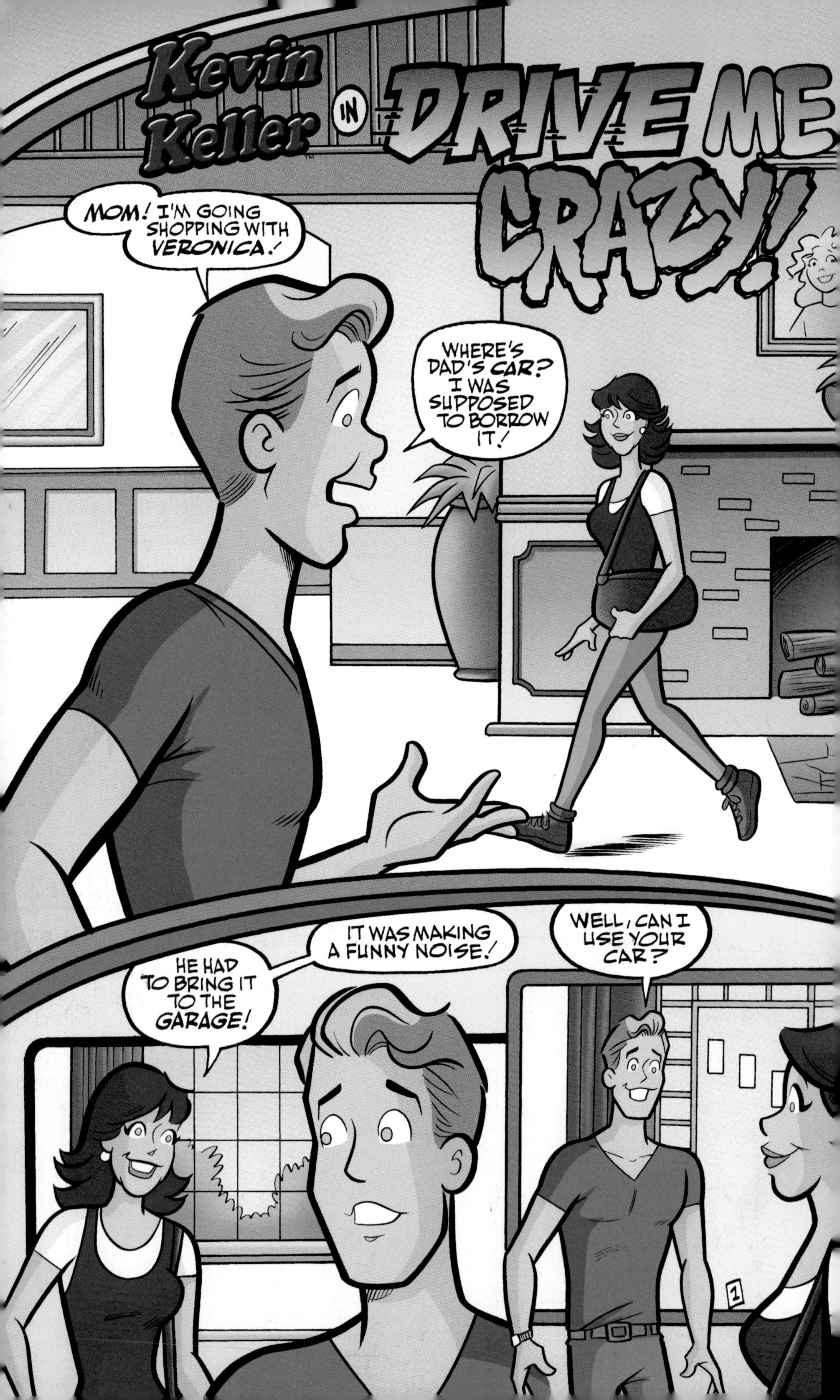
Kevin Keller
IN
DRIVE ME CRAZY!
MOM! I'M GOING SHOPPING WITH VERONICA!
WHERE'S DAD'S CAR? I WAS SUPPOSED TO BORROW IT!
IT WAS MAKING A FUNNY NOISE!
HE HAD TO BRING IT TO THE GARAGE!
WELL, CAN I USE YOUR CAR?
1

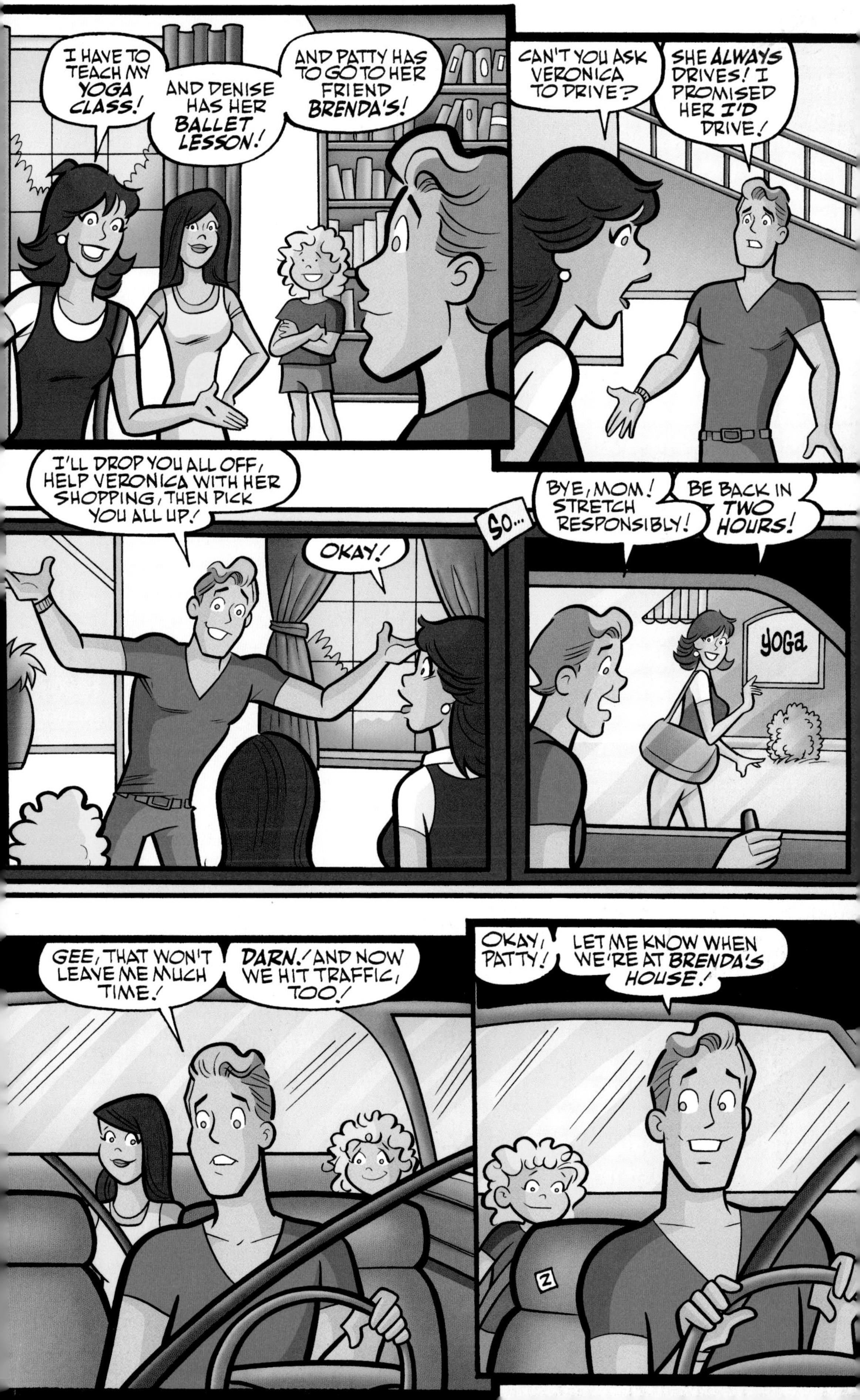

I HAVE TO TEACH MY YOGA CLASS!
AND DENISE HAS HER BALLET LESSON!
AND PATTY HAS TO GO TO HER FRIEND BRENDA'S!
CAN'T YOU ASK VERONICA TO DRIVE?
SHE ALWAYS DRIVES! I PROMISED HER I'D DRIVE!
I'LL DROP YOU ALL OFF, HELP VERONICA WITH HER SHOPPING, THEN PICK YOU ALL UP!
OKAY!
SO...
BYE, MOM! STRETCH RESPONSIBLY!
BE BACK IN TWO HOURS!
YOGA
GEE, THAT WON'T LEAVE ME MUCH TIME!
DARN! AND NOW WE HIT TRAFFIC, TOO!
OKAY, PATTY!
LET ME KNOW WHEN WE'RE AT BRENDA'S HOUSE!

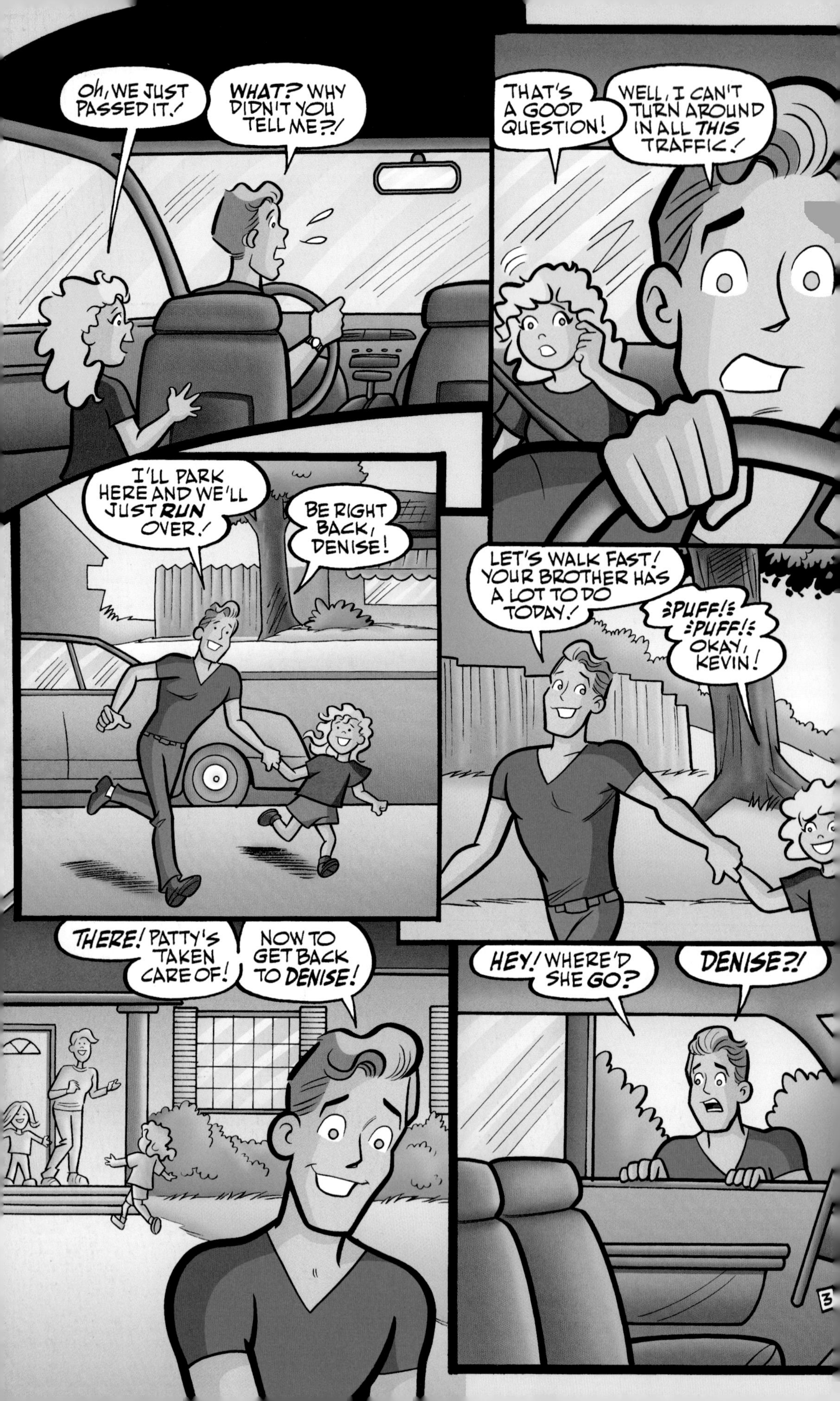
Oh, WE JUST PASSED IT!
WHAT? WHY DIDN'T YOU TELL ME?!
THAT'S A GOOD QUESTION!
WELL, I CAN'T TURN AROUND IN ALL THIS TRAFFIC!
I'LL PARK HERE AND WE'LL JUST RUN OVER!
BE RIGHT BACK, DENISE!
LET'S WALK FAST! YOUR BROTHER HAS A LOT TO DO TODAY!
PUFF! PUFF! OKAY, KEVIN!
THERE! PATTY'S TAKEN CARE OF!
NOW TO GET BACK TO DENISE!
HEY! WHERE'D SHE GO?
DENISE?!
3

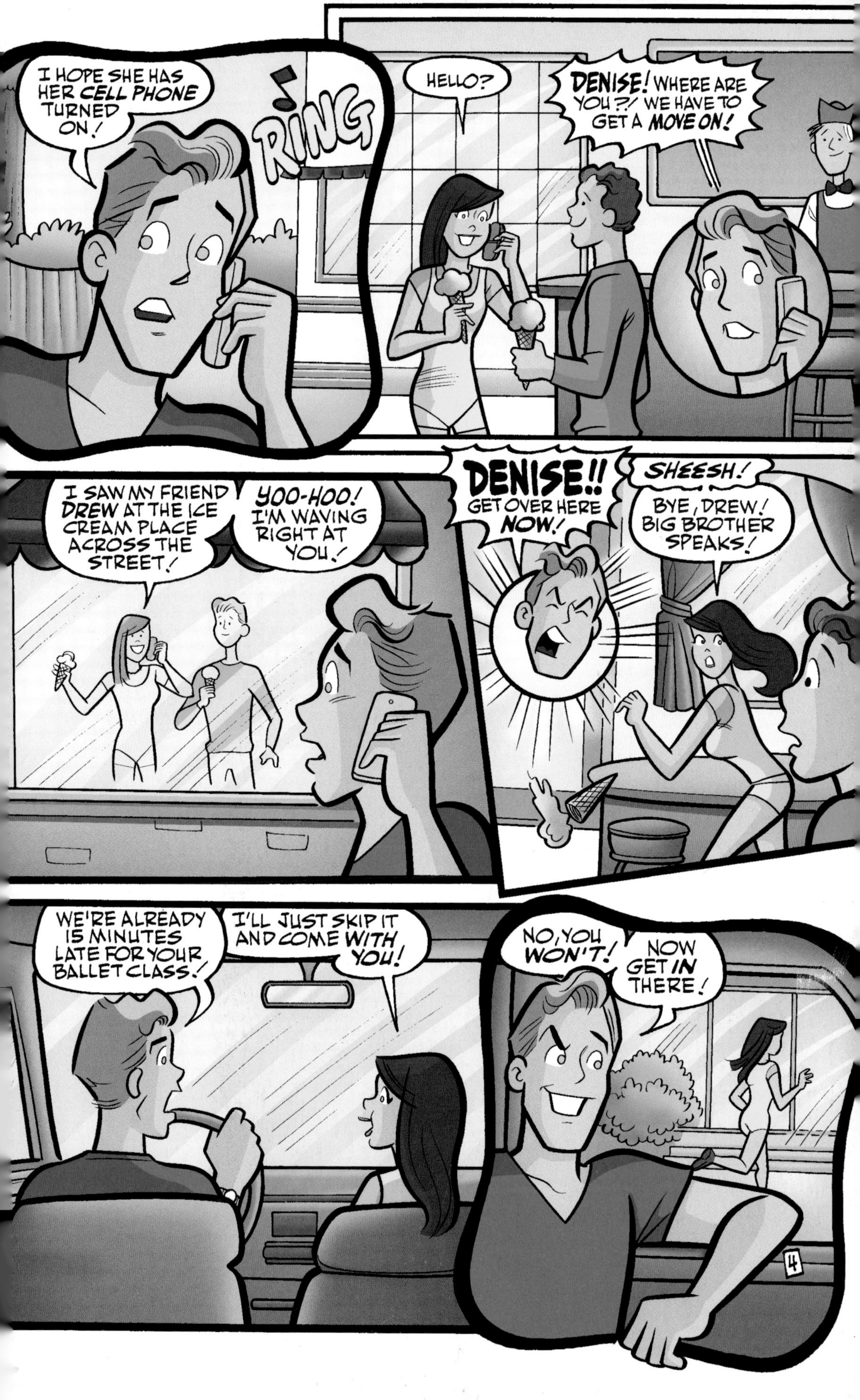
I HOPE SHE HAS HER CELL PHONE TURNED ON!
RING
HELLO?
DENISE! WHERE ARE YOU?! WE HAVE TO GET A MOVE ON!
I SAW MY FRIEND DREW AT THE ICE CREAM PLACE ACROSS THE STREET!
YOO-HOO! I'M WAVING RIGHT AT YOU!
DENISE!! GET OVER HERE NOW!
SHEESH!
BYE, DREW! BIG BROTHER SPEAKS!
WE'RE ALREADY 15 MINUTES LATE FOR YOUR BALLET CLASS!
I'LL JUST SKIP IT AND COME WITH YOU!
NO, YOU WON'T!
NOW GET IN THERE!
4

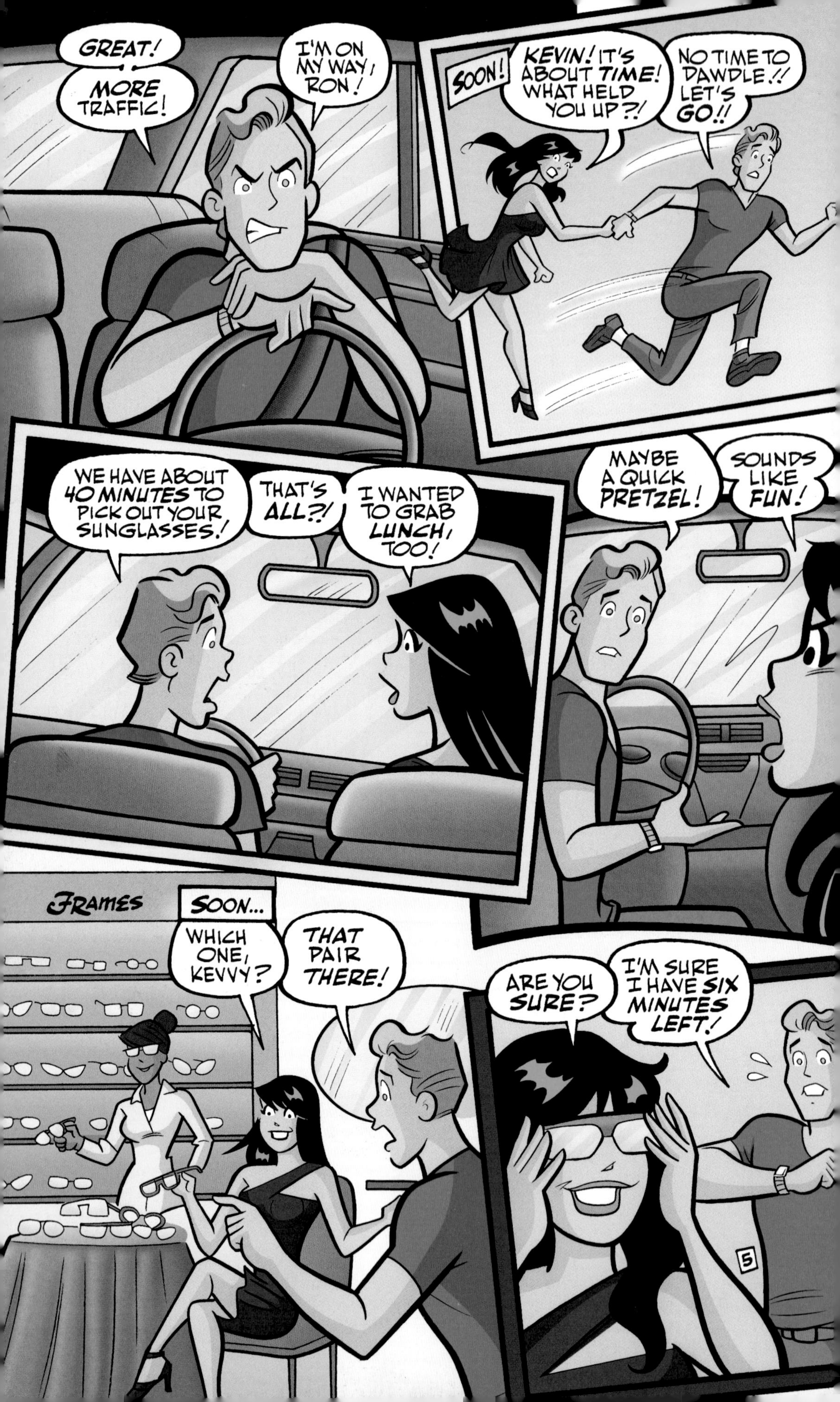

GREAT!
MORE TRAFFIC!
I'M ON MY WAY, RON!
SOON!
KEVIN! IT'S ABOUT TIME! WHAT HELD YOU UP?!
NO TIME TO DAWDLE!! LET'S GO!!
WE HAVE ABOUT 40 MINUTES TO PICK OUT YOUR SUNGLASSES!
THAT'S ALL?!
I WANTED TO GRAB LUNCH, TOO!
MAYBE A QUICK PRETZEL!
SOUNDS LIKE FUN!
FRAMES
SOON...
WHICH ONE, KEVVY?
THAT PAIR THERE!
ARE YOU SURE?
I'M SURE I HAVE SIX MINUTES LEFT!

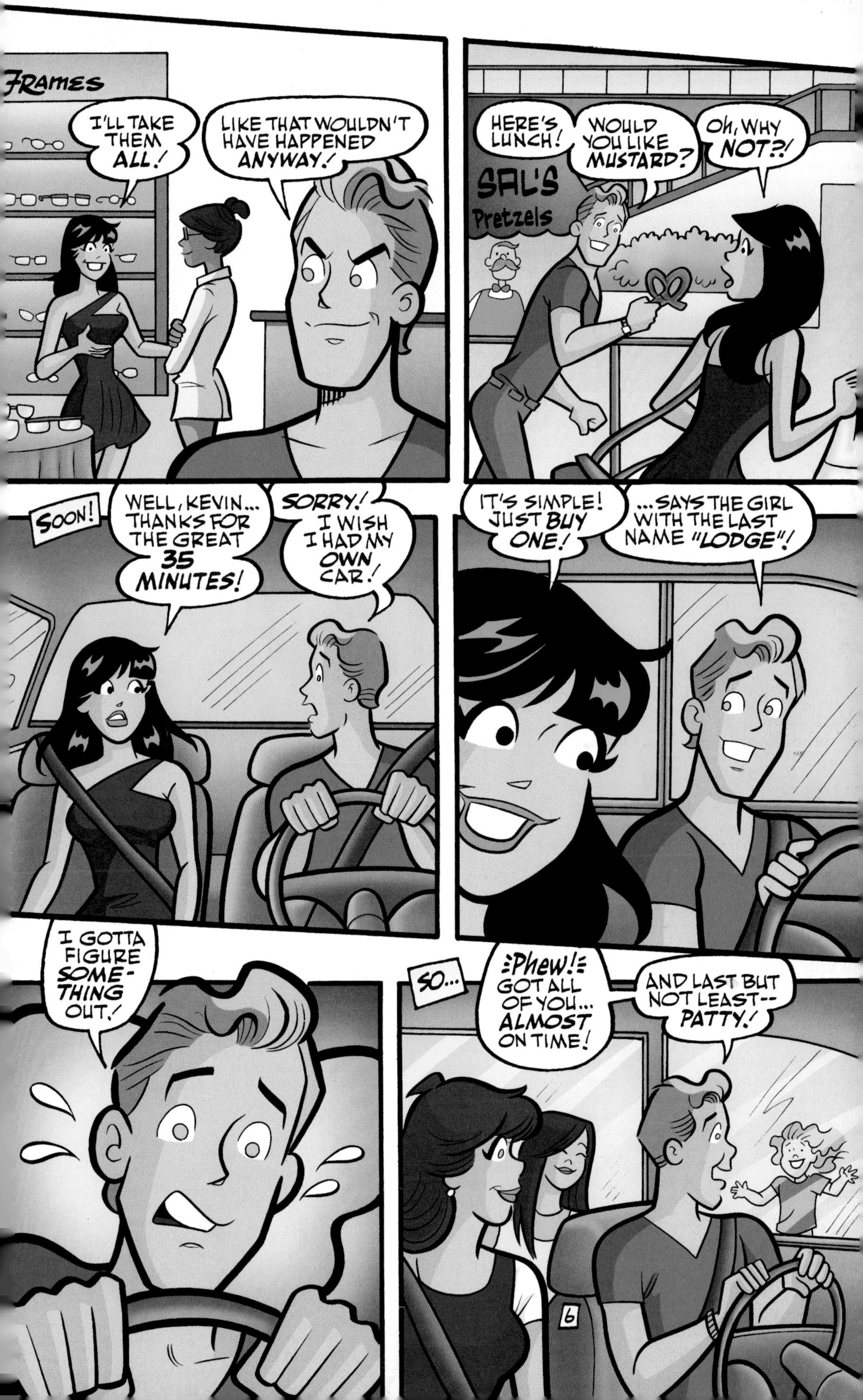
FRAMES
I'LL TAKE THEM ALL!
LIKE THAT WOULDN'T HAVE HAPPENED ANYWAY!
SAL'S Pretzels
HERE'S LUNCH!
WOULD YOU LIKE MUSTARD?
Oh, WHY NOT?!
SOON!
WELL, KEVIN... THANKS FOR THE GREAT 35 MINUTES!
SORRY! I WISH I HAD MY OWN CAR!
IT'S SIMPLE! JUST BUY ONE!
...SAYS THE GIRL WITH THE LAST NAME "LODGE"!
I GOTTA FIGURE SOME-THING OUT!
SO...
Phew! GOT ALL OF YOU... ALMOST ON TIME!
AND LAST BUT NOT LEAST-- PATTY!
6

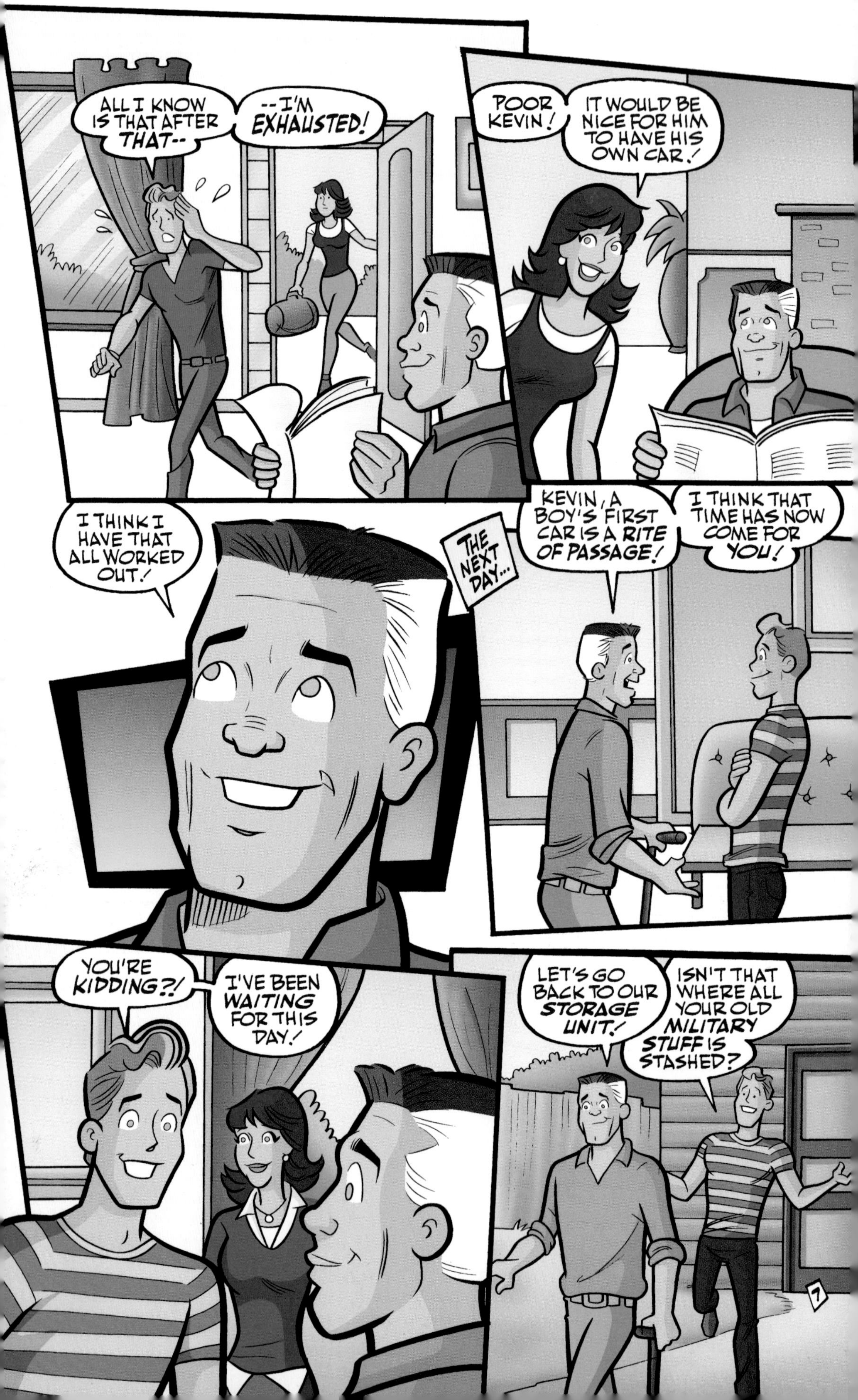
ALL I KNOW IS THAT AFTER THAT--
--I'M EXHAUSTED!
POOR KEVIN!
IT WOULD BE NICE FOR HIM TO HAVE HIS OWN CAR!
I THINK I HAVE THAT ALL WORKED OUT!
THE NEXT DAY...
KEVIN, A BOY'S FIRST CAR IS A RITE OF PASSAGE!
I THINK THAT TIME HAS NOW COME FOR YOU!
YOU'RE KIDDING?!
I'VE BEEN WAITING FOR THIS DAY!
LET'S GO BACK TO OUR STORAGE UNIT!
ISN'T THAT WHERE ALL YOUR OLD MILITARY STUFF IS STASHED?
7

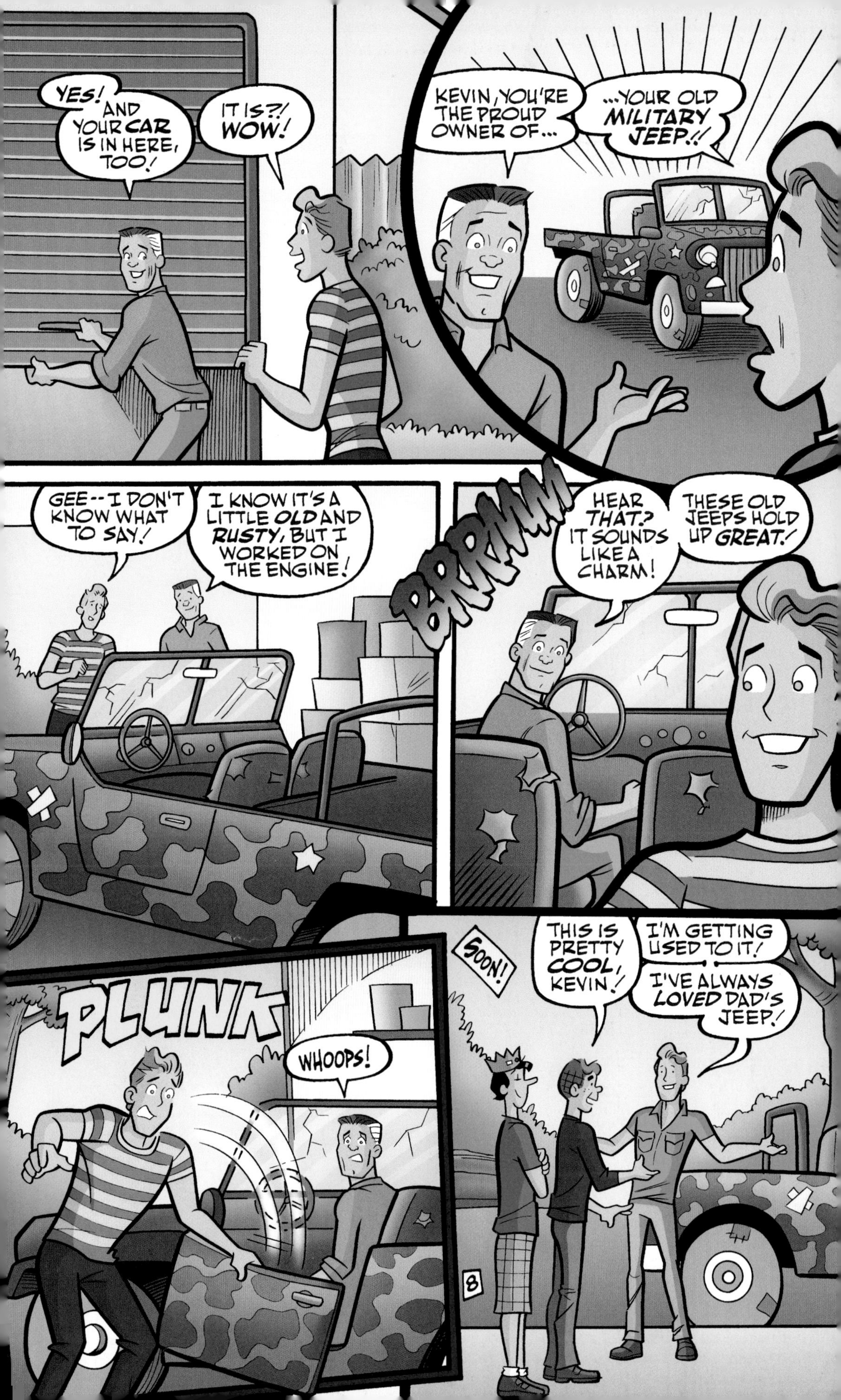

YES! AND YOUR CAR IS IN HERE, TOO!
IT IS?! WOW!
KEVIN, YOU'RE THE PROUD OWNER OF...
...YOUR OLD MILITARY JEEP!!
GEE--I DON'T KNOW WHAT TO SAY!
I KNOW IT'S A LITTLE OLD AND RUSTY, BUT I WORKED ON THE ENGINE!
BRRMM
HEAR THAT? IT SOUNDS LIKE A CHARM!
THESE OLD JEEPS HOLD UP GREAT!
PLUNK
WHOOPS!
SOON!
THIS IS PRETTY COOL, KEVIN!
I'M GETTING USED TO IT!
I'VE ALWAYS LOVED DAD'S JEEP!
8

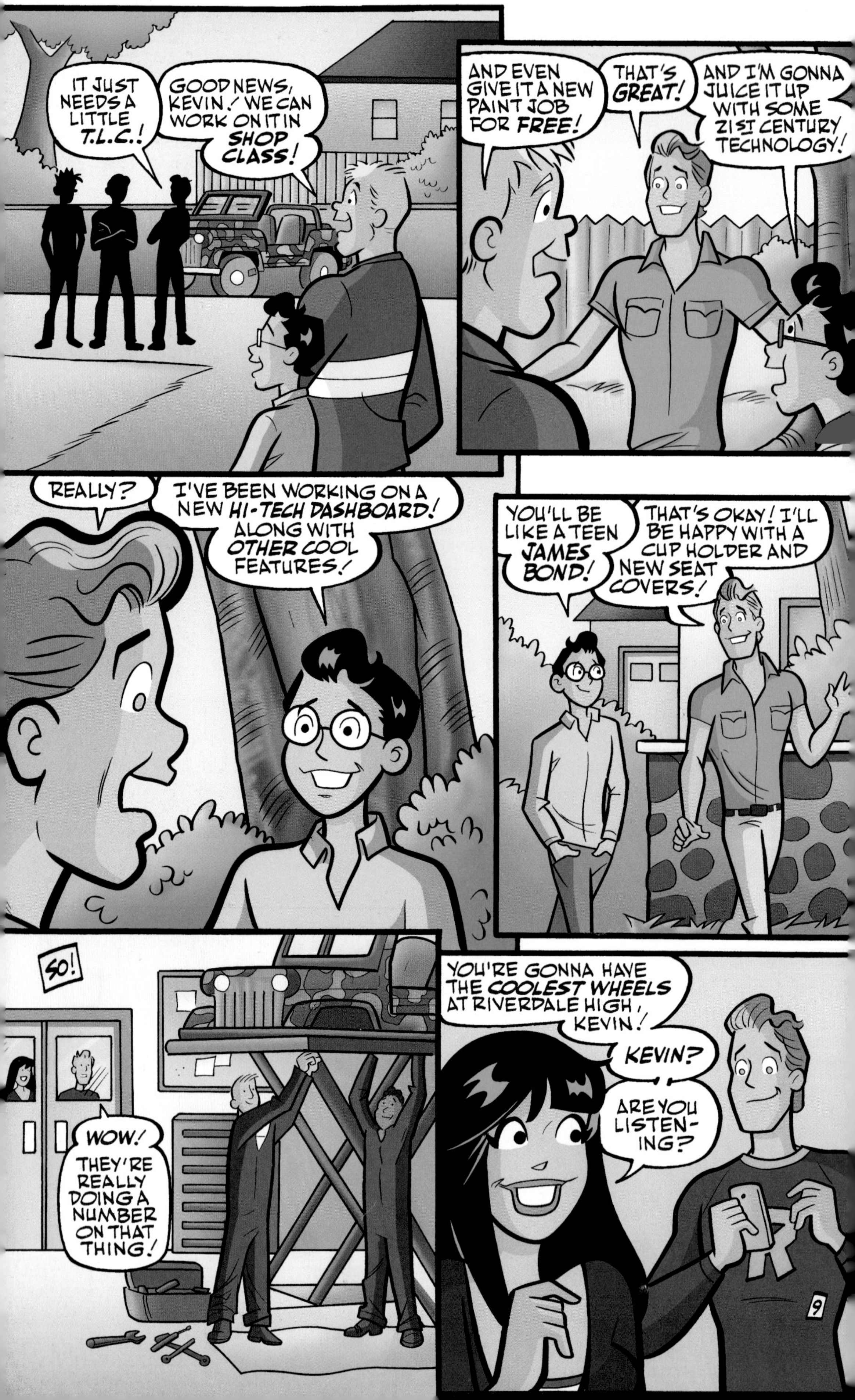

IT JUST NEEDS A LITTLE T.L.C.!
GOOD NEWS, KEVIN! WE CAN WORK ON IT IN SHOP CLASS!
AND EVEN GIVE IT A NEW PAINT JOB FOR FREE!
THAT'S GREAT!
AND I'M GONNA JUICE IT UP WITH SOME 21ST CENTURY TECHNOLOGY!
REALLY?
I'VE BEEN WORKING ON A NEW HI-TECH DASHBOARD! ALONG WITH OTHER COOL FEATURES!
YOU'LL BE LIKE A TEEN JAMES BOND!
THAT'S OKAY! I'LL BE HAPPY WITH A CUP HOLDER AND NEW SEAT COVERS!
SO!
WOW! THEY'RE REALLY DOING A NUMBER ON THAT THING!
YOU'RE GONNA HAVE THE COOLEST WHEELS AT RIVERDALE HIGH, KEVIN!
KEVIN?
ARE YOU LISTEN-ING?
9

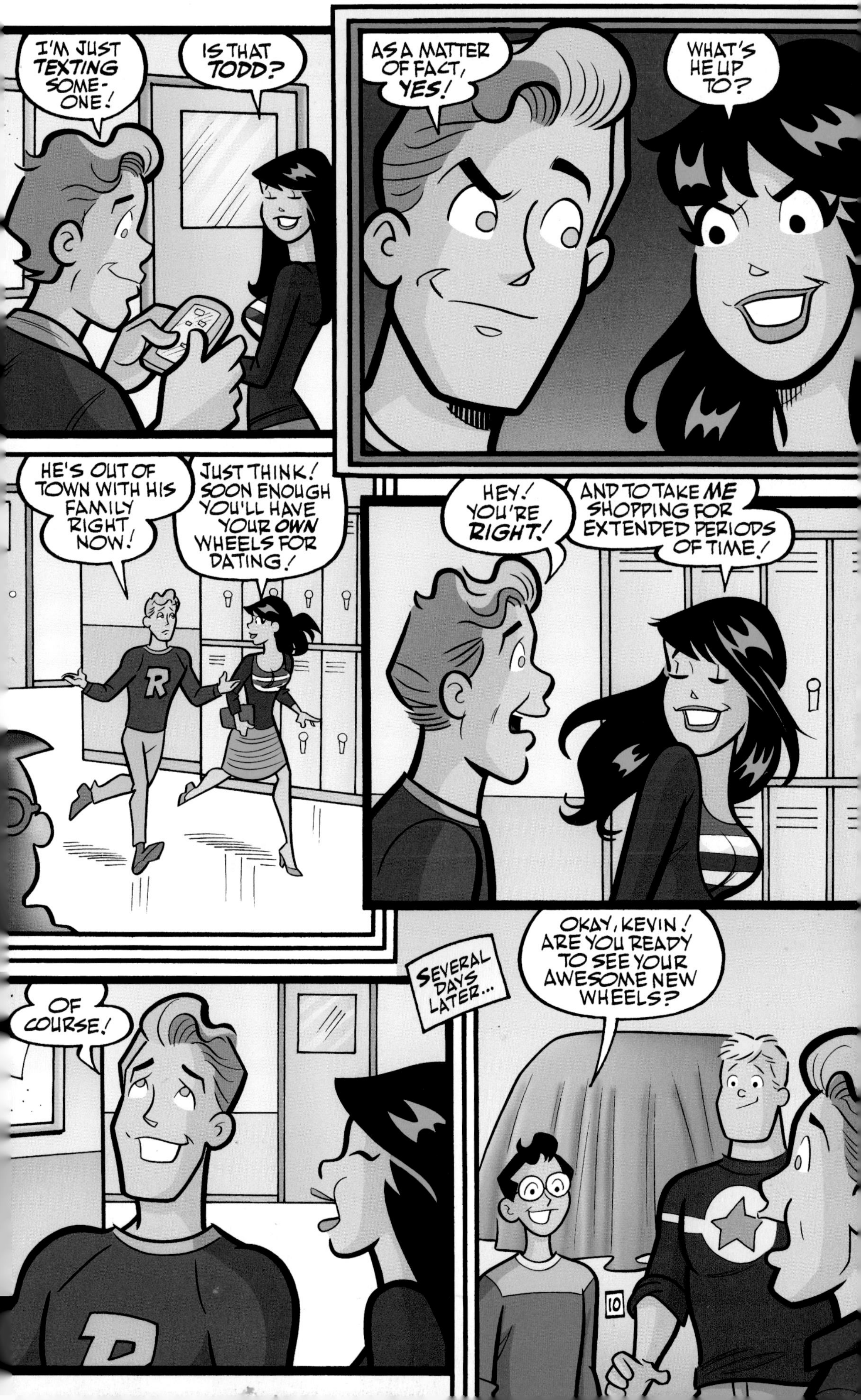
I'M JUST TEXTING SOME-ONE!
IS THAT TODD?
AS A MATTER OF FACT, YES!
WHAT'S HE UP TO?
HE'S OUT OF TOWN WITH HIS FAMILY RIGHT NOW!
JUST THINK! SOON ENOUGH YOU'LL HAVE YOUR OWN WHEELS FOR DATING!
HEY! YOU'RE RIGHT!
AND TO TAKE ME SHOPPING FOR EXTENDED PERIODS OF TIME!
OF COURSE!
SEVERAL DAYS LATER...
OKAY, KEVIN! ARE YOU READY TO SEE YOUR AWESOME NEW WHEELS?
10

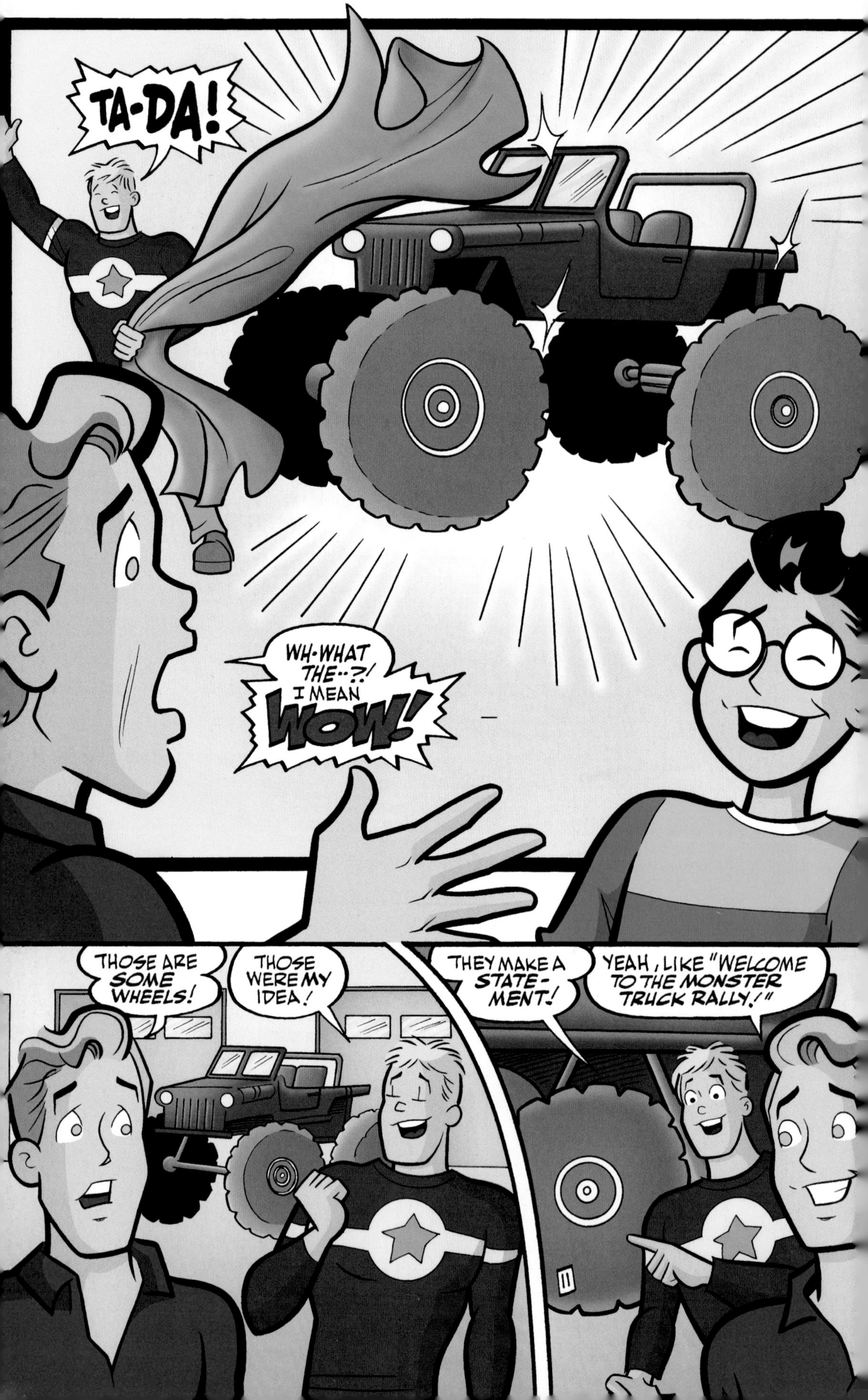
TA-DA!
WH-WHAT THE--?! I MEAN WOW!
THOSE ARE SOME WHEELS!
THOSE WERE MY IDEA!
THEY MAKE A STATE-MENT!
YEAH, LIKE "WELCOME TO THE MONSTER TRUCK RALLY!"

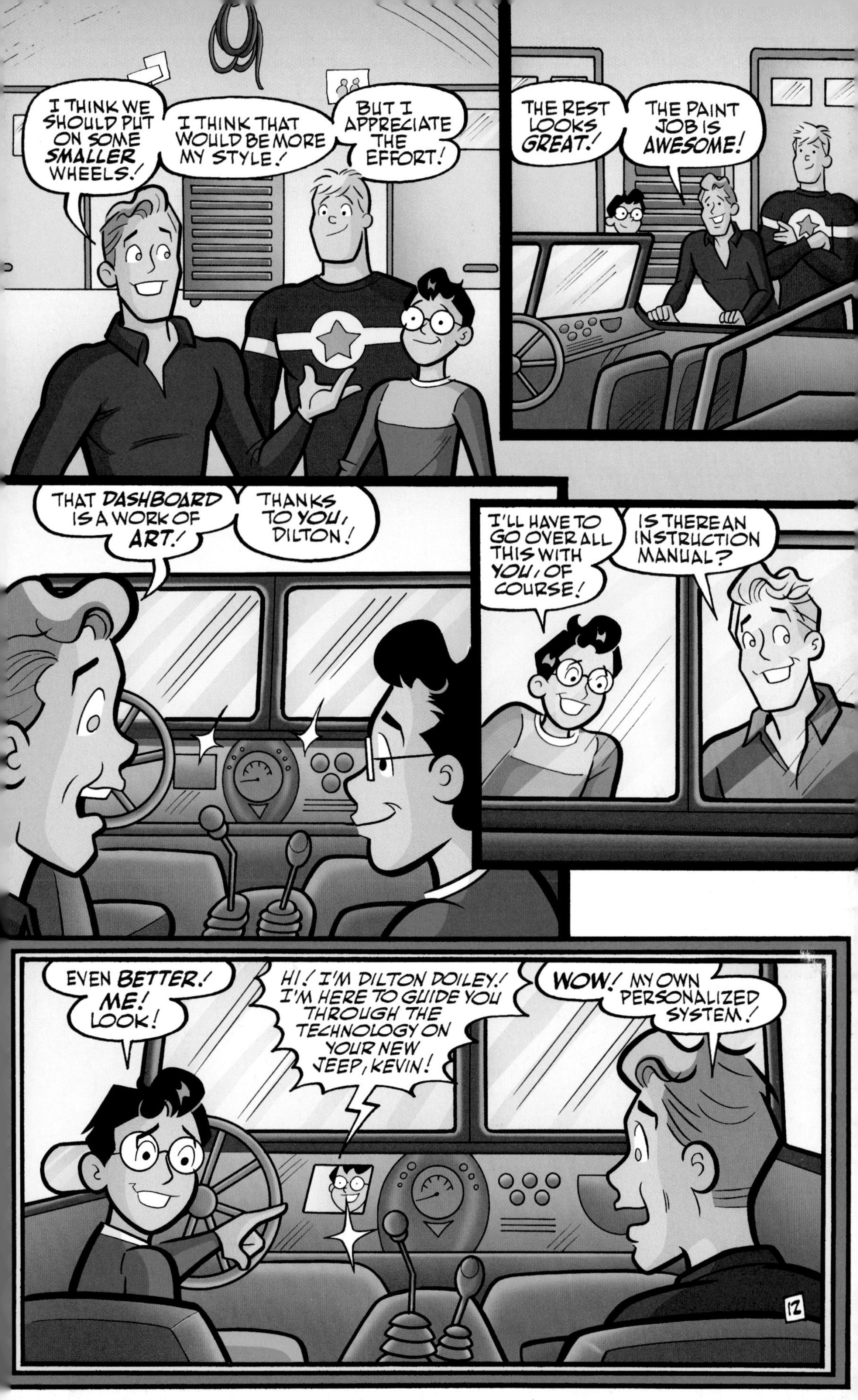
I THINK WE SHOULD PUT ON SOME SMALLER WHEELS!
I THINK THAT WOULD BE MORE MY STYLE!
BUT I APPRECIATE THE EFFORT!
THE REST LOOKS GREAT!
THE PAINT JOB IS AWESOME!
THAT DASHBOARD IS A WORK OF ART!
THANKS TO YOU, DILTON!
I'LL HAVE TO GO OVER ALL THIS WITH YOU, OF COURSE!
IS THERE AN INSTRUCTION MANUAL?
EVEN BETTER! ME! LOOK!
HI! I'M DILTON DOILEY! I'M HERE TO GUIDE YOU THROUGH THE TECHNOLOGY ON YOUR NEW JEEP, KEVIN!
WOW! MY OWN PERSONALIZED SYSTEM!
12

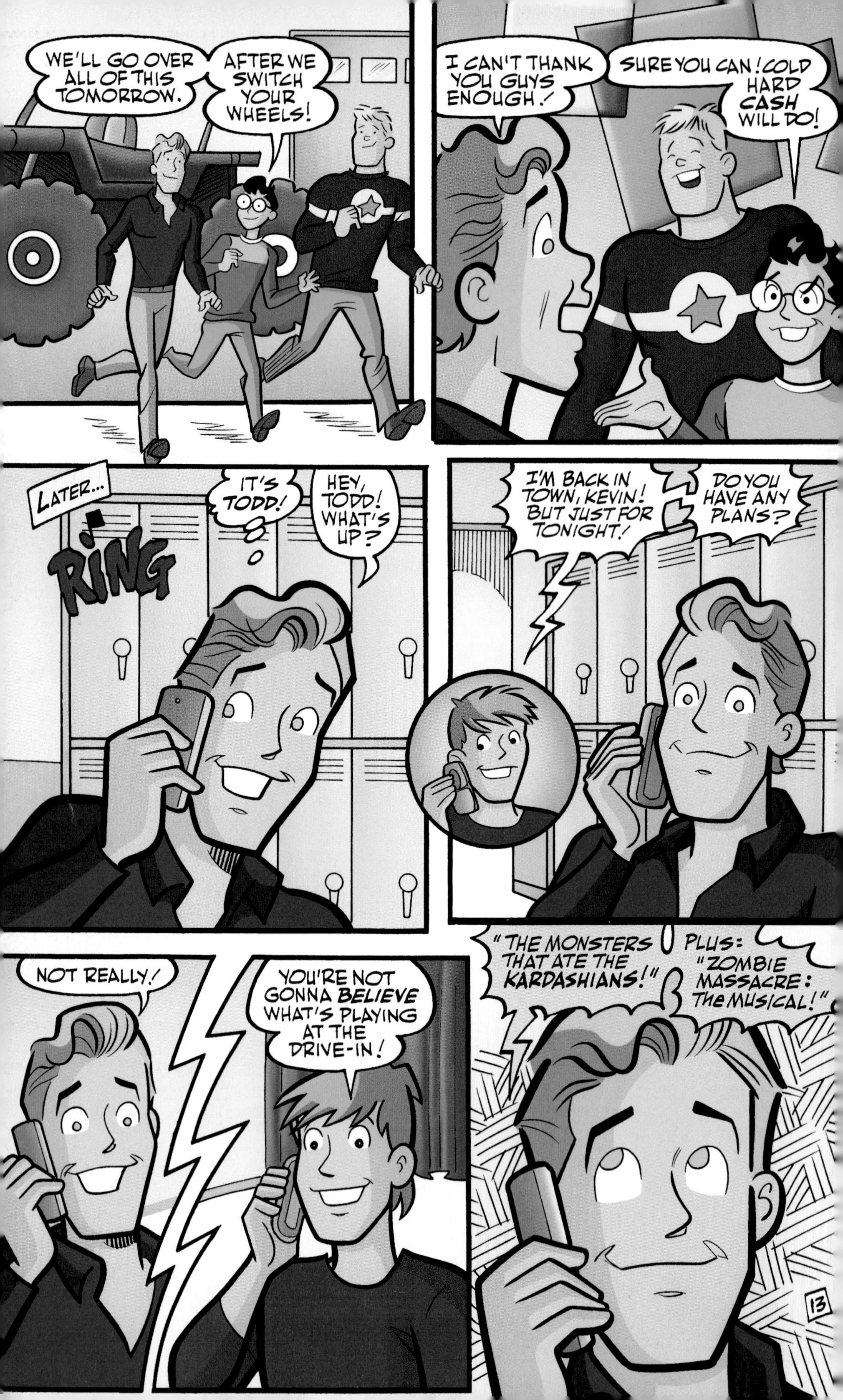

WE'LL GO OVER ALL OF THIS TOMORROW.
AFTER WE SWITCH YOUR WHEELS!
I CAN'T THANK YOU GUYS ENOUGH!
SURE YOU CAN! COLD HARD CASH WILL DO!
LATER...
RING
IT'S TODD!
HEY, TODD! WHAT'S UP?
I'M BACK IN TOWN, KEVIN! BUT JUST FOR TONIGHT!
DO YOU HAVE ANY PLANS?
NOT REALLY!
YOU'RE NOT GONNA BELIEVE WHAT'S PLAYING AT THE DRIVE-IN!
"THE MONSTERS THAT ATE THE KARDASHIANS!"
PLUS: "ZOMBIE MASSACRE: The MUSICAL!"
13

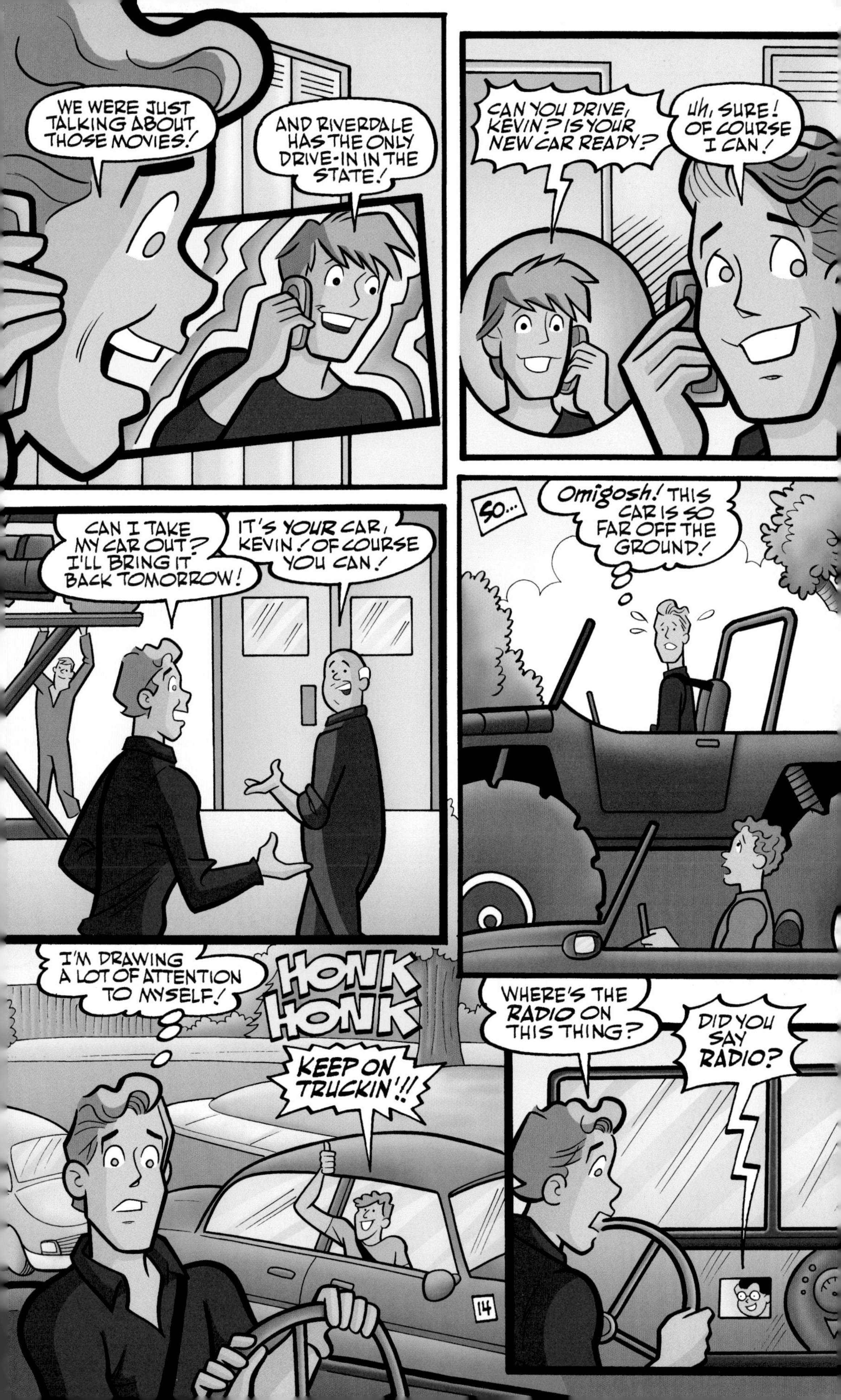
WE WERE JUST TALKING ABOUT THOSE MOVIES!
AND RIVERDALE HAS THE ONLY DRIVE-IN IN THE STATE!
CAN YOU DRIVE, KEVIN? IS YOUR NEW CAR READY?
UH, SURE! OF COURSE I CAN!
CAN I TAKE MY CAR OUT? I'LL BRING IT BACK TOMORROW!
IT'S YOUR CAR, KEVIN! OF COURSE YOU CAN!
SO...
Omigosh! THIS CAR IS SO FAR OFF THE GROUND!
I'M DRAWING A LOT OF ATTENTION TO MYSELF!
HONK HONK
KEEP ON TRUCKIN'!!
14
WHERE'S THE RADIO ON THIS THING?
DID YOU SAY RADIO?

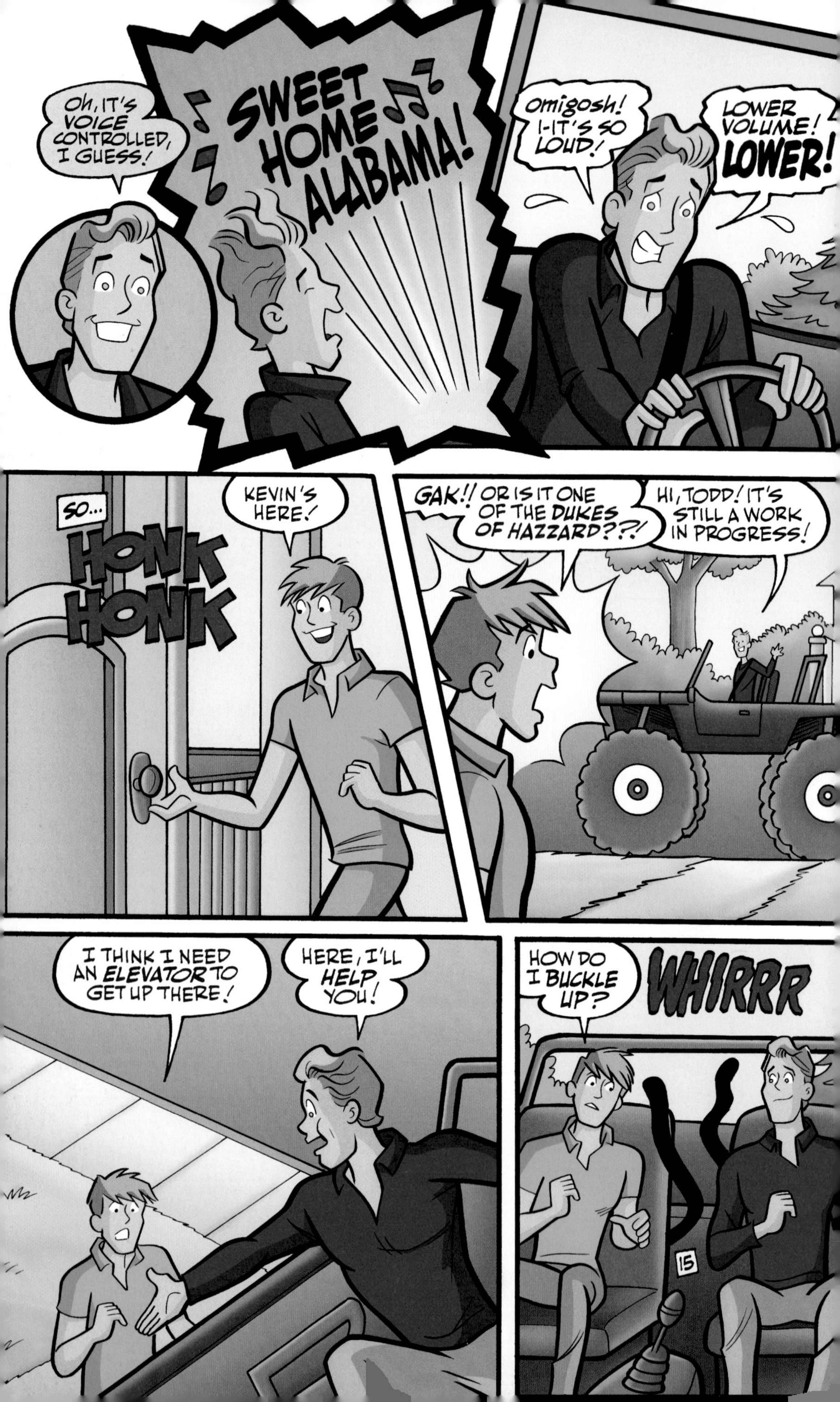
Oh, IT'S VOICE CONTROLLED, I GUESS!
SWEET HOME ALABAMA!
Omigosh! I-IT'S SO LOUD!
LOWER VOLUME! LOWER!
SO...
HONK HONK
KEVIN'S HERE!
GAK!! OR IS IT ONE OF THE DUKES OF HAZZARD?!?!
HI, TODD! IT'S STILL A WORK IN PROGRESS!
I THINK I NEED AN ELEVATOR TO GET UP THERE!
HERE, I'LL HELP YOU!
HOW DO I BUCKLE UP?
WHIRRR
15

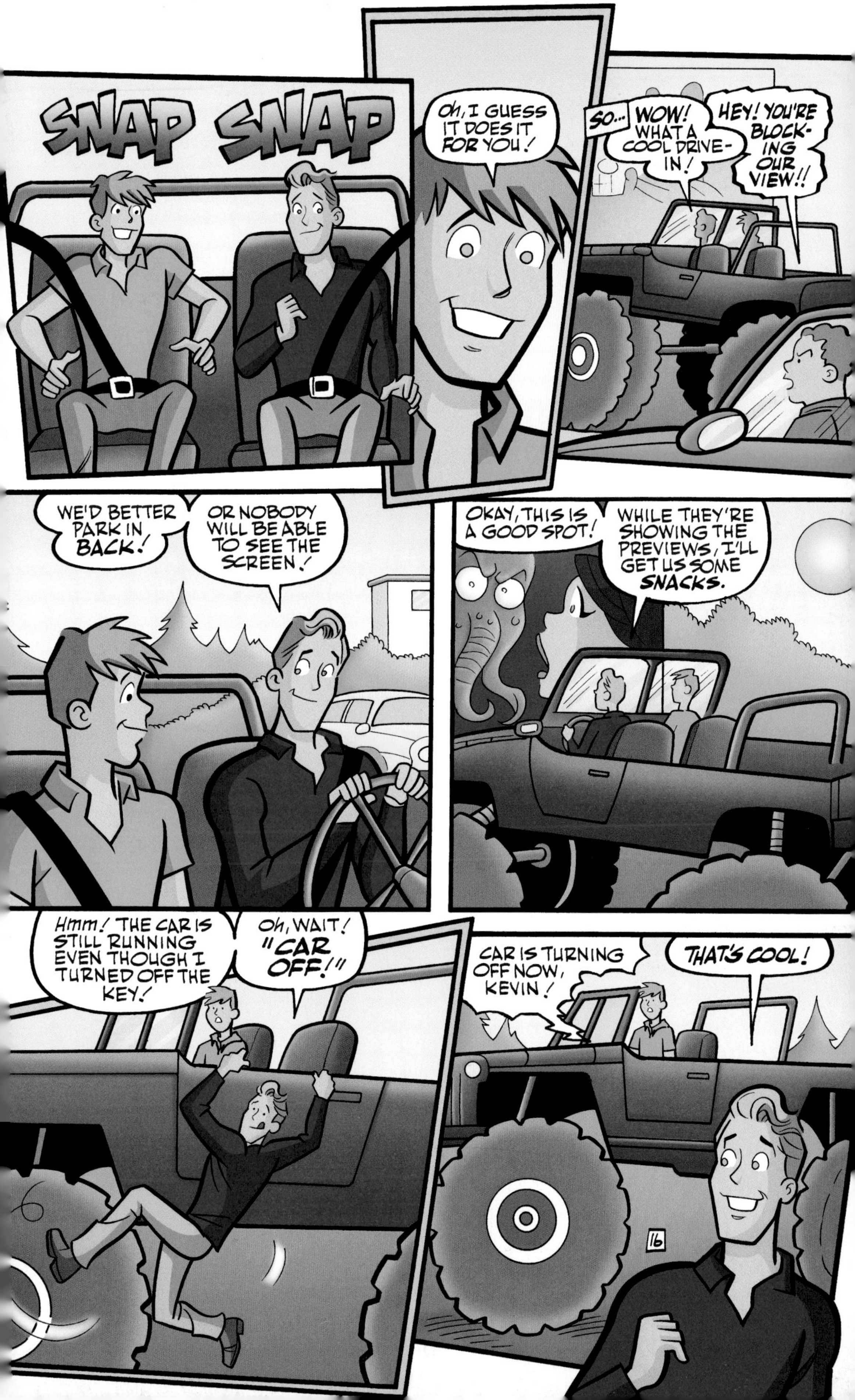
SNAP SNAP
Oh, I GUESS IT DOES IT FOR YOU!
SO...
WOW! WHAT A COOL DRIVE-IN!
HEY! YOU'RE BLOCKING OUR VIEW!!
WE'D BETTER PARK IN BACK!
OR NOBODY WILL BE ABLE TO SEE THE SCREEN!
OKAY, THIS IS A GOOD SPOT!
WHILE THEY'RE SHOWING THE PREVIEWS, I'LL GET US SOME SNACKS.
Hmm! THE CAR IS STILL RUNNING EVEN THOUGH I TURNED OFF THE KEY!
Oh, WAIT! "CAR OFF!"
CAR IS TURNING OFF NOW, KEVIN!
THAT'S COOL!
16

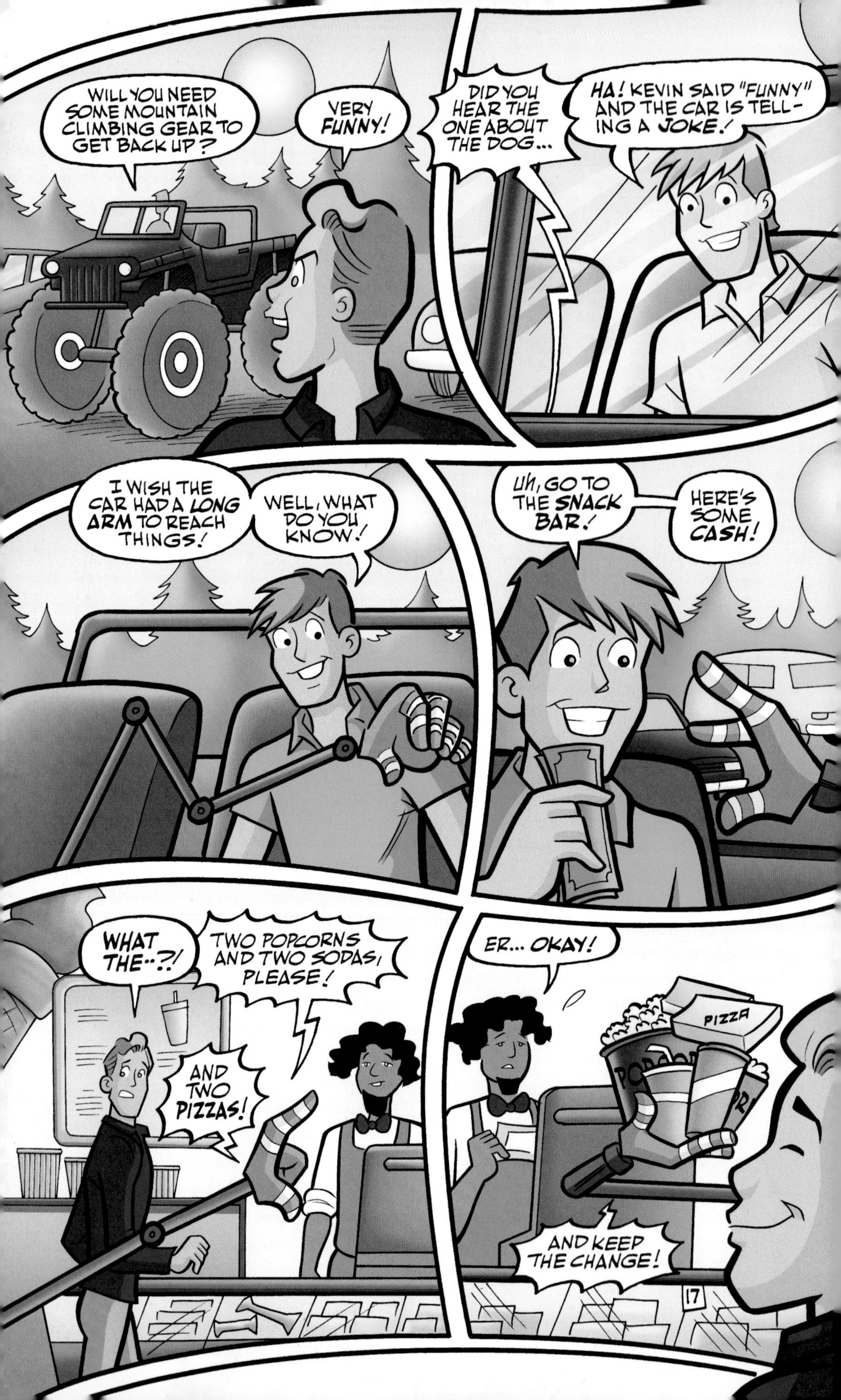

WILL YOU NEED SOME MOUNTAIN CLIMBING GEAR TO GET BACK UP?
VERY FUNNY!
DID YOU HEAR THE ONE ABOUT THE DOG...
HA! KEVIN SAID "FUNNY" AND THE CAR IS TELL-ING A JOKE!
I WISH THE CAR HAD A LONG ARM TO REACH THINGS!
WELL, WHAT DO YOU KNOW!
UH, GO TO THE SNACK BAR!
HERE'S SOME CASH!
WHAT THE--?!
TWO POPCORNS AND TWO SODAS, PLEASE!
AND TWO PIZZAS!
ER... OKAY!
PIZZA
AND KEEP THE CHANGE!

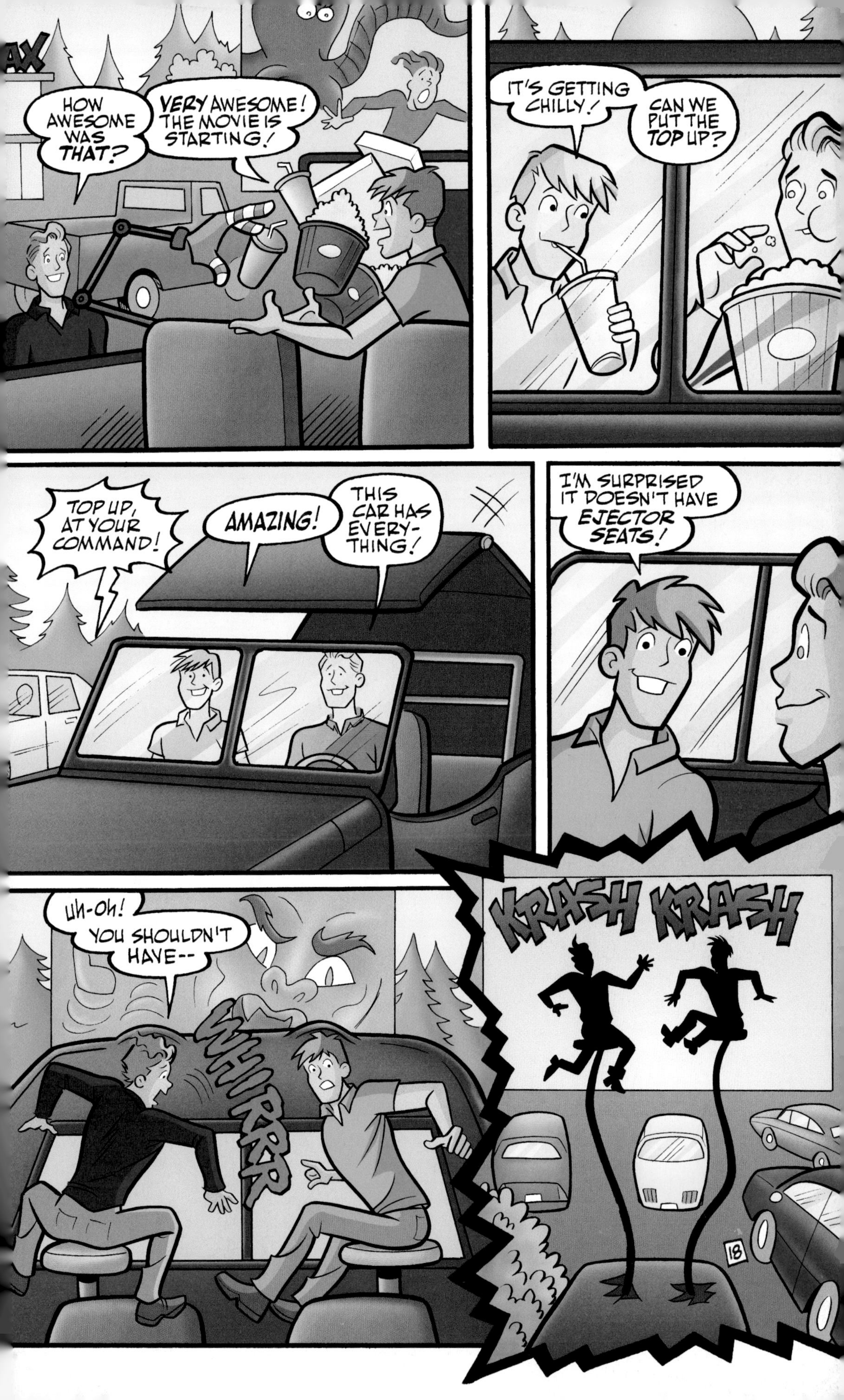
HOW AWESOME WAS THAT?
VERY AWESOME! THE MOVIE IS STARTING!
IT'S GETTING CHILLY!
CAN WE PUT THE TOP UP?
TOP UP, AT YOUR COMMAND!
AMAZING!
THIS CAR HAS EVERY-THING!
I'M SURPRISED IT DOESN'T HAVE EJECTOR SEATS!
UH-OH!
YOU SHOULDN'T HAVE--
WHIRRR
KRASH KRASH
18

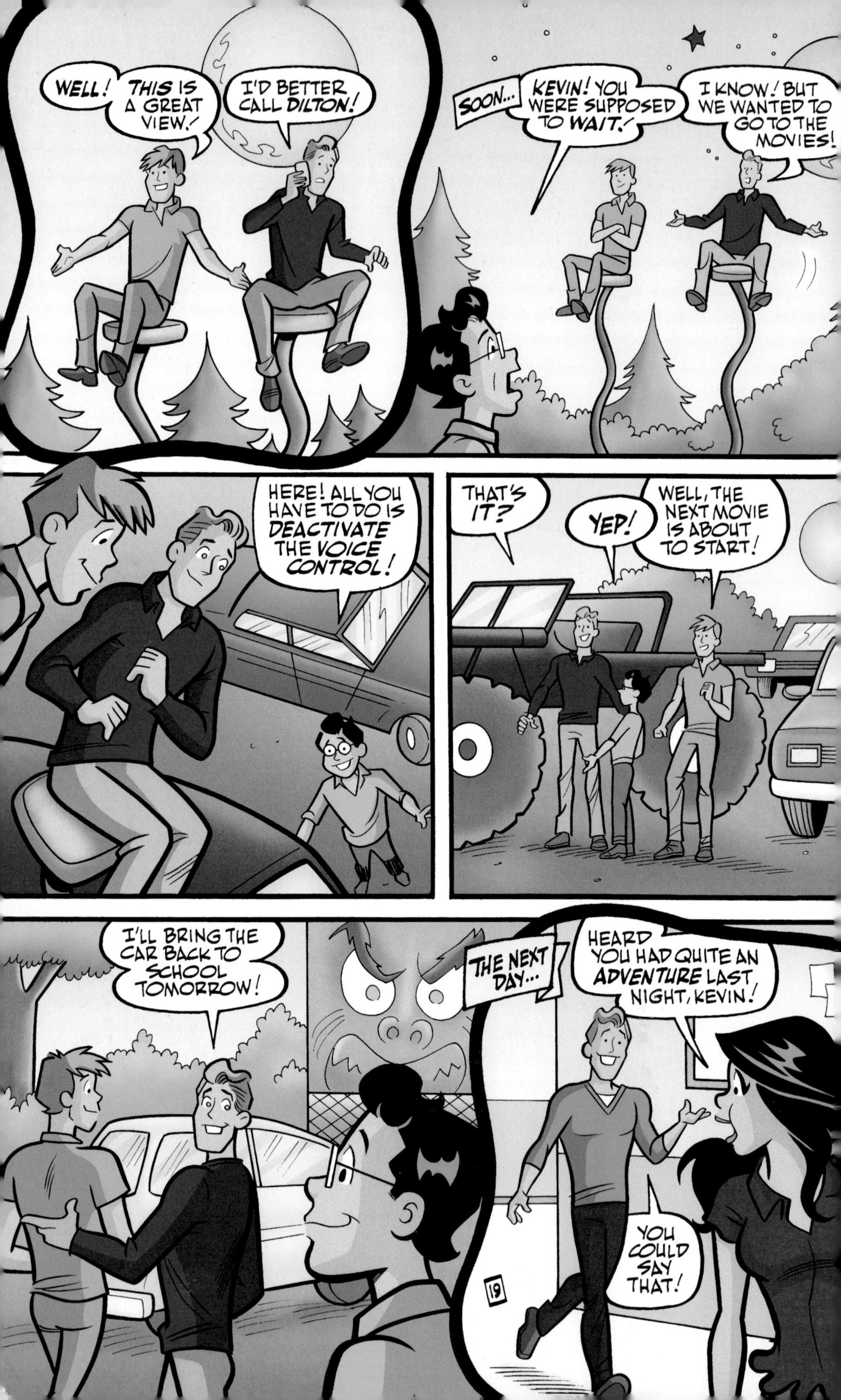
WELL!
THIS IS A GREAT VIEW!
I'D BETTER CALL DILTON!
SOON...
KEVIN! YOU WERE SUPPOSED TO WAIT!
I KNOW! BUT WE WANTED TO GO TO THE MOVIES!
HERE! ALL YOU HAVE TO DO IS DEACTIVATE THE VOICE CONTROL!
THAT'S IT?
YEP!
WELL, THE NEXT MOVIE IS ABOUT TO START!
I'LL BRING THE CAR BACK TO SCHOOL TOMORROW!
THE NEXT DAY...
HEARD YOU HAD QUITE AN ADVENTURE LAST NIGHT, KEVIN!
YOU COULD SAY THAT!
19

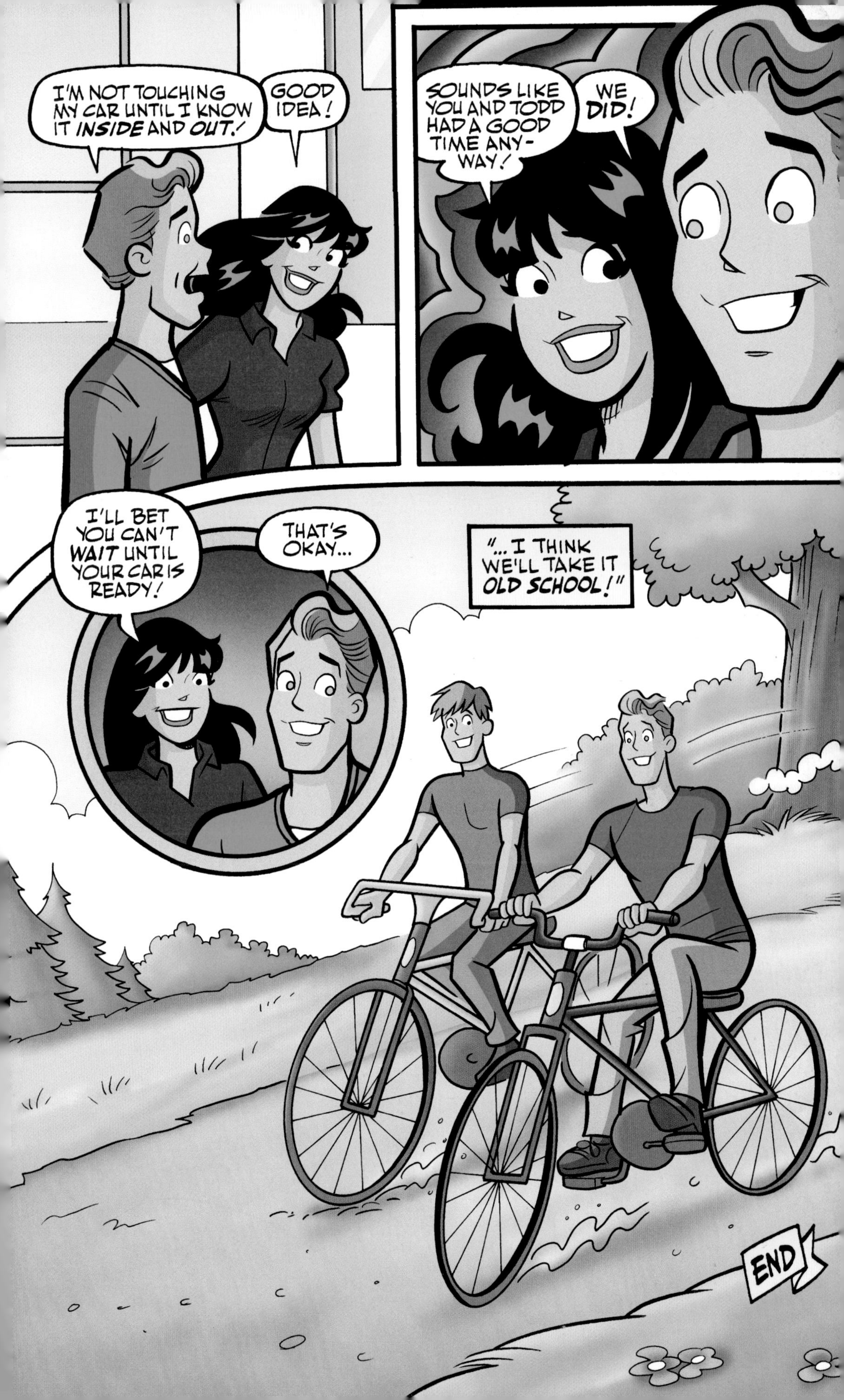

I'M NOT TOUCHING MY CAR UNTIL I KNOW IT INSIDE AND OUT!
GOOD IDEA!
SOUNDS LIKE YOU AND TODD HAD A GOOD TIME ANY-WAY!
WE DID!
I'LL BET YOU CAN'T WAIT UNTIL YOUR CAR IS READY!
THAT'S OKAY...
"... I THINK WE'LL TAKE IT OLD SCHOOL!"
END

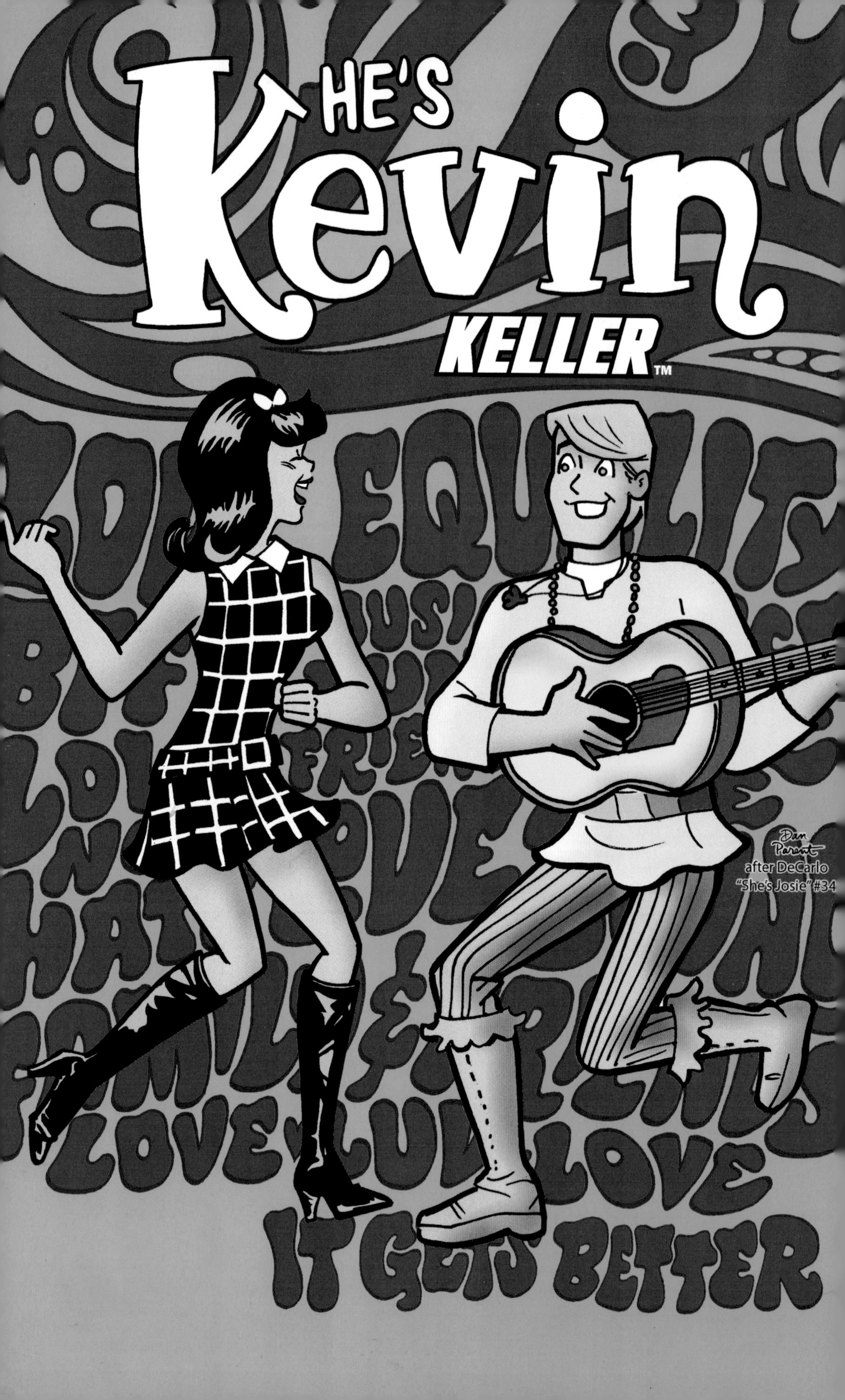
HE'S
Kevin
KELLER™
IT GETS BETTER
Dan Parent
after DeCarlo
"She's Josie" #34

Chapter 3

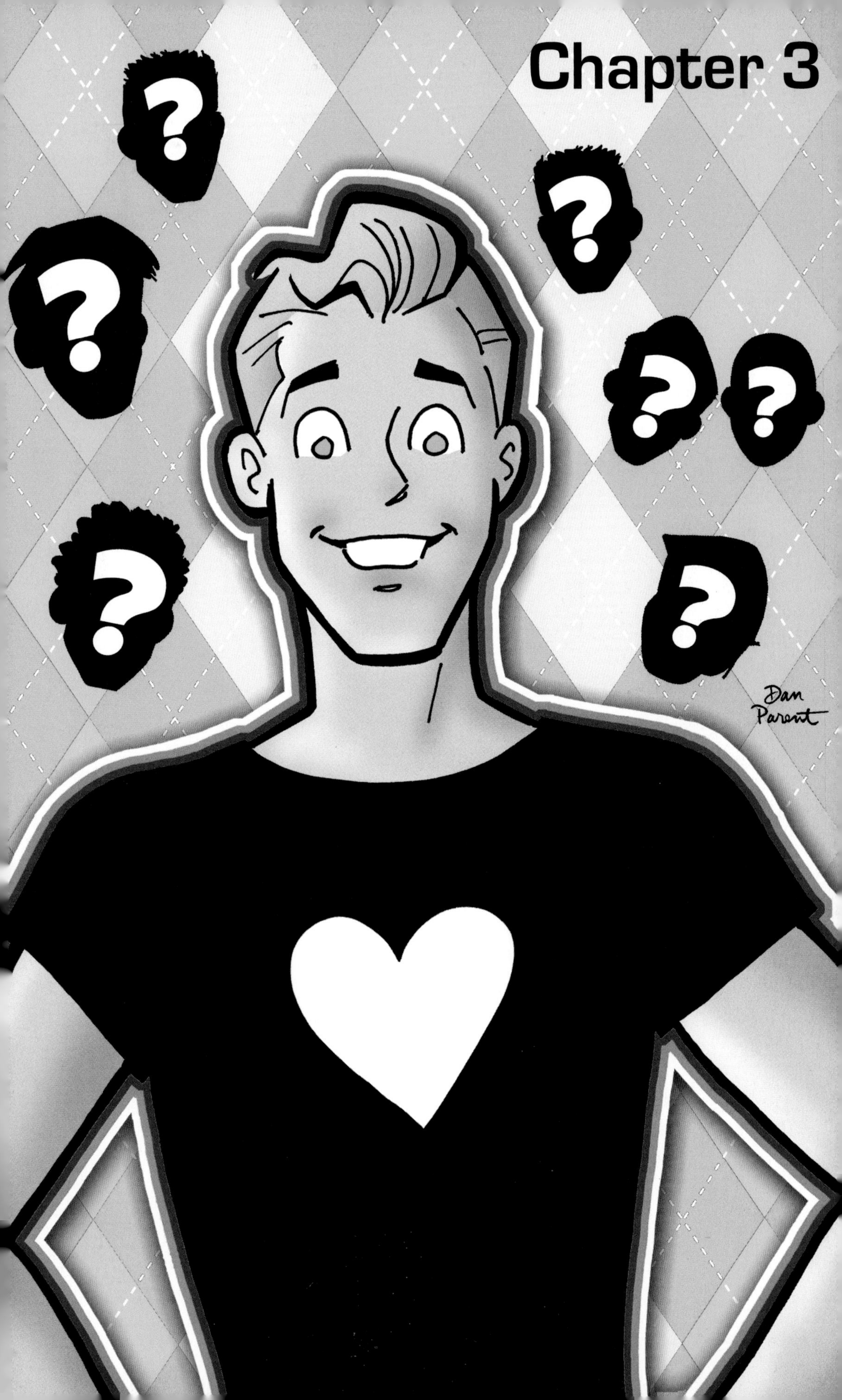
Dan Parent

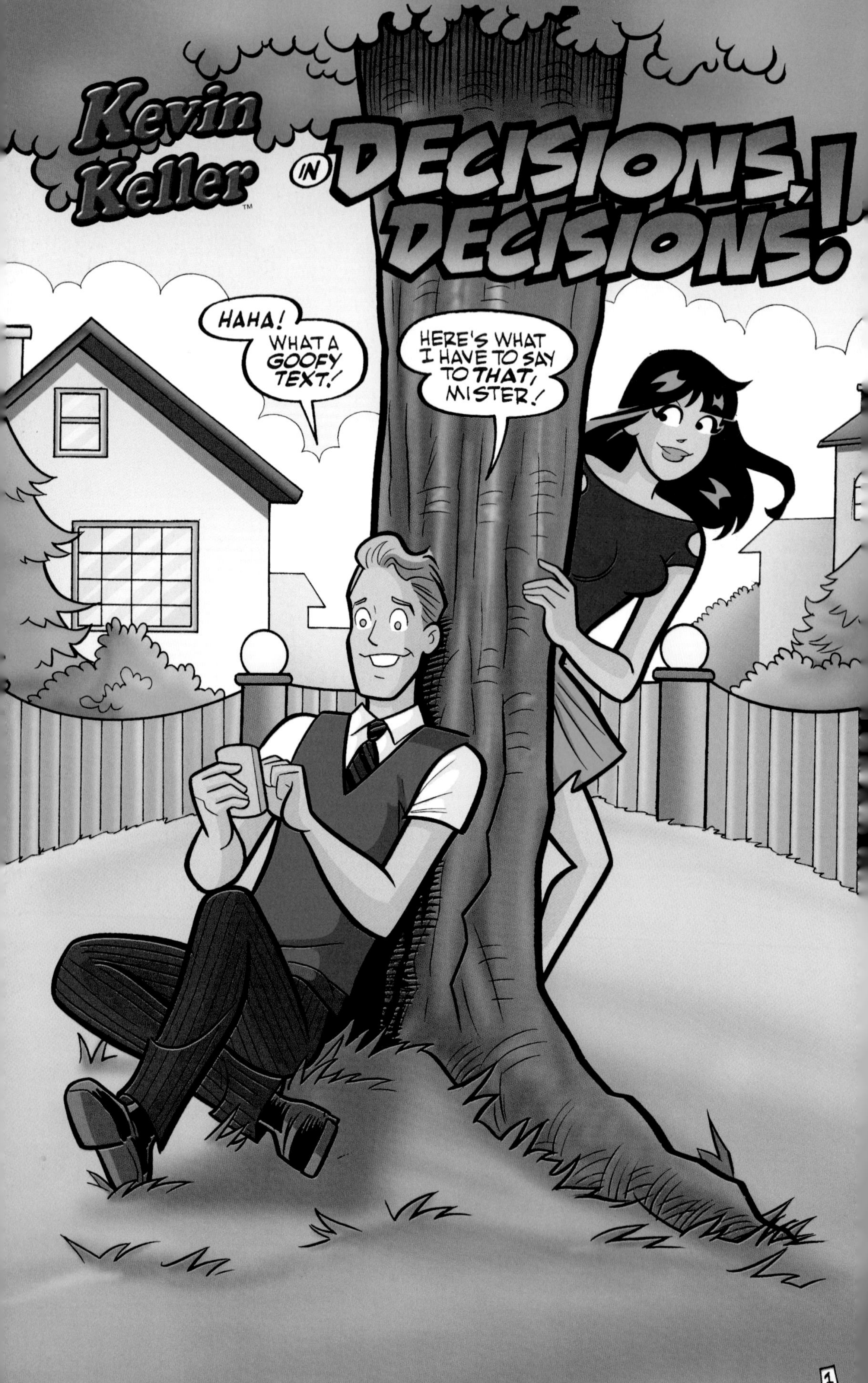

Kevin Keller™ IN DECISIONS, DECISIONS!
HAHA! WHAT A GOOFY TEXT!
HERE'S WHAT I HAVE TO SAY TO THAT, MISTER!

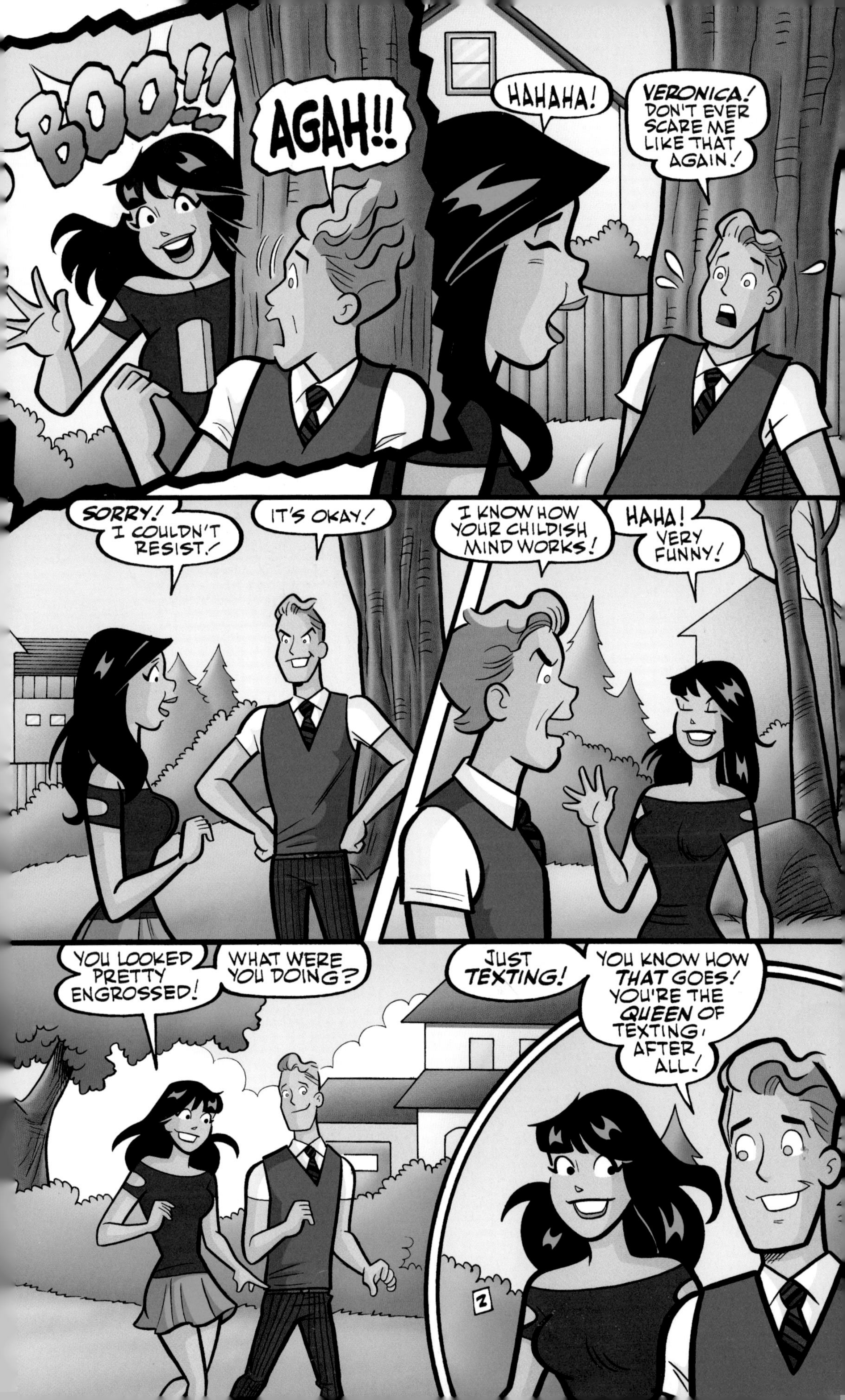
BOO!!
AGAH!!
HAHAHA!
VERONICA! DON'T EVER SCARE ME LIKE THAT AGAIN!
SORRY! I COULDN'T RESIST!
IT'S OKAY!
I KNOW HOW YOUR CHILDISH MIND WORKS!
HAHA! VERY FUNNY!
YOU LOOKED PRETTY ENGROSSED!
WHAT WERE YOU DOING?
JUST TEXTING!
YOU KNOW HOW THAT GOES! YOU'RE THE QUEEN OF TEXTING, AFTER ALL!
2

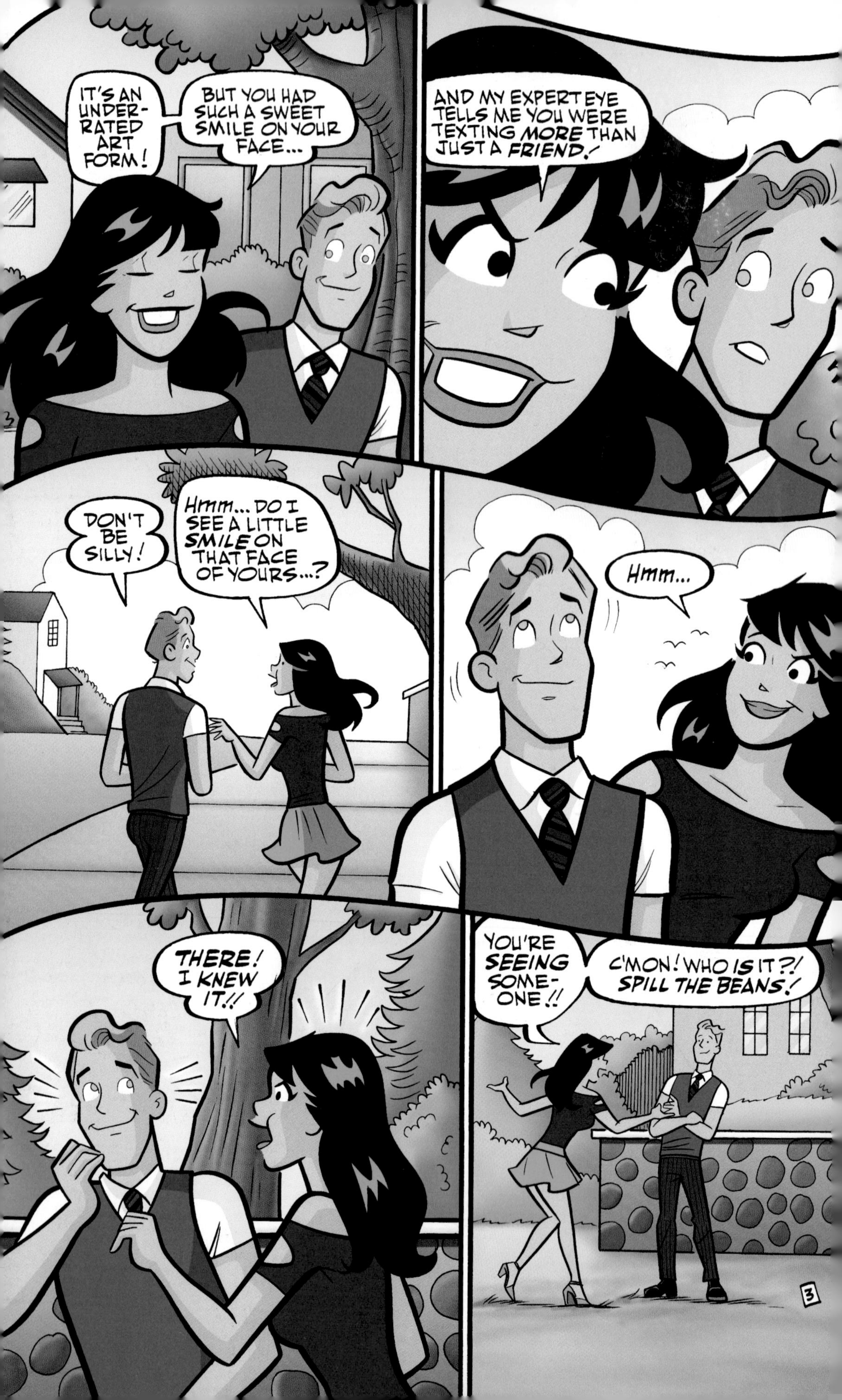
IT'S AN UNDER-RATED ART FORM!
BUT YOU HAD SUCH A SWEET SMILE ON YOUR FACE...
AND MY EXPERT EYE TELLS ME YOU WERE TEXTING MORE THAN JUST A FRIEND!
DON'T BE SILLY!
Hmm... DO I SEE A LITTLE SMILE ON THAT FACE OF YOURS...?
Hmm...
THERE! I KNEW IT!!
YOU'RE SEEING SOME-ONE!!
C'MON! WHO IS IT?! SPILL THE BEANS!
3

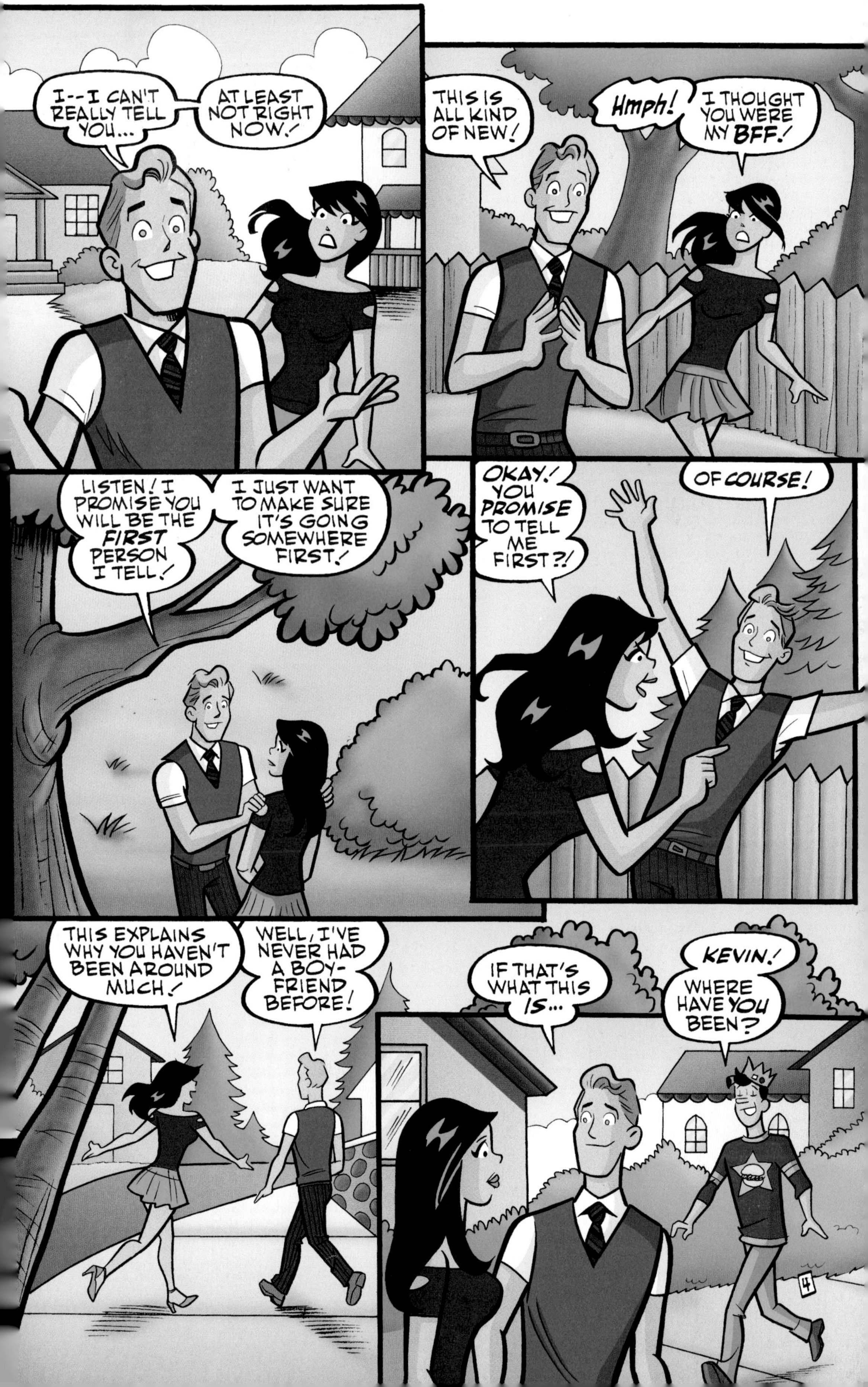
I--I CAN'T REALLY TELL YOU...
AT LEAST NOT RIGHT NOW!
THIS IS ALL KIND OF NEW!
Hmph!
I THOUGHT YOU WERE MY BFF!
LISTEN! I PROMISE YOU WILL BE THE FIRST PERSON I TELL!
I JUST WANT TO MAKE SURE IT'S GOING SOMEWHERE FIRST!
OKAY! YOU PROMISE TO TELL ME FIRST?!
OF COURSE!
THIS EXPLAINS WHY YOU HAVEN'T BEEN AROUND MUCH!
WELL, I'VE NEVER HAD A BOY-FRIEND BEFORE!
IF THAT'S WHAT THIS IS...
KEVIN!
WHERE HAVE YOU BEEN?
4

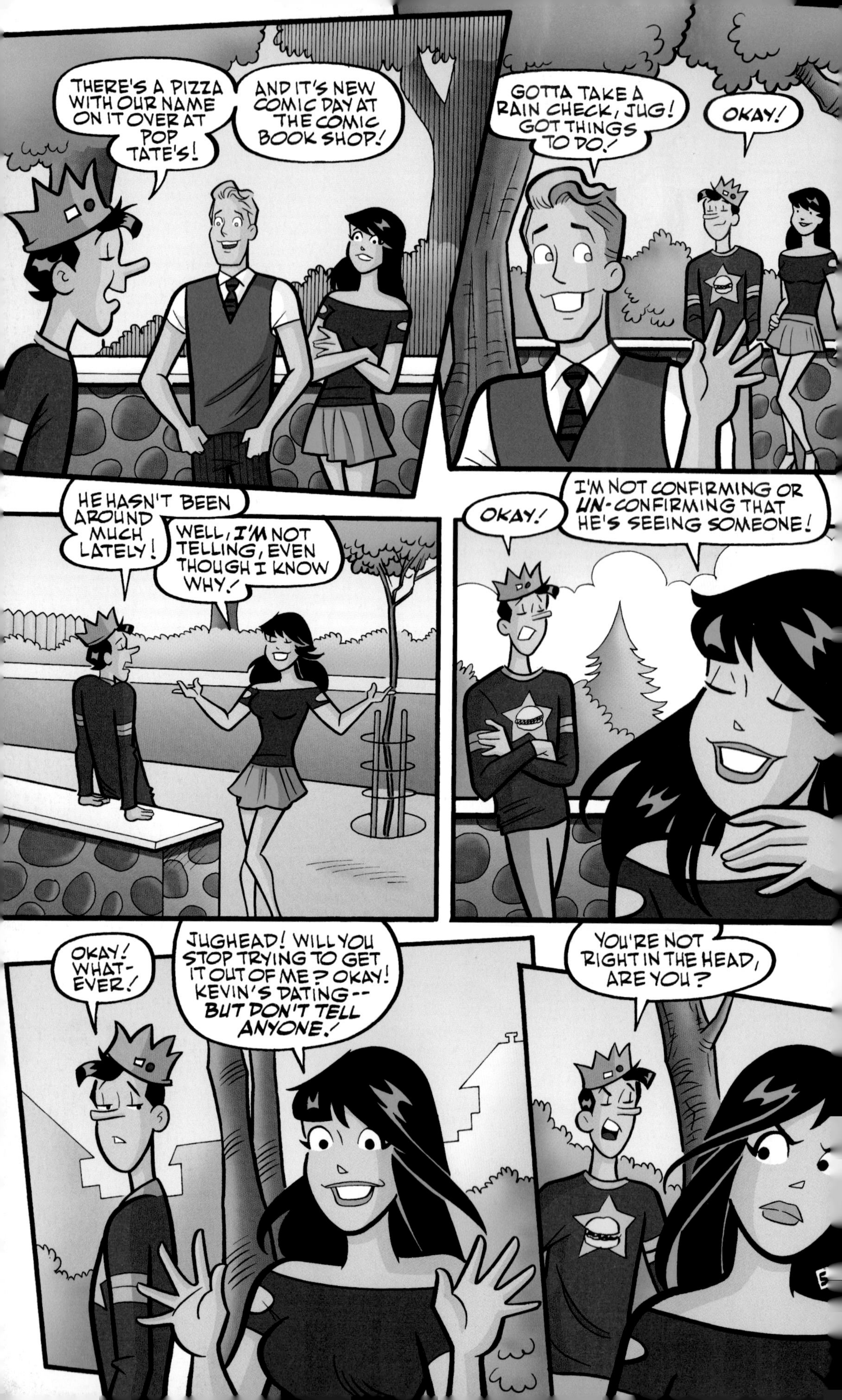

THERE'S A PIZZA WITH OUR NAME ON IT OVER AT POP TATE'S!
AND IT'S NEW COMIC DAY AT THE COMIC BOOK SHOP!
GOTTA TAKE A RAIN CHECK, JUG! GOT THINGS TO DO!
OKAY!
HE HASN'T BEEN AROUND MUCH LATELY!
WELL, I'M NOT TELLING, EVEN THOUGH I KNOW WHY!
OKAY!
I'M NOT CONFIRMING OR UN-CONFIRMING THAT HE'S SEEING SOMEONE!
OKAY! WHAT-EVER!
JUGHEAD! WILL YOU STOP TRYING TO GET IT OUT OF ME? OKAY! KEVIN'S DATING-- BUT DON'T TELL ANYONE!
YOU'RE NOT RIGHT IN THE HEAD, ARE YOU?
5

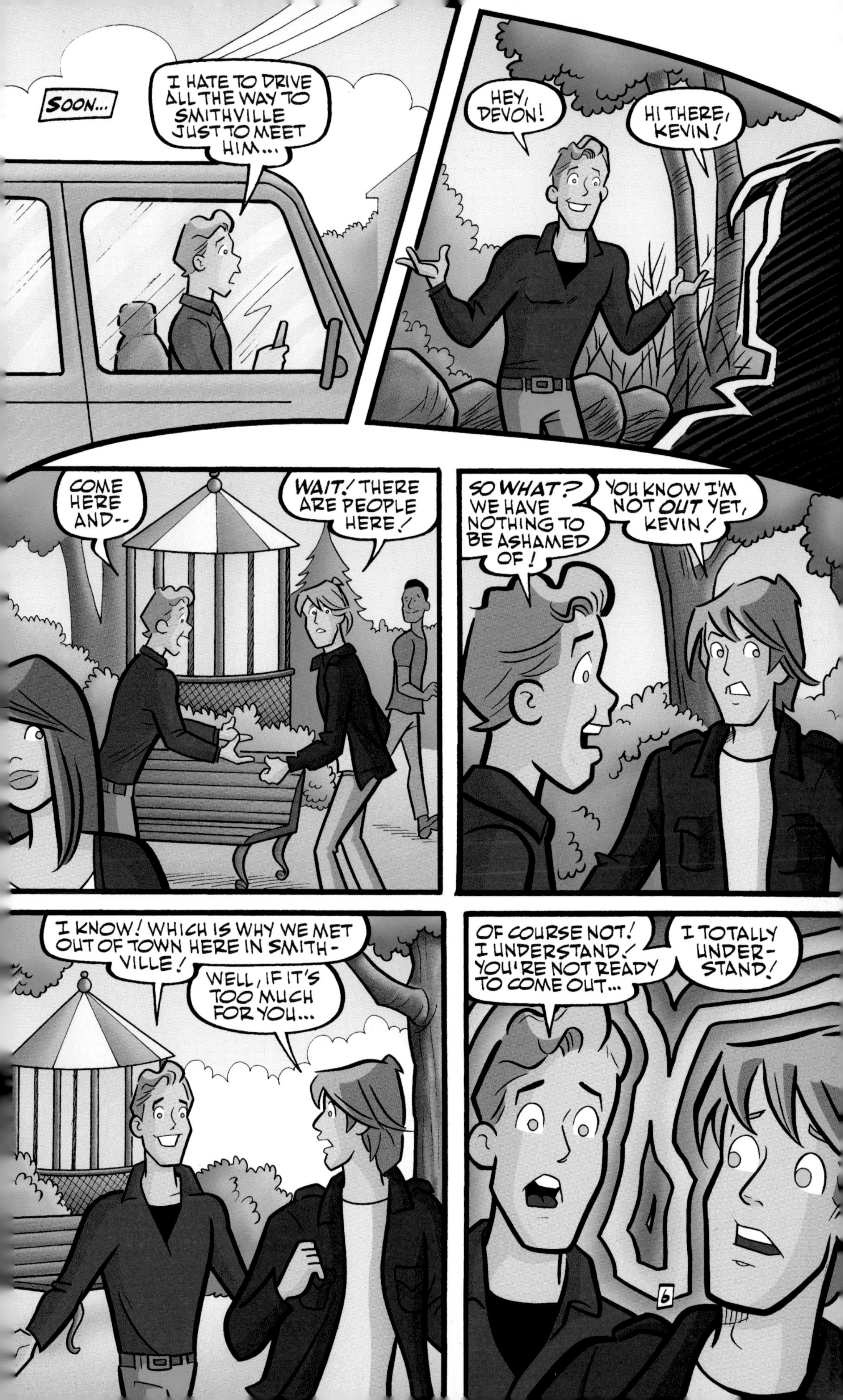
SOON...
I HATE TO DRIVE ALL THE WAY TO SMITHVILLE JUST TO MEET HIM...
HEY, DEVON!
HI THERE, KEVIN!
COME HERE AND--
WAIT! THERE ARE PEOPLE HERE!
SO WHAT? WE HAVE NOTHING TO BE ASHAMED OF!
YOU KNOW I'M NOT OUT YET, KEVIN!
I KNOW! WHICH IS WHY WE MET OUT OF TOWN HERE IN SMITH-VILLE!
WELL, IF IT'S TOO MUCH FOR YOU...
OF COURSE NOT! I UNDERSTAND! YOU'RE NOT READY TO COME OUT...
I TOTALLY UNDER-STAND!
6

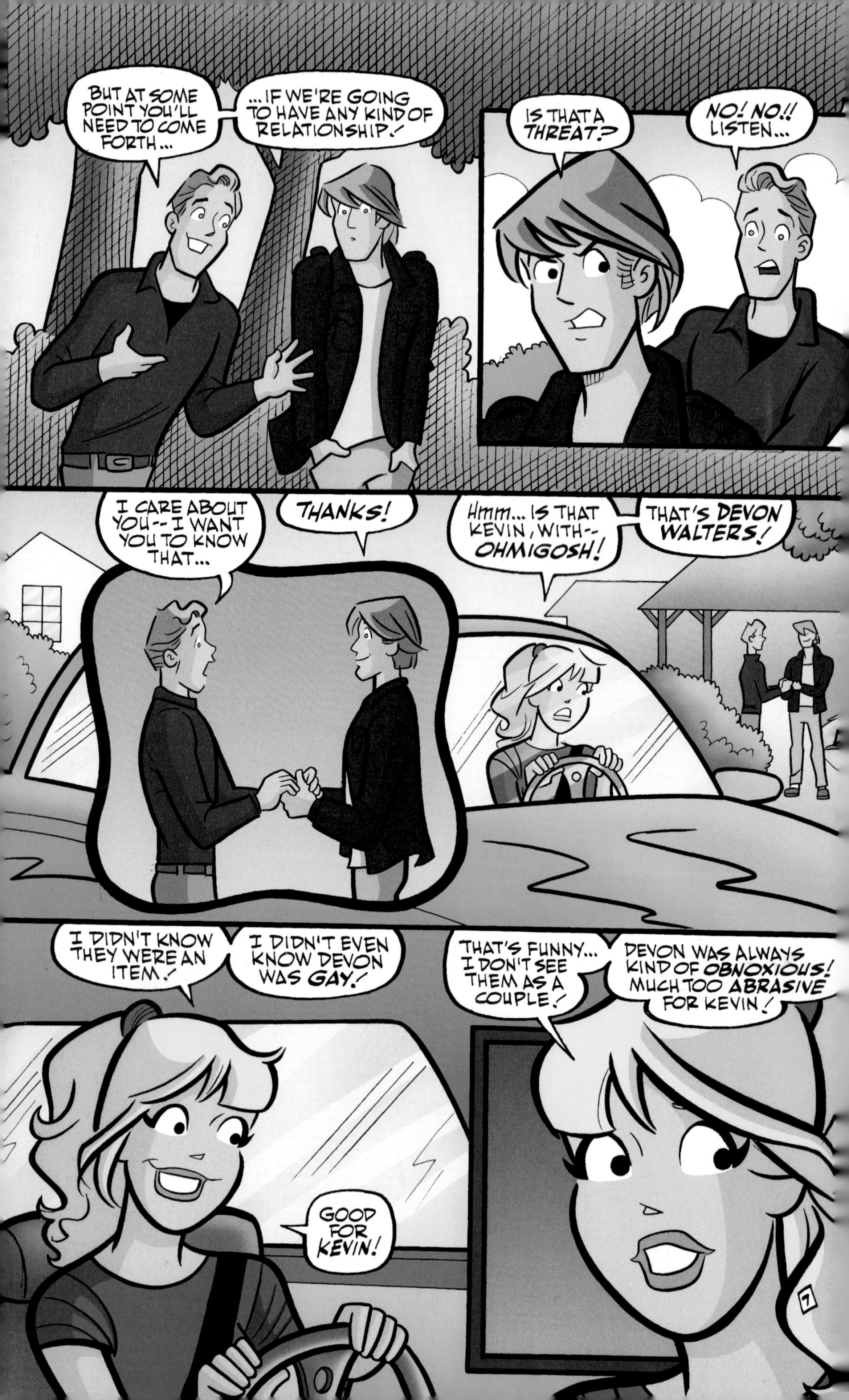
BUT AT SOME POINT YOU'LL NEED TO COME FORTH...
...IF WE'RE GOING TO HAVE ANY KIND OF RELATIONSHIP!
IS THAT A THREAT?
NO! NO!! LISTEN...
I CARE ABOUT YOU-- I WANT YOU TO KNOW THAT...
THANKS!
Hmm... IS THAT KEVIN, WITH-- OHMIGOSH!
THAT'S DEVON WALTERS!
I DIDN'T KNOW THEY WERE AN ITEM!
I DIDN'T EVEN KNOW DEVON WAS GAY!
GOOD FOR KEVIN!
THAT'S FUNNY... I DON'T SEE THEM AS A COUPLE!
DEVON WAS ALWAYS KIND OF OBNOXIOUS! MUCH TOO ABRASIVE FOR KEVIN!
7

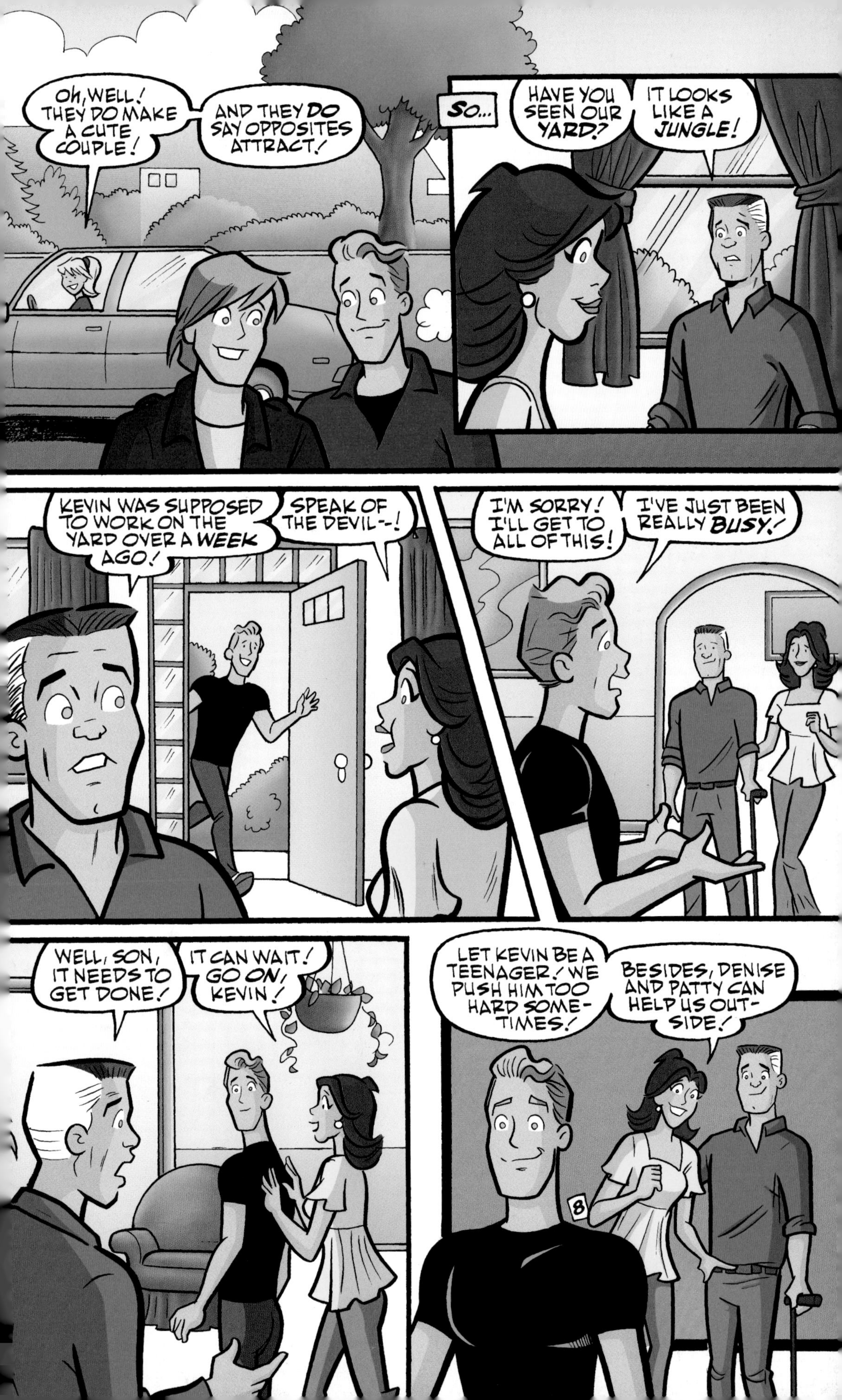

Oh, WELL! THEY DO MAKE A CUTE COUPLE!
AND THEY DO SAY OPPOSITES ATTRACT!
SO...
HAVE YOU SEEN OUR YARD?
IT LOOKS LIKE A JUNGLE!
KEVIN WAS SUPPOSED TO WORK ON THE YARD OVER A WEEK AGO!
SPEAK OF THE DEVIL--!
I'M SORRY! I'LL GET TO ALL OF THIS!
I'VE JUST BEEN REALLY BUSY!
WELL, SON, IT NEEDS TO GET DONE!
IT CAN WAIT! GO ON, KEVIN!
LET KEVIN BE A TEENAGER! WE PUSH HIM TOO HARD SOME-TIMES!
BESIDES, DENISE AND PATTY CAN HELP US OUT-SIDE!
8

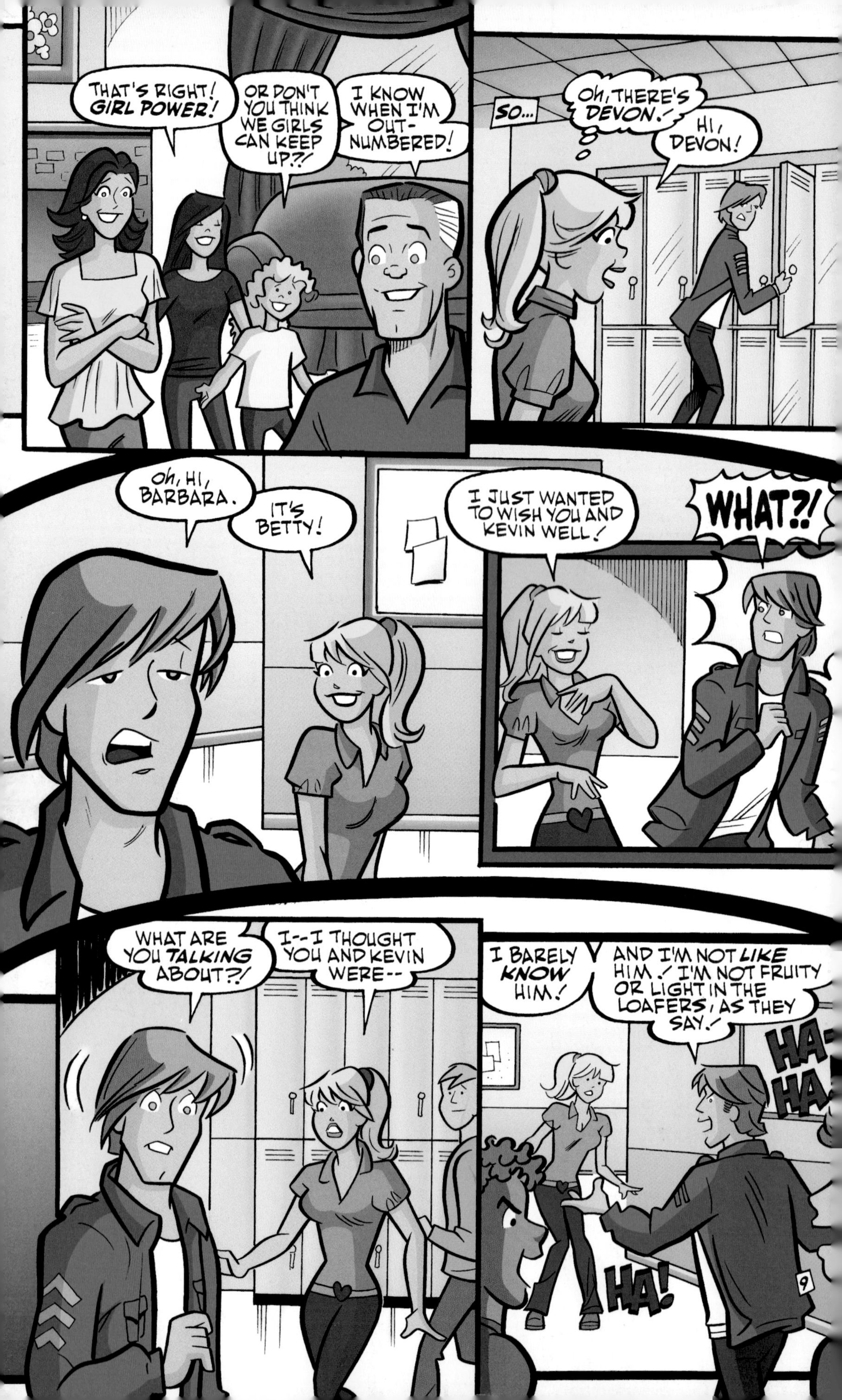

THAT'S RIGHT! GIRL POWER!
OR DON'T YOU THINK WE GIRLS CAN KEEP UP?!
I KNOW WHEN I'M OUT-NUMBERED!
SO...
Oh, THERE'S DEVON.!
HI, DEVON!
Oh, HI, BARBARA.
IT'S BETTY!
I JUST WANTED TO WISH YOU AND KEVIN WELL!
WHAT?!
WHAT ARE YOU TALKING ABOUT?!
I--I THOUGHT YOU AND KEVIN WERE--
I BARELY KNOW HIM!
AND I'M NOT LIKE HIM.! I'M NOT FRUITY OR LIGHT IN THE LOAFERS, AS THEY SAY.!
HA-HA!
HA!
9

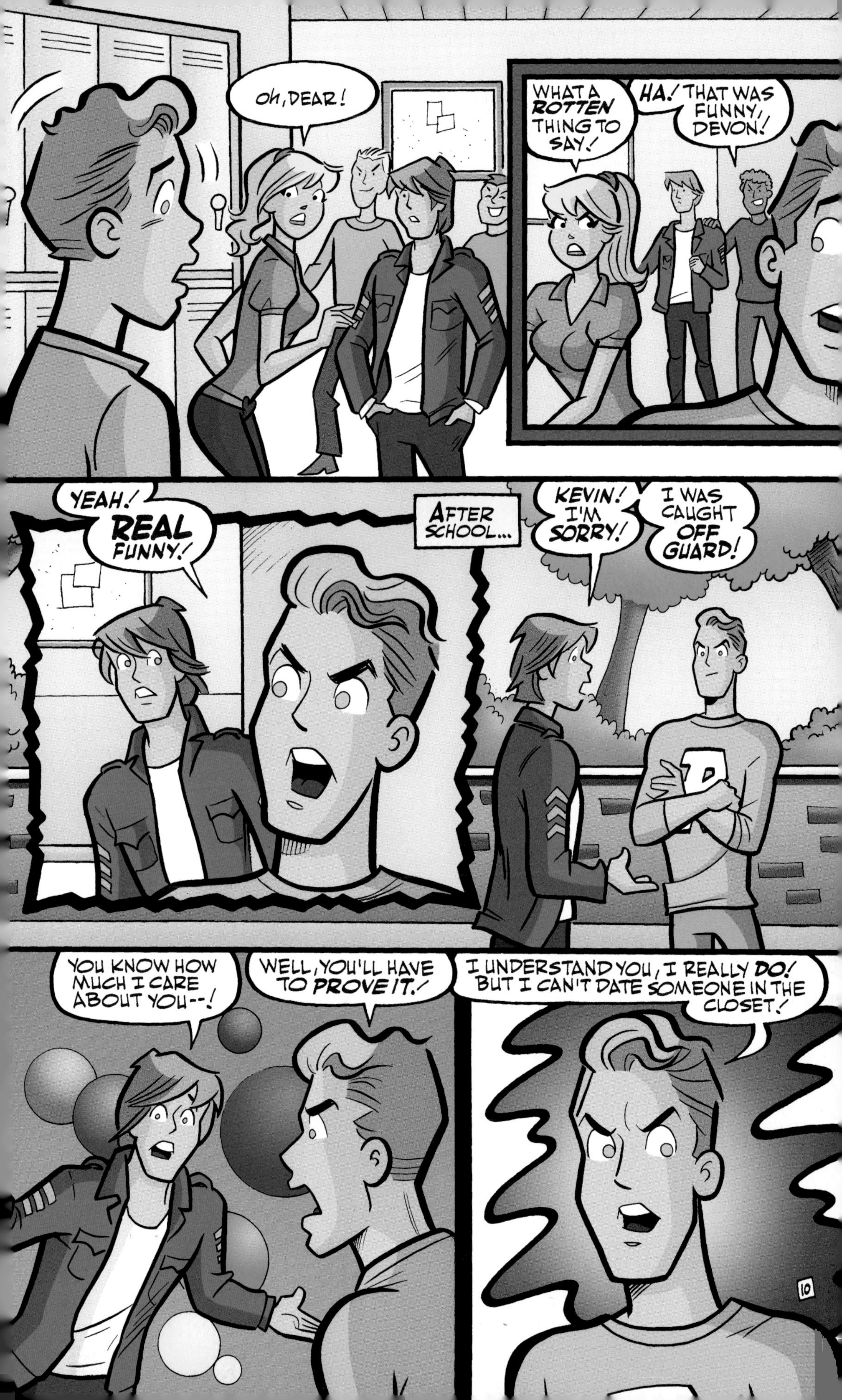

OH, DEAR!
WHAT A ROTTEN THING TO SAY!
HA! THAT WAS FUNNY, DEVON!
YEAH! REAL FUNNY!
AFTER SCHOOL...
KEVIN! I'M SORRY!
I WAS CAUGHT OFF GUARD!
YOU KNOW HOW MUCH I CARE ABOUT YOU--!
WELL, YOU'LL HAVE TO PROVE IT.!
I UNDERSTAND YOU, I REALLY DO! BUT I CAN'T DATE SOMEONE IN THE CLOSET!
10

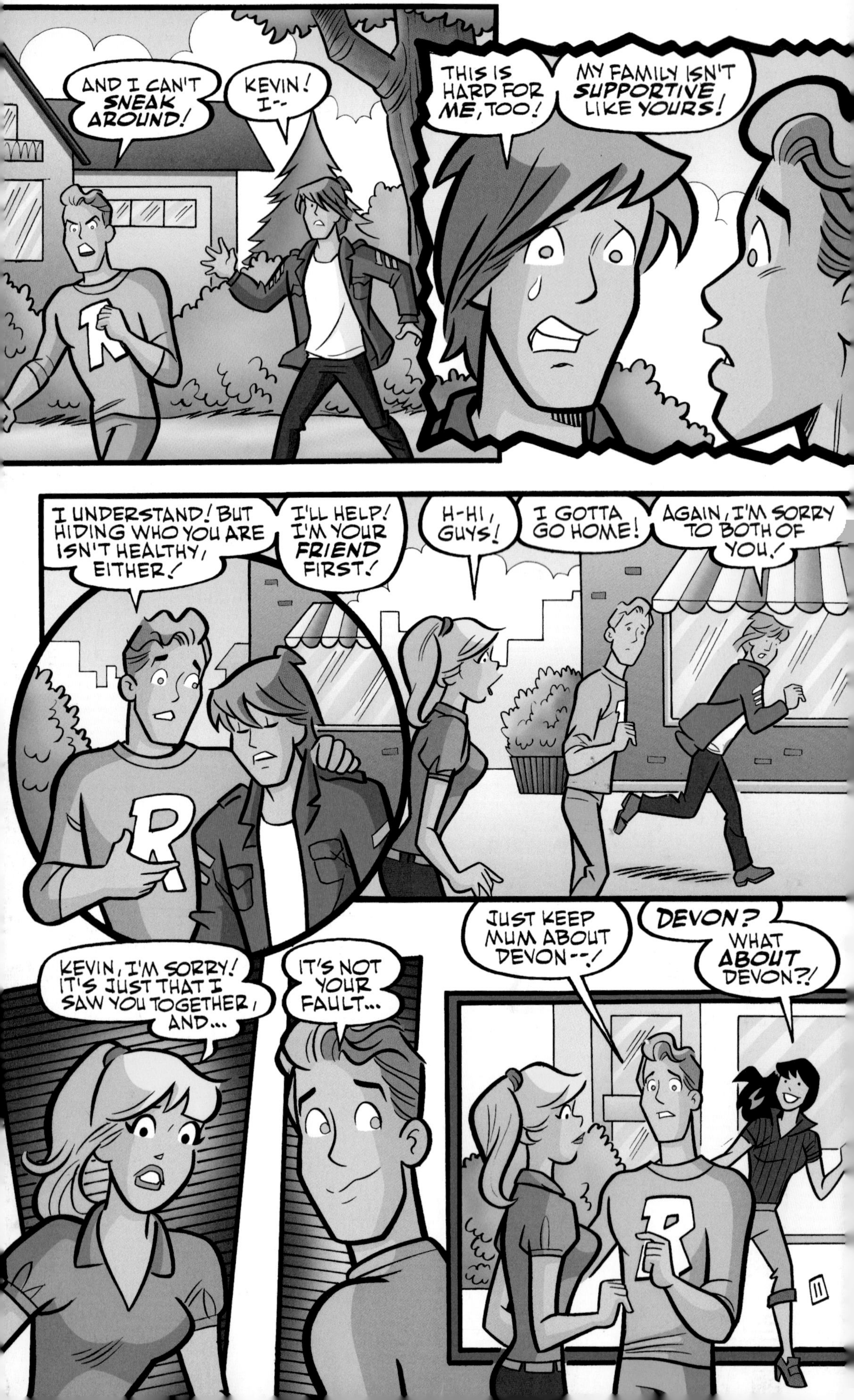
AND I CAN'T SNEAK AROUND!
KEVIN! I--
THIS IS HARD FOR ME, TOO!
MY FAMILY ISN'T SUPPORTIVE LIKE YOURS!
I UNDERSTAND! BUT HIDING WHO YOU ARE ISN'T HEALTHY, EITHER!
I'LL HELP! I'M YOUR FRIEND FIRST!
H-HI, GUYS!
I GOTTA GO HOME!
AGAIN, I'M SORRY TO BOTH OF YOU!
KEVIN, I'M SORRY! IT'S JUST THAT I SAW YOU TOGETHER, AND...
IT'S NOT YOUR FAULT...
JUST KEEP MUM ABOUT DEVON--!
DEVON? WHAT ABOUT DEVON?!
11

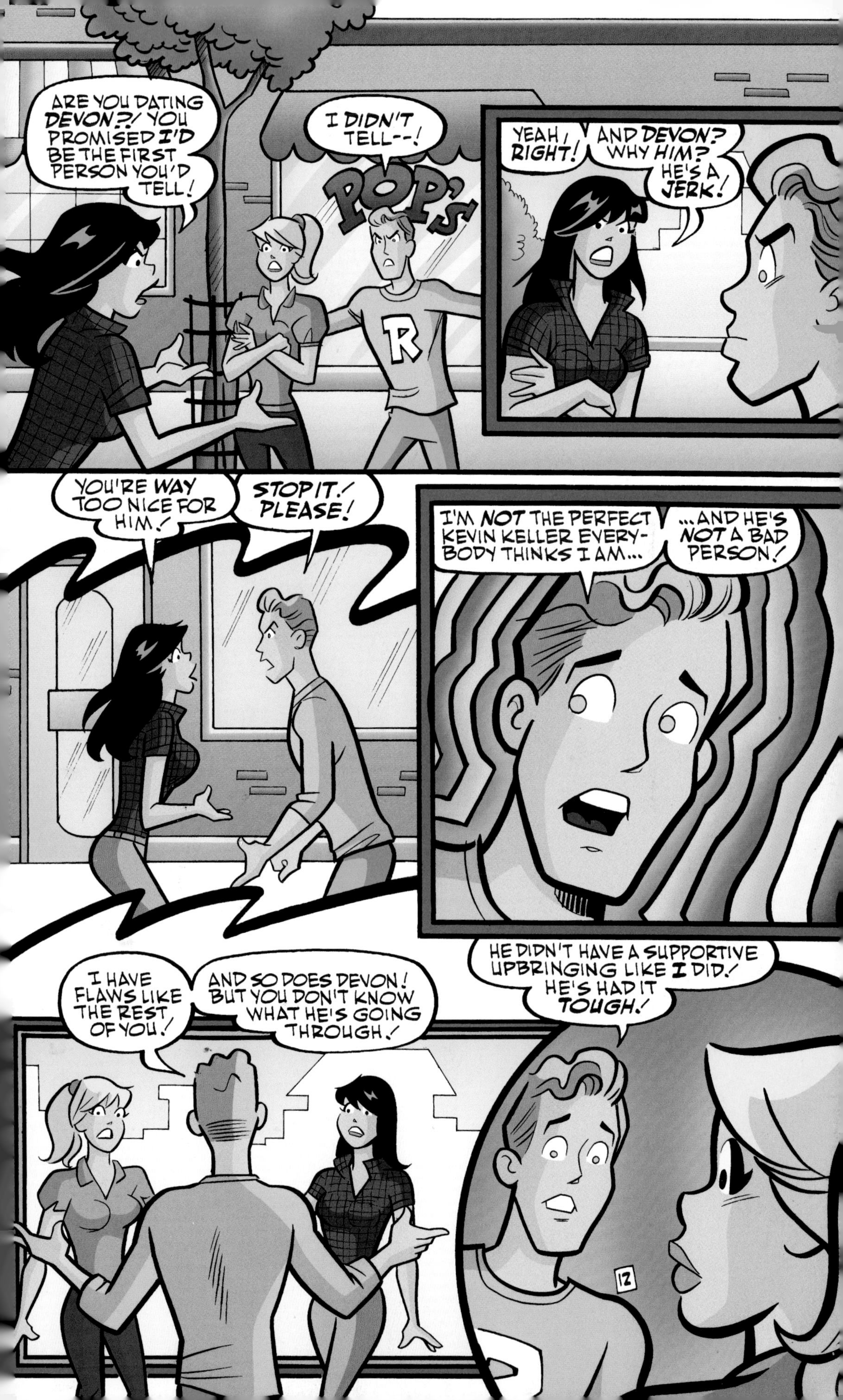
ARE YOU DATING DEVON?! YOU PROMISED I'D BE THE FIRST PERSON YOU'D TELL!
I DIDN'T TELL--!
POP'S
YEAH, RIGHT!
AND DEVON? WHY HIM? HE'S A JERK!
YOU'RE WAY TOO NICE FOR HIM!
STOP IT! PLEASE!
I'M NOT THE PERFECT KEVIN KELLER EVERYBODY THINKS I AM...
...AND HE'S NOT A BAD PERSON!
I HAVE FLAWS LIKE THE REST OF YOU!
AND SO DOES DEVON! BUT YOU DON'T KNOW WHAT HE'S GOING THROUGH!
HE DIDN'T HAVE A SUPPORTIVE UPBRINGING LIKE I DID! HE'S HAD IT TOUGH!
12

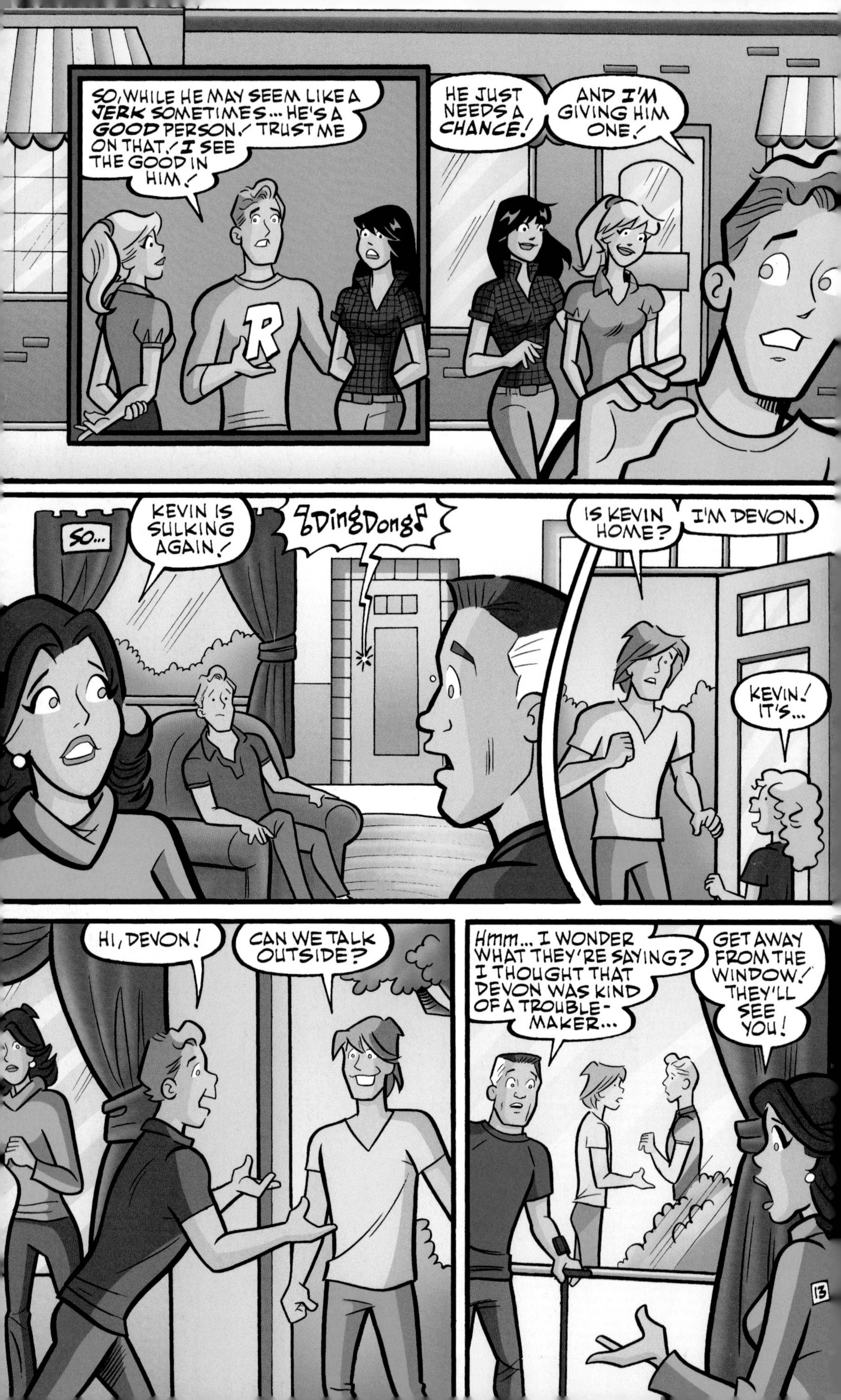
SO, WHILE HE MAY SEEM LIKE A JERK SOMETIMES... HE'S A GOOD PERSON! TRUST ME ON THAT! I SEE THE GOOD IN HIM!
HE JUST NEEDS A CHANCE!
AND I'M GIVING HIM ONE!
SO...
KEVIN IS SULKING AGAIN!
DING DONG
IS KEVIN HOME?
I'M DEVON.
KEVIN! IT'S...
HI, DEVON!
CAN WE TALK OUTSIDE?
Hmm... I WONDER WHAT THEY'RE SAYING? I THOUGHT THAT DEVON WAS KIND OF A TROUBLE-MAKER...
GET AWAY FROM THE WINDOW! THEY'LL SEE YOU!
13

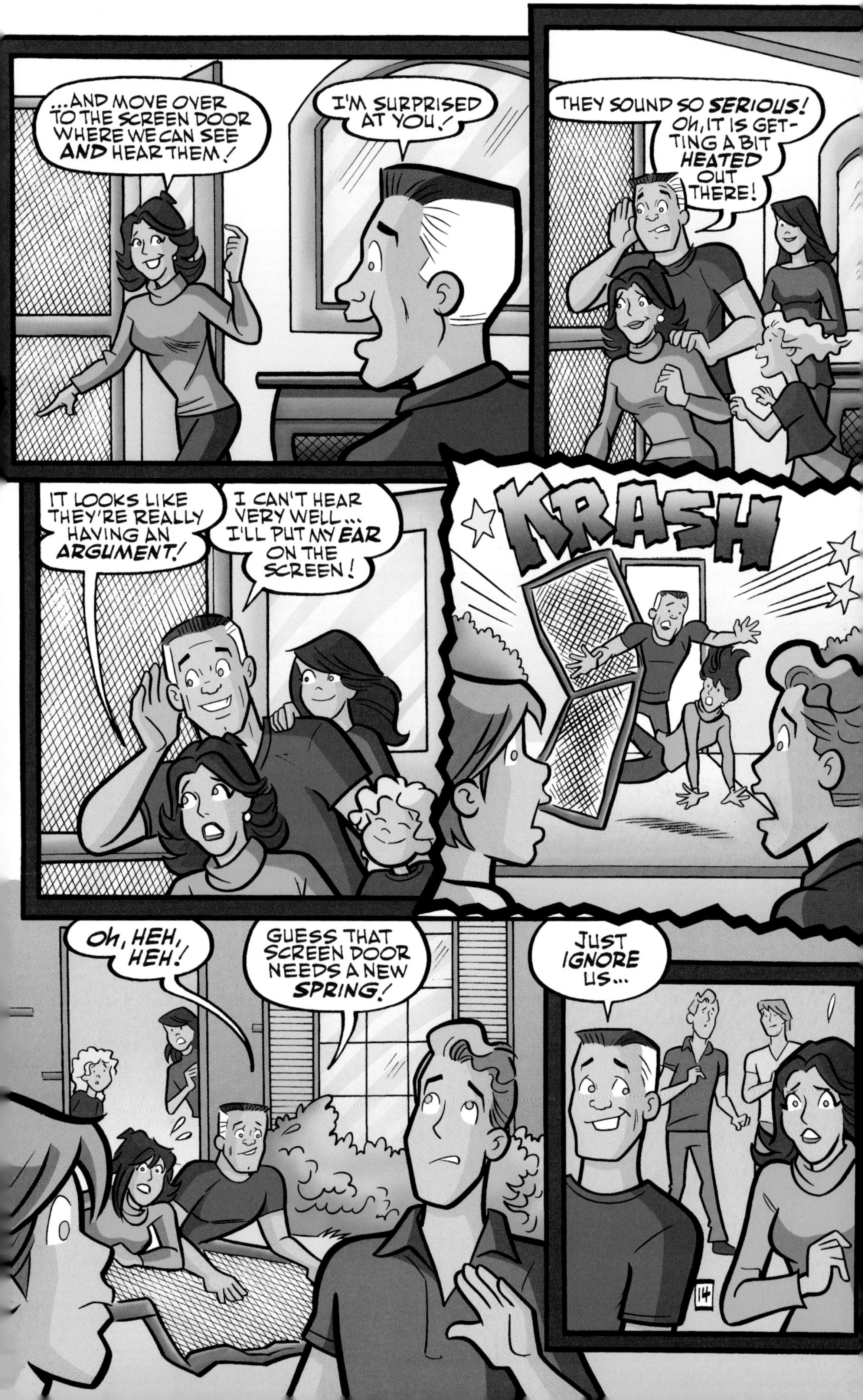

...AND MOVE OVER TO THE SCREEN DOOR WHERE WE CAN SEE AND HEAR THEM!
I'M SURPRISED AT YOU!
THEY SOUND SO SERIOUS!
Oh, IT IS GETTING A BIT HEATED OUT THERE!
IT LOOKS LIKE THEY'RE REALLY HAVING AN ARGUMENT!
I CAN'T HEAR VERY WELL... I'LL PUT MY EAR ON THE SCREEN!
KRASH
Oh, HEH, HEH!
GUESS THAT SCREEN DOOR NEEDS A NEW SPRING!
JUST IGNORE US...
14

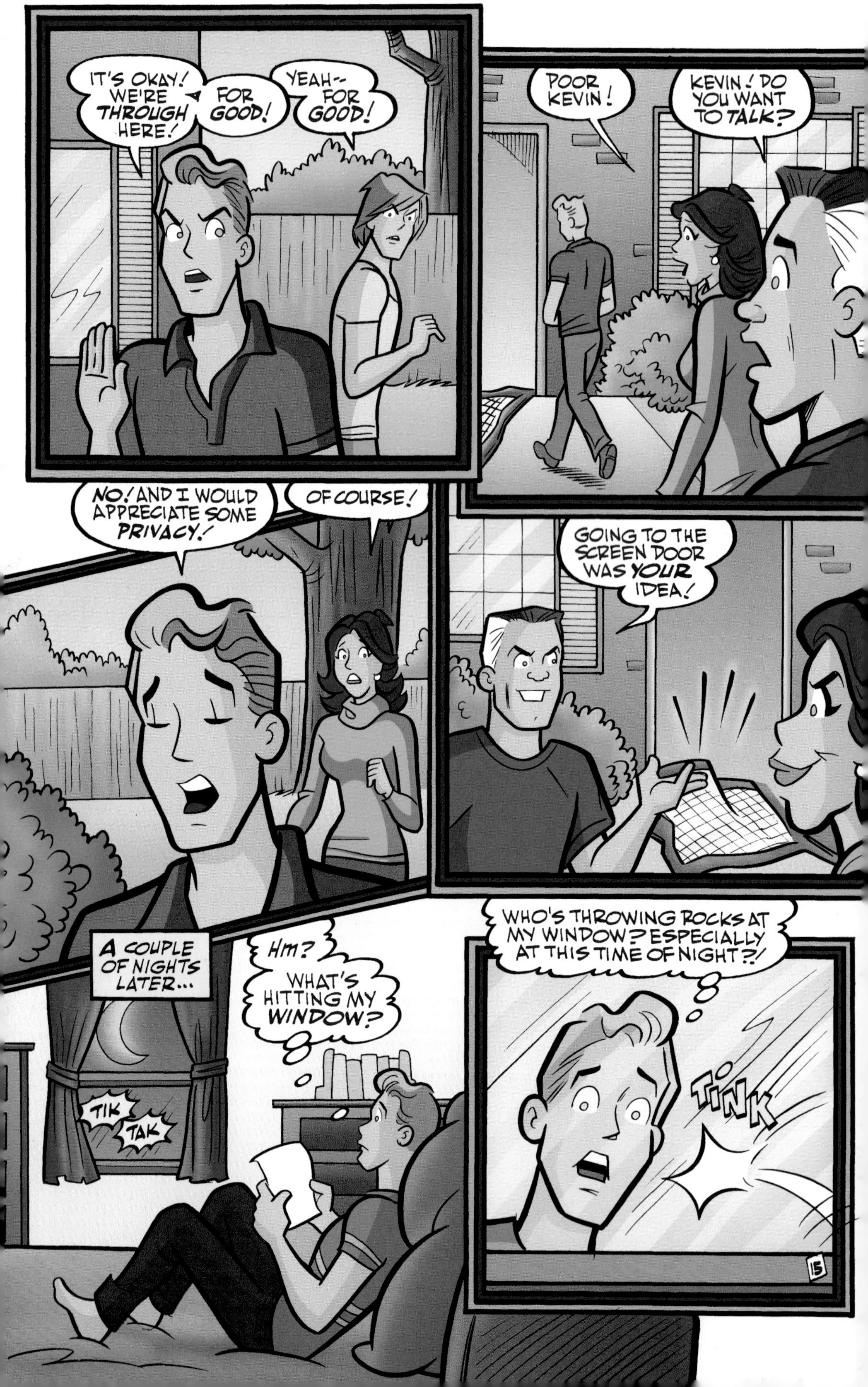
IT'S OKAY! WE'RE THROUGH HERE!
FOR GOOD!
YEAH-- FOR GOOD!
POOR KEVIN!
KEVIN! DO YOU WANT TO TALK?
NO! AND I WOULD APPRECIATE SOME PRIVACY!
OF COURSE!
GOING TO THE SCREEN DOOR WAS YOUR IDEA!
A COUPLE OF NIGHTS LATER...
Hm? WHAT'S HITTING MY WINDOW?
TIK
TAK
WHO'S THROWING ROCKS AT MY WINDOW? ESPECIALLY AT THIS TIME OF NIGHT?!
TINK
15

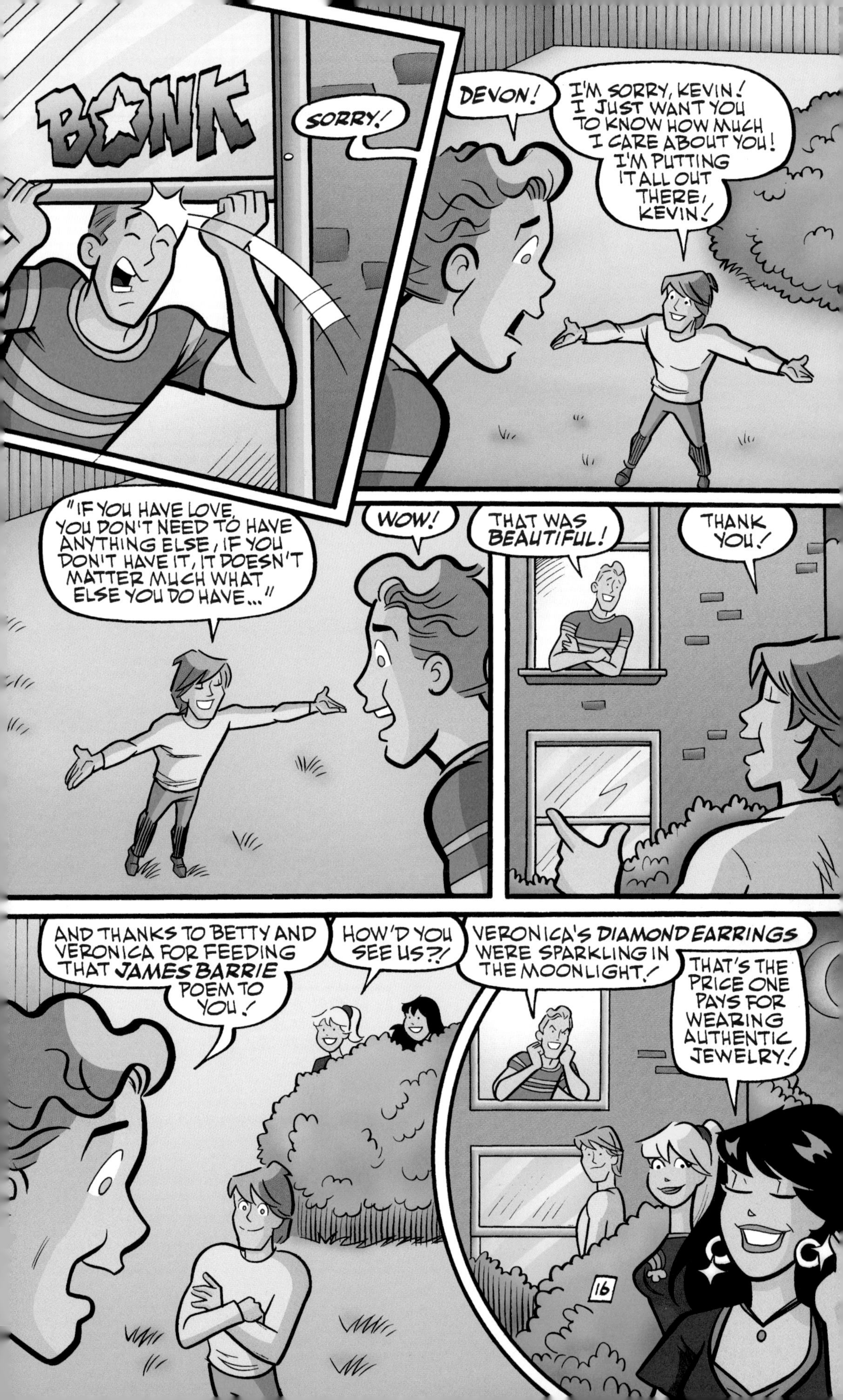
BONK
SORRY!
DEVON!
I'M SORRY, KEVIN! I JUST WANT YOU TO KNOW HOW MUCH I CARE ABOUT YOU! I'M PUTTING IT ALL OUT THERE, KEVIN!
"IF YOU HAVE LOVE, YOU DON'T NEED TO HAVE ANYTHING ELSE, IF YOU DON'T HAVE IT, IT DOESN'T MATTER MUCH WHAT ELSE YOU DO HAVE..."
WOW!
THAT WAS BEAUTIFUL!
THANK YOU!
AND THANKS TO BETTY AND VERONICA FOR FEEDING THAT JAMES BARRIE POEM TO YOU!
HOW'D YOU SEE US?!
VERONICA'S DIAMOND EARRINGS WERE SPARKLING IN THE MOONLIGHT!
THAT'S THE PRICE ONE PAYS FOR WEARING AUTHENTIC JEWELRY!
16

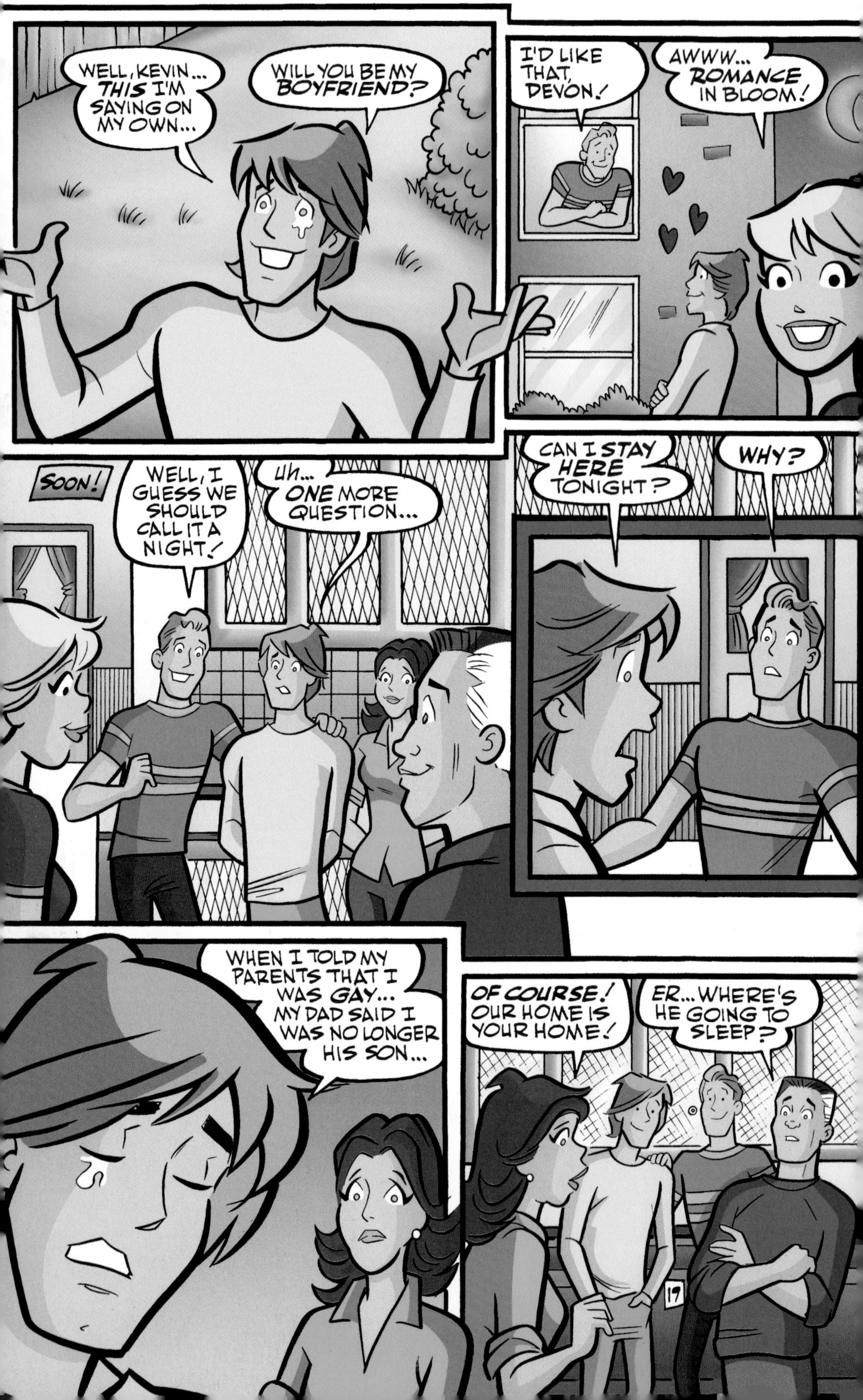

WELL, KEVIN... THIS I'M SAYING ON MY OWN...
WILL YOU BE MY BOYFRIEND?
I'D LIKE THAT, DEVON!
AWWW... ROMANCE IN BLOOM!
SOON!
WELL, I GUESS WE SHOULD CALL IT A NIGHT!
UH... ONE MORE QUESTION...
CAN I STAY HERE TONIGHT?
WHY?
WHEN I TOLD MY PARENTS THAT I WAS GAY... MY DAD SAID I WAS NO LONGER HIS SON...
OF COURSE! OUR HOME IS YOUR HOME!
ER... WHERE'S HE GOING TO SLEEP?

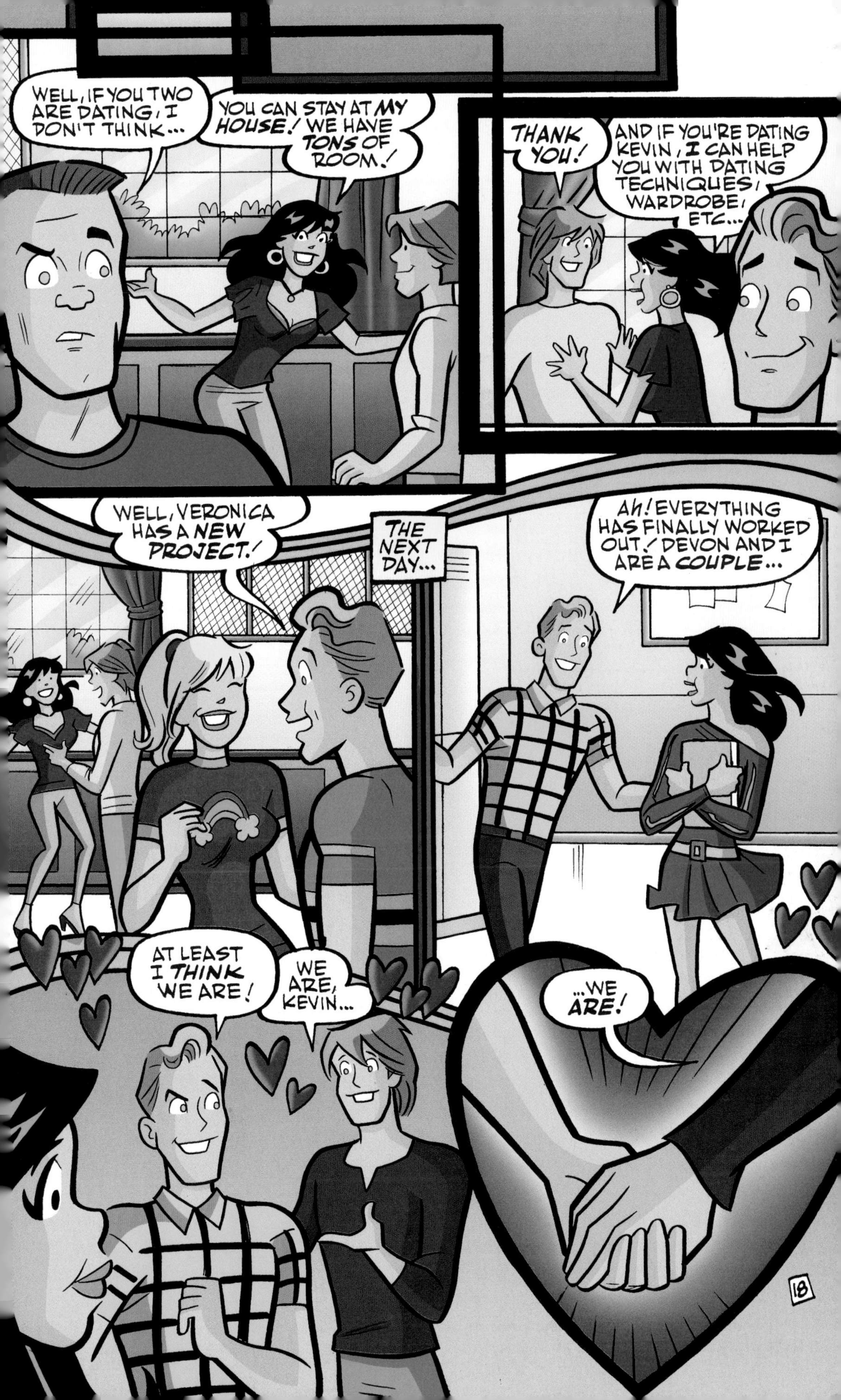
WELL, IF YOU TWO ARE DATING, I DON'T THINK...
YOU CAN STAY AT MY HOUSE! WE HAVE TONS OF ROOM!
THANK YOU!
AND IF YOU'RE DATING KEVIN, I CAN HELP YOU WITH DATING TECHNIQUES, WARDROBE, ETC...
WELL, VERONICA HAS A NEW PROJECT!
THE NEXT DAY...
AH! EVERYTHING HAS FINALLY WORKED OUT! DEVON AND I ARE A COUPLE...
AT LEAST I THINK WE ARE!
WE ARE, KEVIN...
...WE ARE!
18

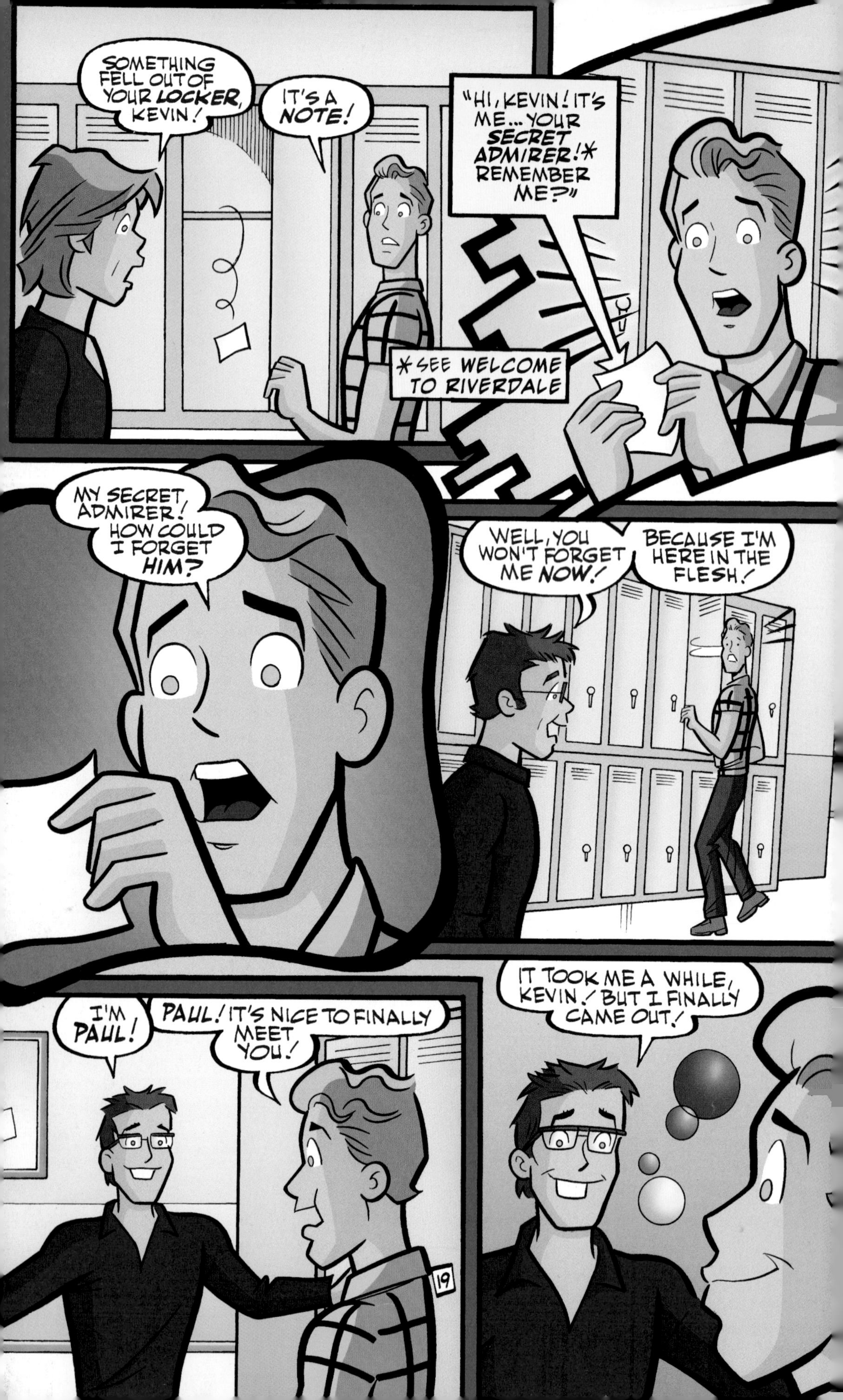
SOMETHING FELL OUT OF YOUR LOCKER, KEVIN!
IT'S A NOTE!
"HI, KEVIN! IT'S ME... YOUR SECRET ADMIRER!* REMEMBER ME?"
*SEE WELCOME TO RIVERDALE
MY SECRET ADMIRER! HOW COULD I FORGET HIM?
WELL, YOU WON'T FORGET ME NOW!
BECAUSE I'M HERE IN THE FLESH!
I'M PAUL!
PAUL! IT'S NICE TO FINALLY MEET YOU!
IT TOOK ME A WHILE, KEVIN! BUT I FINALLY CAME OUT!
19

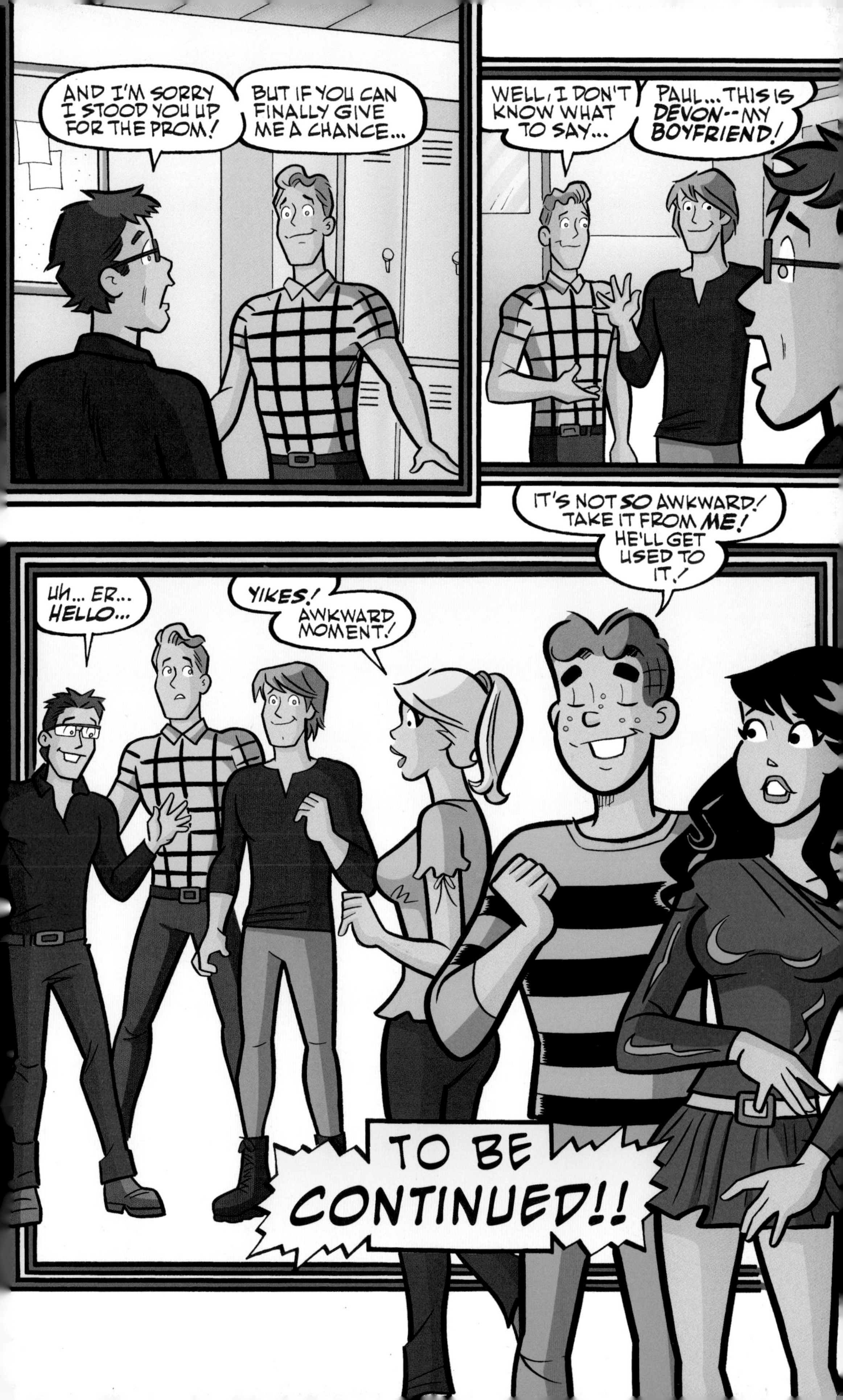

AND I'M SORRY I STOOD YOU UP FOR THE PROM!
BUT IF YOU CAN FINALLY GIVE ME A CHANCE...
WELL, I DON'T KNOW WHAT TO SAY...
PAUL... THIS IS DEVON--MY BOYFRIEND!
UH... ER... HELLO...
YIKES! AWKWARD MOMENT!
IT'S NOT SO AWKWARD! TAKE IT FROM ME! HE'LL GET USED TO IT!
TO BE CONTINUED!!

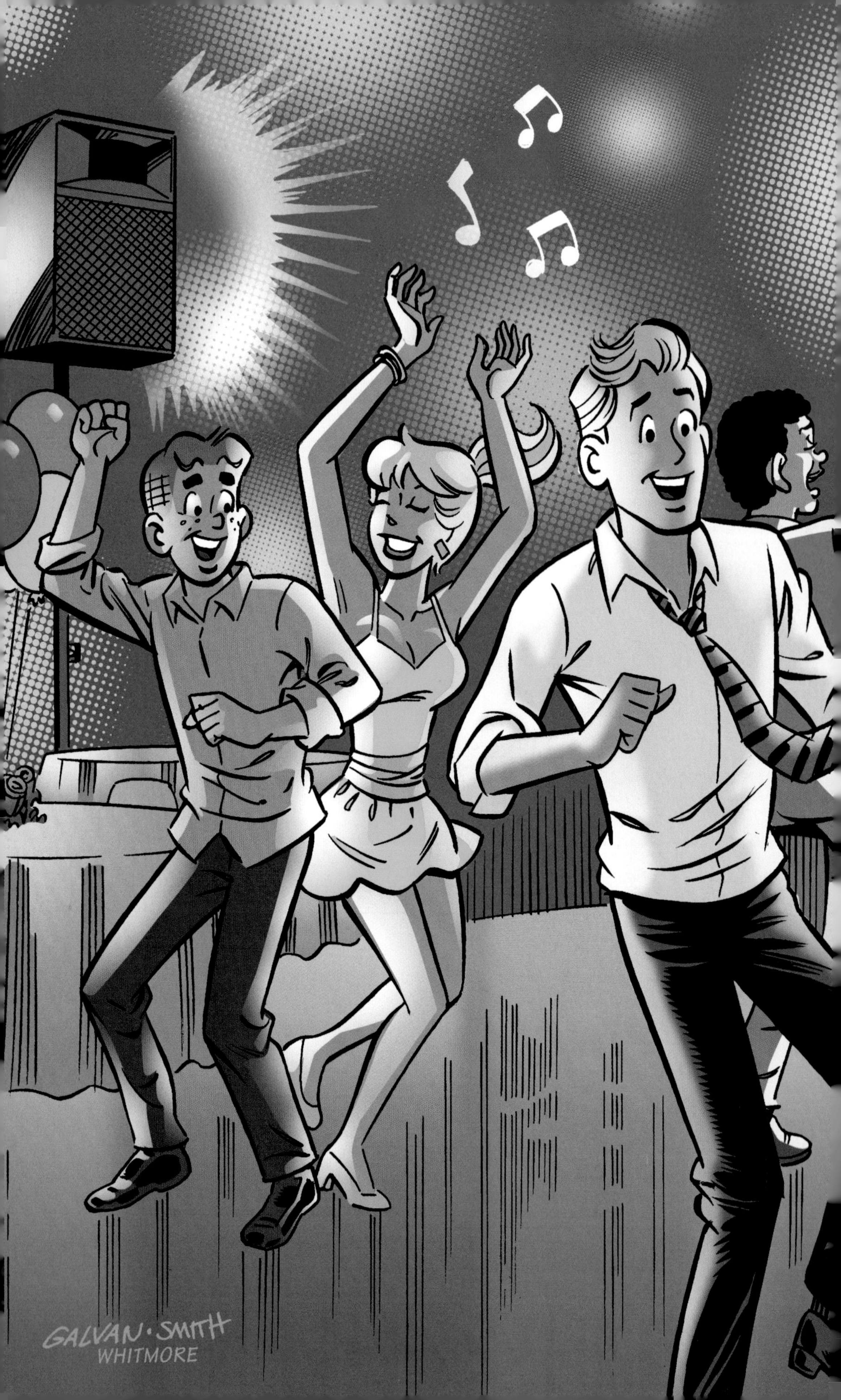
GALVAN • SMITH
WHITMORE

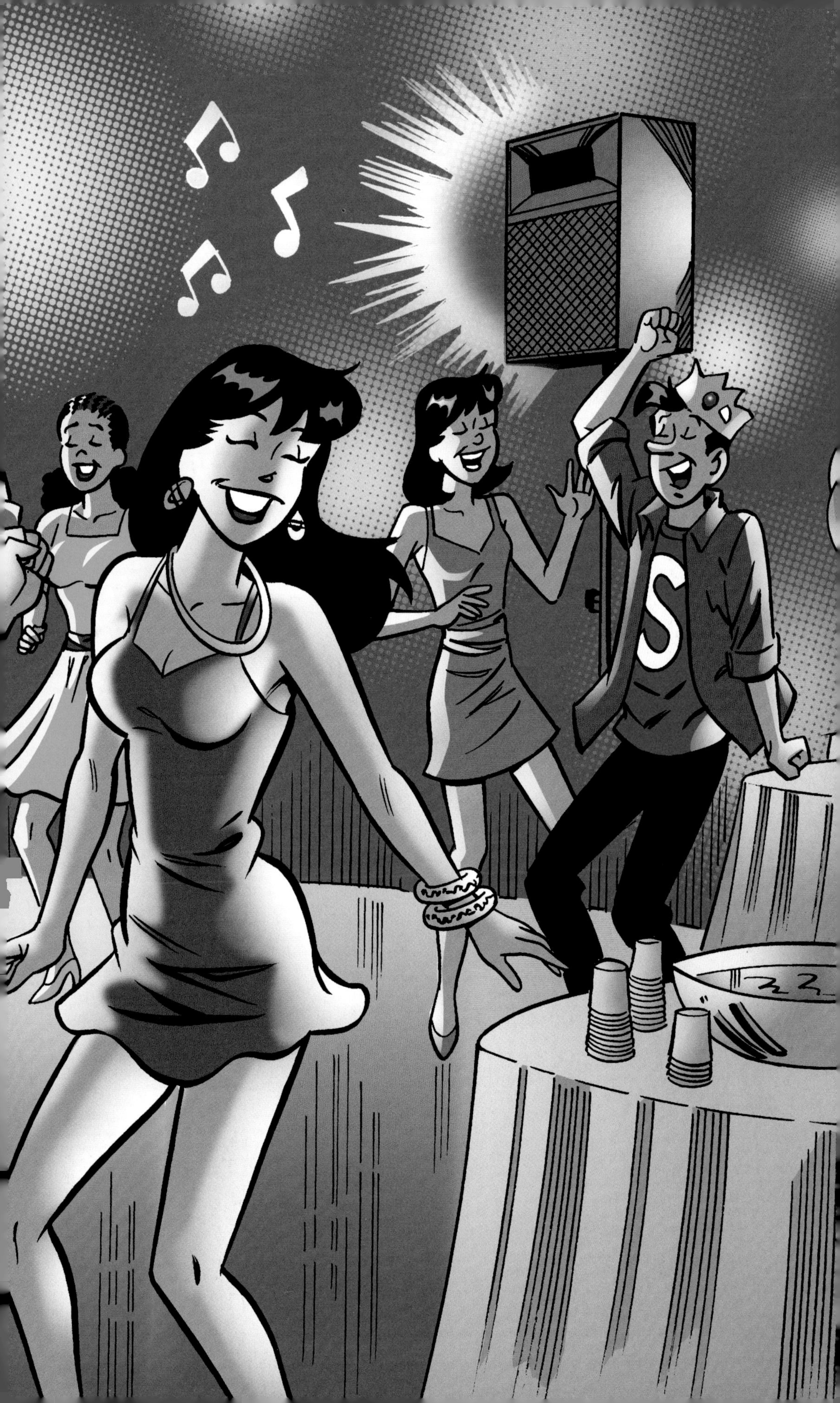

Chapter 4

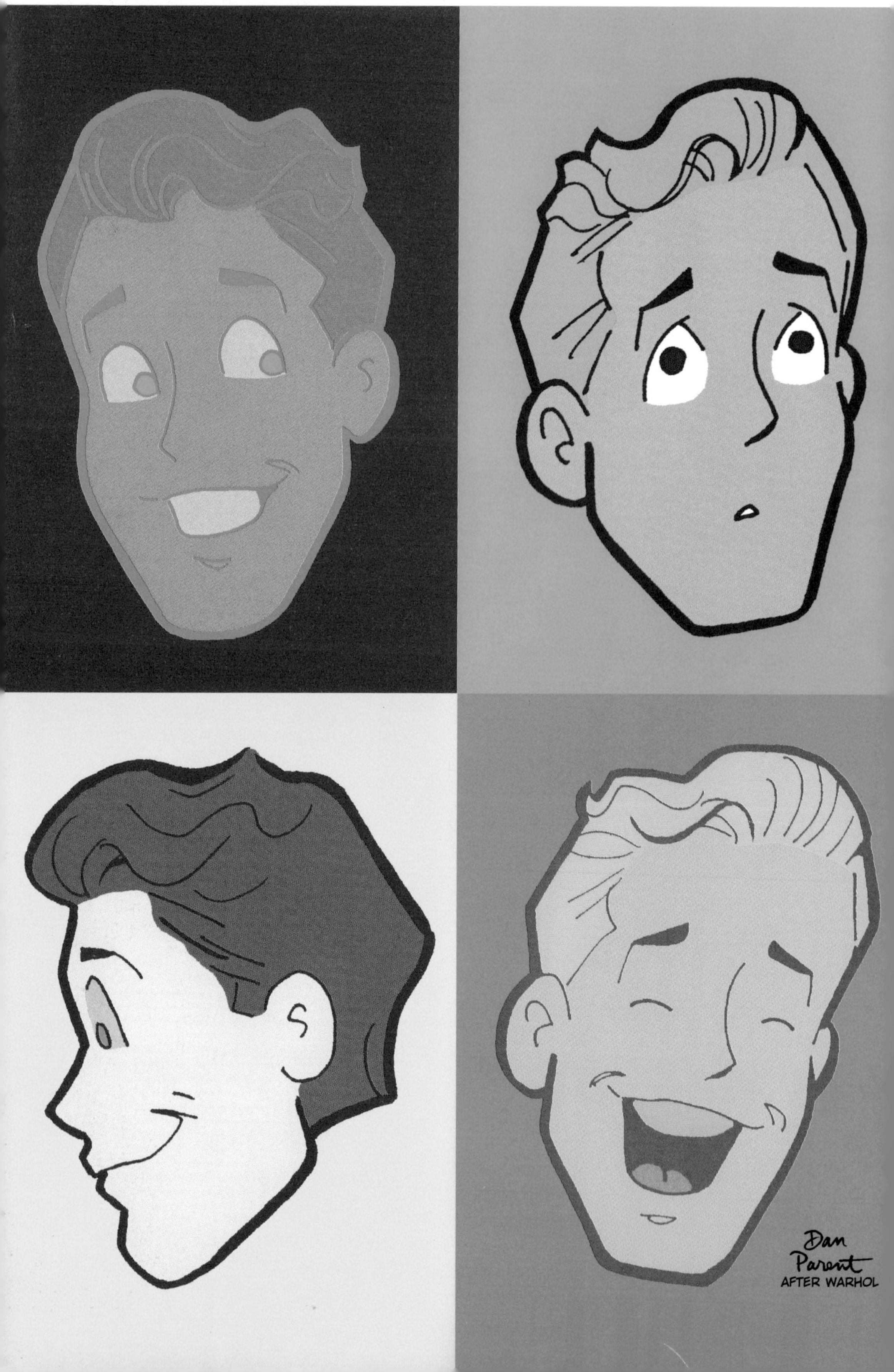
Dan Parent
AFTER WARHOL

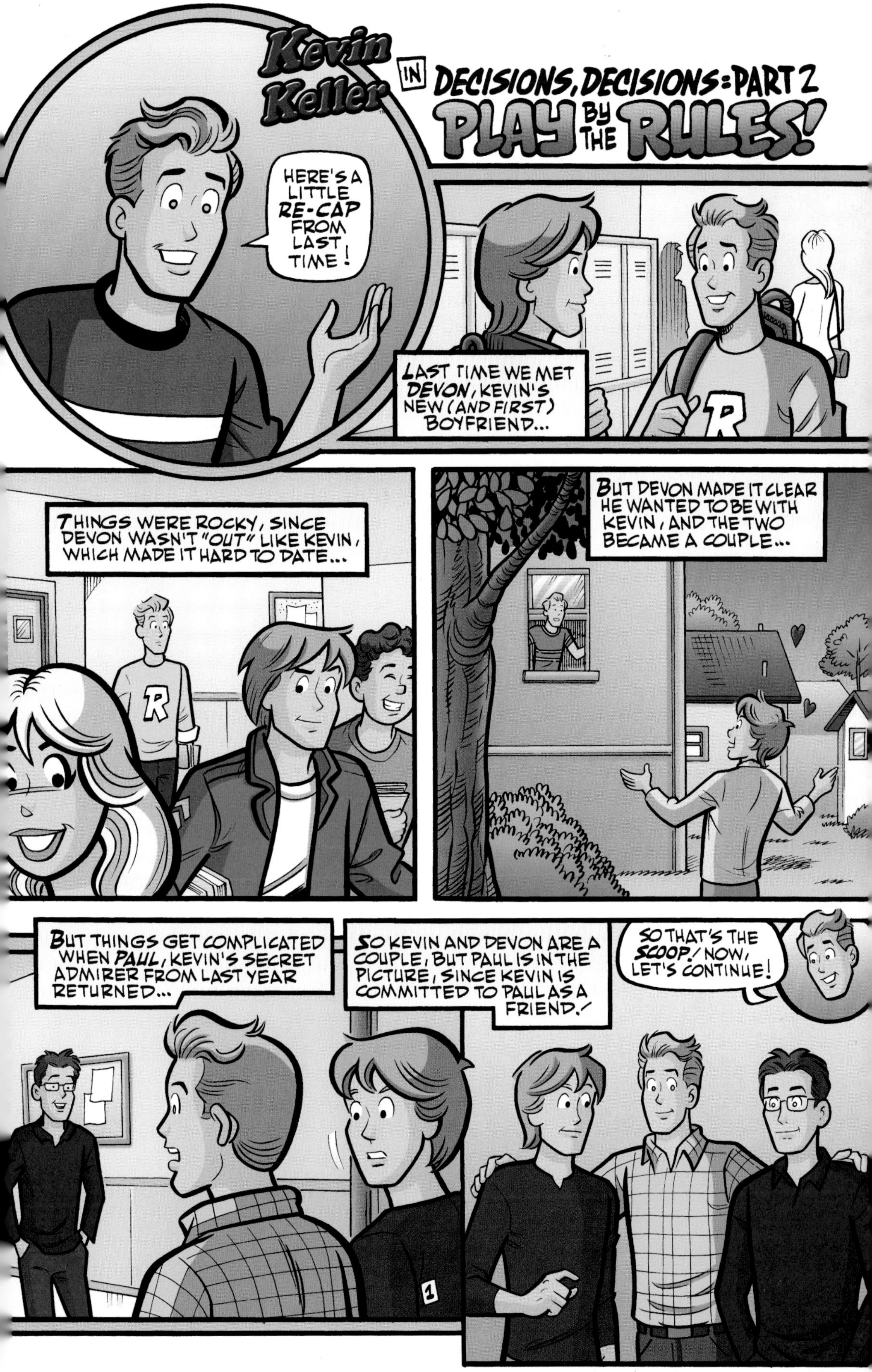
Kevin Keller
IN
DECISIONS, DECISIONS: PART 2
PLAY BY THE RULES!
HERE'S A LITTLE RE-CAP FROM LAST TIME!
LAST TIME WE MET DEVON, KEVIN'S NEW (AND FIRST) BOYFRIEND...
THINGS WERE ROCKY, SINCE DEVON WASN'T "OUT" LIKE KEVIN, WHICH MADE IT HARD TO DATE...
BUT DEVON MADE IT CLEAR HE WANTED TO BE WITH KEVIN, AND THE TWO BECAME A COUPLE...
BUT THINGS GET COMPLICATED WHEN PAUL, KEVIN'S SECRET ADMIRER FROM LAST YEAR RETURNED...
SO KEVIN AND DEVON ARE A COUPLE, BUT PAUL IS IN THE PICTURE, SINCE KEVIN IS COMMITTED TO PAUL AS A FRIEND!
SO THAT'S THE SCOOP! NOW, LET'S CONTINUE!

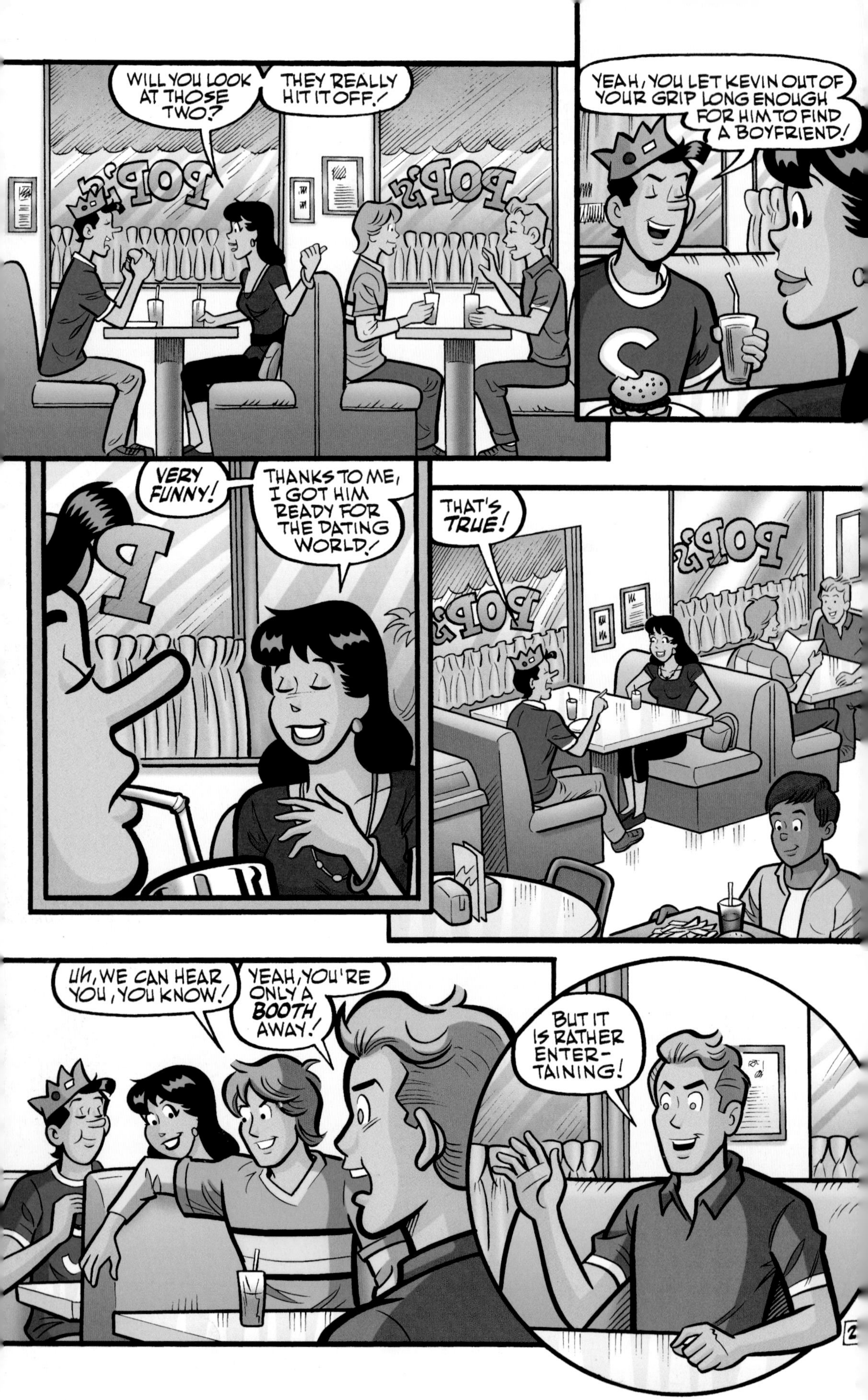
WILL YOU LOOK AT THOSE TWO?
THEY REALLY HIT IT OFF!
POP'S
YEAH, YOU LET KEVIN OUT OF YOUR GRIP LONG ENOUGH FOR HIM TO FIND A BOYFRIEND!
VERY FUNNY!
THANKS TO ME, I GOT HIM READY FOR THE DATING WORLD!
THAT'S TRUE!
UH, WE CAN HEAR YOU, YOU KNOW!
YEAH, YOU'RE ONLY A BOOTH AWAY!
BUT IT IS RATHER ENTER-TAINING!
2

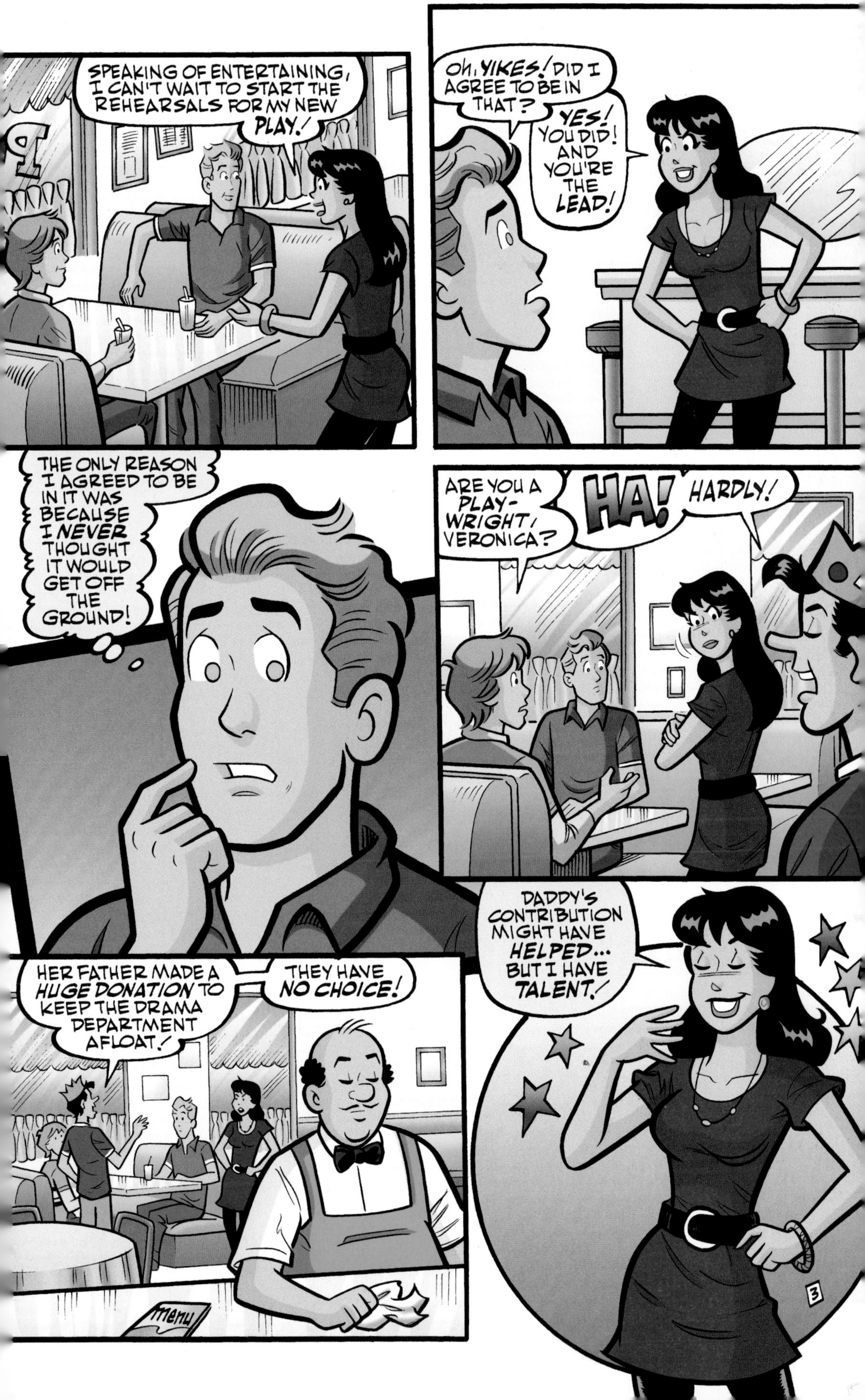
SPEAKING OF ENTERTAINING, I CAN'T WAIT TO START THE REHEARSALS FOR MY NEW PLAY!
Oh, YIKES! DID I AGREE TO BE IN THAT?
YES! YOU DID! AND YOU'RE THE LEAD!
THE ONLY REASON I AGREED TO BE IN IT WAS BECAUSE I NEVER THOUGHT IT WOULD GET OFF THE GROUND!
ARE YOU A PLAY-WRIGHT, VERONICA?
HA!
HARDLY!
HER FATHER MADE A HUGE DONATION TO KEEP THE DRAMA DEPARTMENT AFLOAT!
THEY HAVE NO CHOICE!
DADDY'S CONTRIBUTION MIGHT HAVE HELPED... BUT I HAVE TALENT!
menu
3

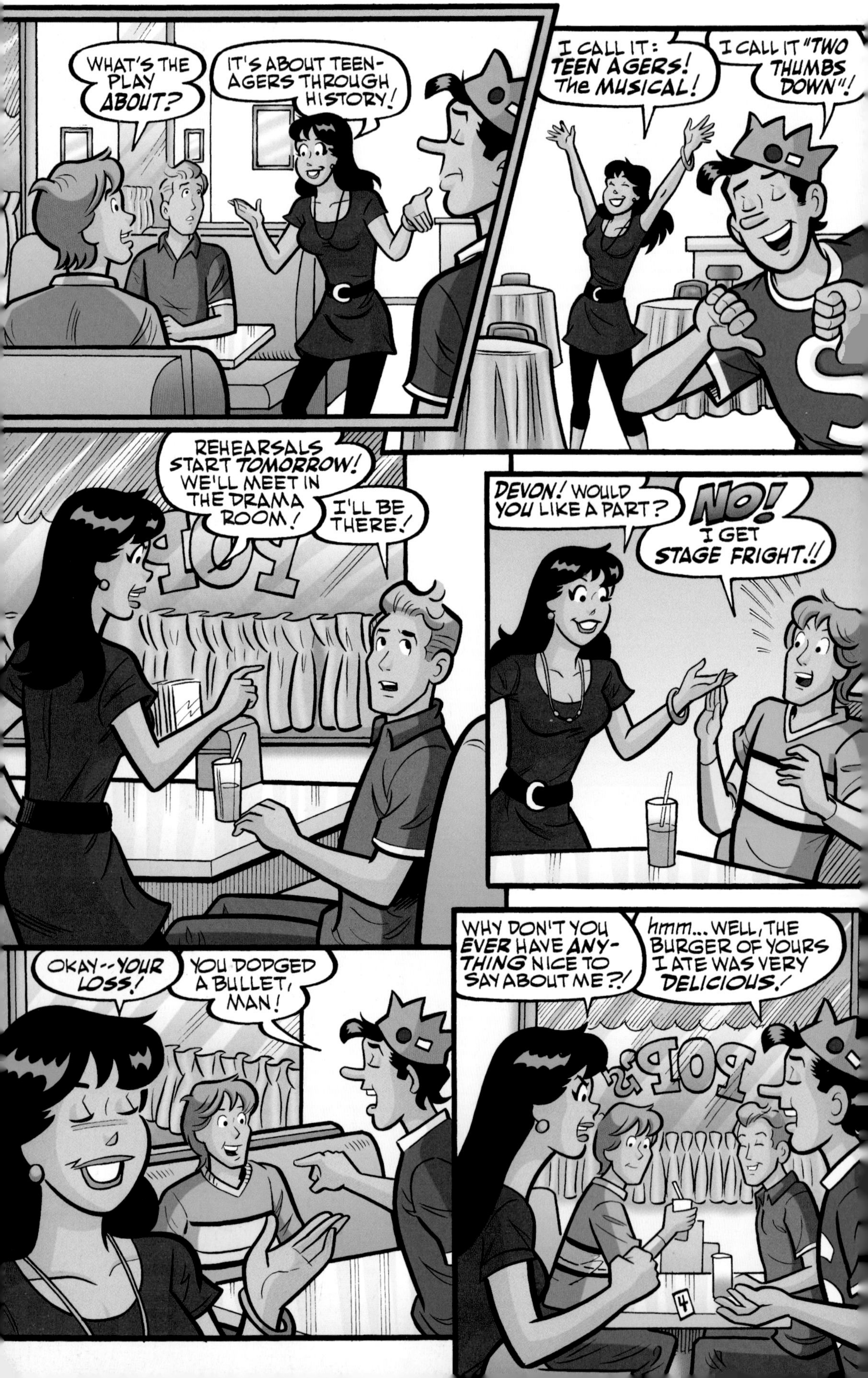

WHAT'S THE PLAY ABOUT?
IT'S ABOUT TEEN-AGERS THROUGH HISTORY!
I CALL IT: TEEN AGERS! The MUSICAL!
I CALL IT "TWO THUMBS DOWN"!
REHEARSALS START TOMORROW! WE'LL MEET IN THE DRAMA ROOM!
I'LL BE THERE!
POP'S
DEVON! WOULD YOU LIKE A PART?
NO! I GET STAGE FRIGHT!!
OKAY--YOUR LOSS!
YOU DODGED A BULLET, MAN!
WHY DON'T YOU EVER HAVE ANY-THING NICE TO SAY ABOUT ME?!
hmm... WELL, THE BURGER OF YOURS I ATE WAS VERY DELICIOUS!
POP'S

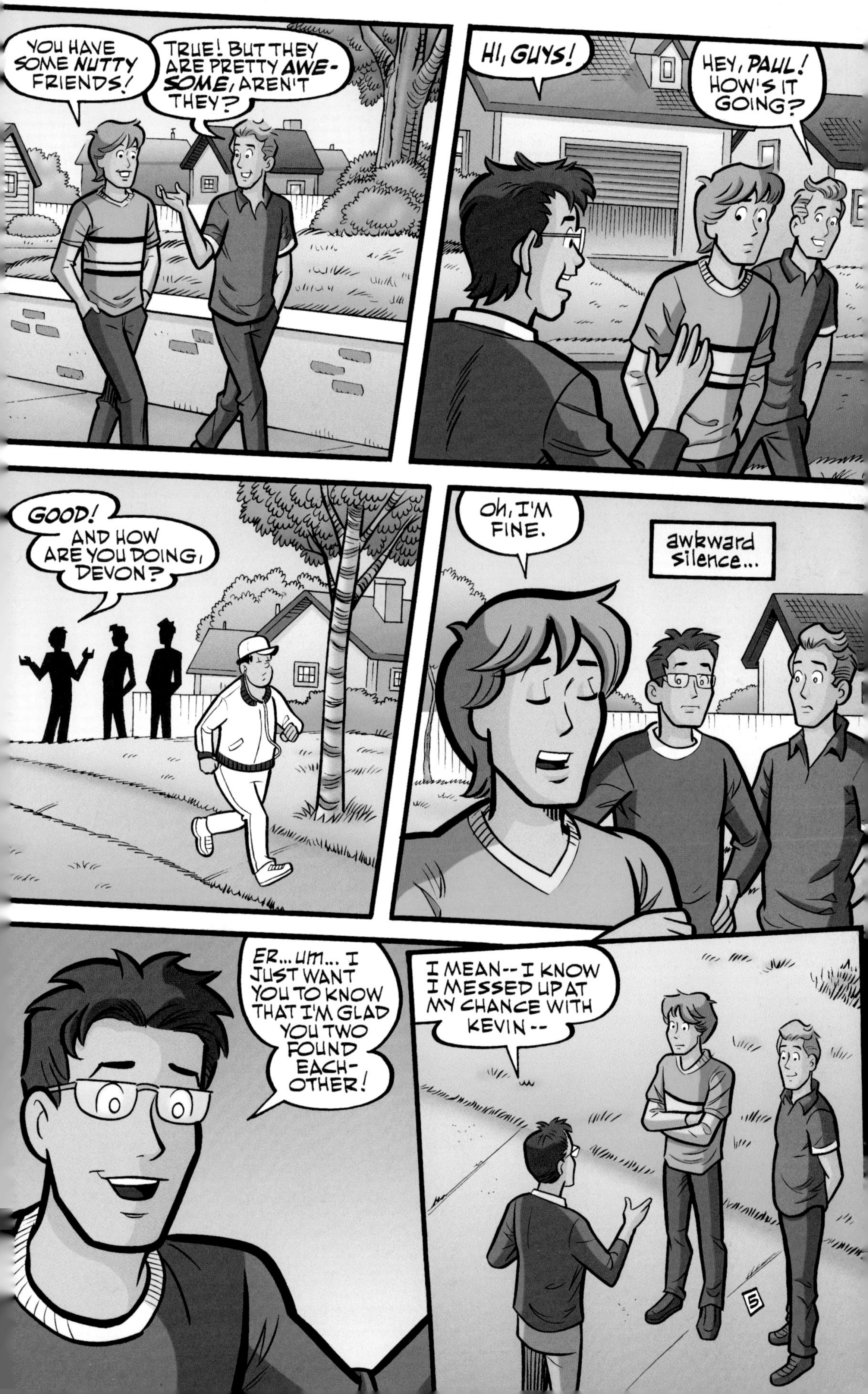
YOU HAVE SOME NUTTY FRIENDS!
TRUE! BUT THEY ARE PRETTY AWESOME, AREN'T THEY?
HI, GUYS!
HEY, PAUL! HOW'S IT GOING?
GOOD! AND HOW ARE YOU DOING, DEVON?
Oh, I'M FINE.
awkward silence...
ER... um... I JUST WANT YOU TO KNOW THAT I'M GLAD YOU TWO FOUND EACH-OTHER!
I MEAN-- I KNOW I MESSED UP AT MY CHANCE WITH KEVIN --
5

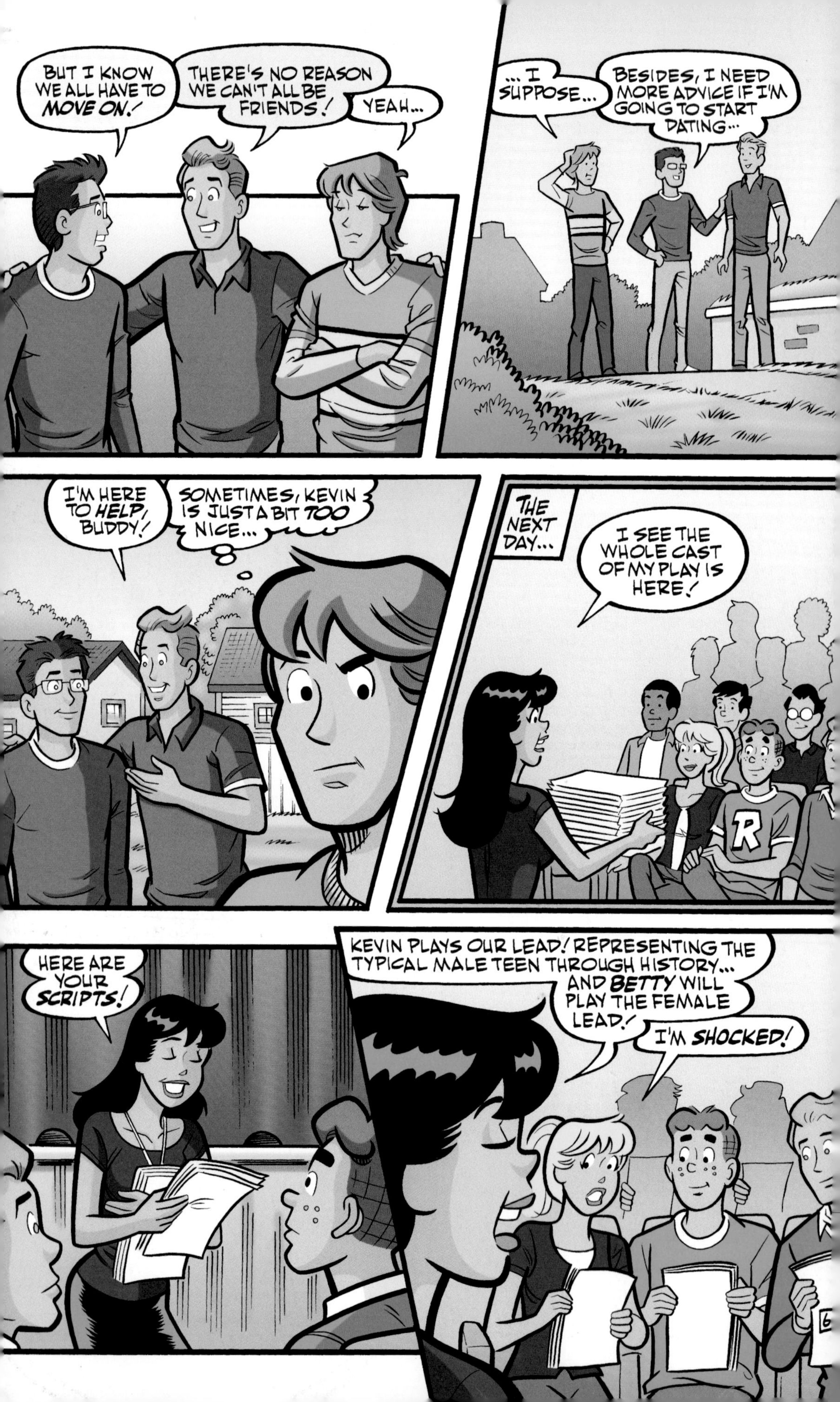
BUT I KNOW WE ALL HAVE TO MOVE ON!
THERE'S NO REASON WE CAN'T ALL BE FRIENDS!
YEAH...
... I SUPPOSE...
BESIDES, I NEED MORE ADVICE IF I'M GOING TO START DATING...
I'M HERE TO HELP, BUDDY!
SOMETIMES, KEVIN IS JUST A BIT TOO NICE...
THE NEXT DAY...
I SEE THE WHOLE CAST OF MY PLAY IS HERE!
HERE ARE YOUR SCRIPTS!
KEVIN PLAYS OUR LEAD! REPRESENTING THE TYPICAL MALE TEEN THROUGH HISTORY...
AND BETTY WILL PLAY THE FEMALE LEAD!
I'M SHOCKED!
6

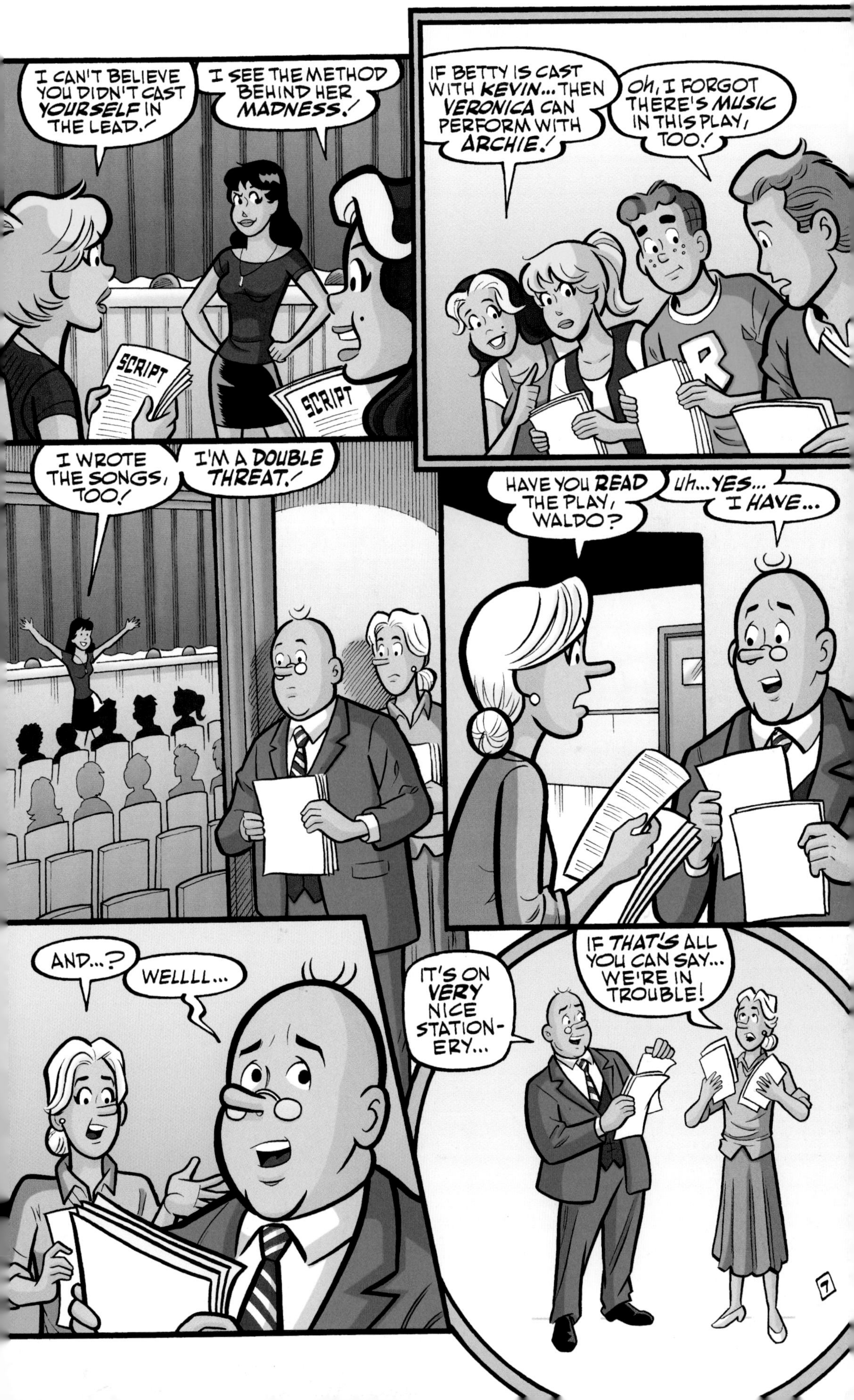

I CAN'T BELIEVE YOU DIDN'T CAST YOURSELF IN THE LEAD.!
I SEE THE METHOD BEHIND HER MADNESS.!
SCRIPT
SCRIPT
IF BETTY IS CAST WITH KEVIN... THEN VERONICA CAN PERFORM WITH ARCHIE.!
Oh, I FORGOT THERE'S MUSIC IN THIS PLAY, TOO.!
I WROTE THE SONGS, TOO!
I'M A DOUBLE THREAT.!
HAVE YOU READ THE PLAY, WALDO?
uh... YES... I HAVE...
AND...?
WELLLL...
IT'S ON VERY NICE STATION-ERY...
IF THAT'S ALL YOU CAN SAY... WE'RE IN TROUBLE!

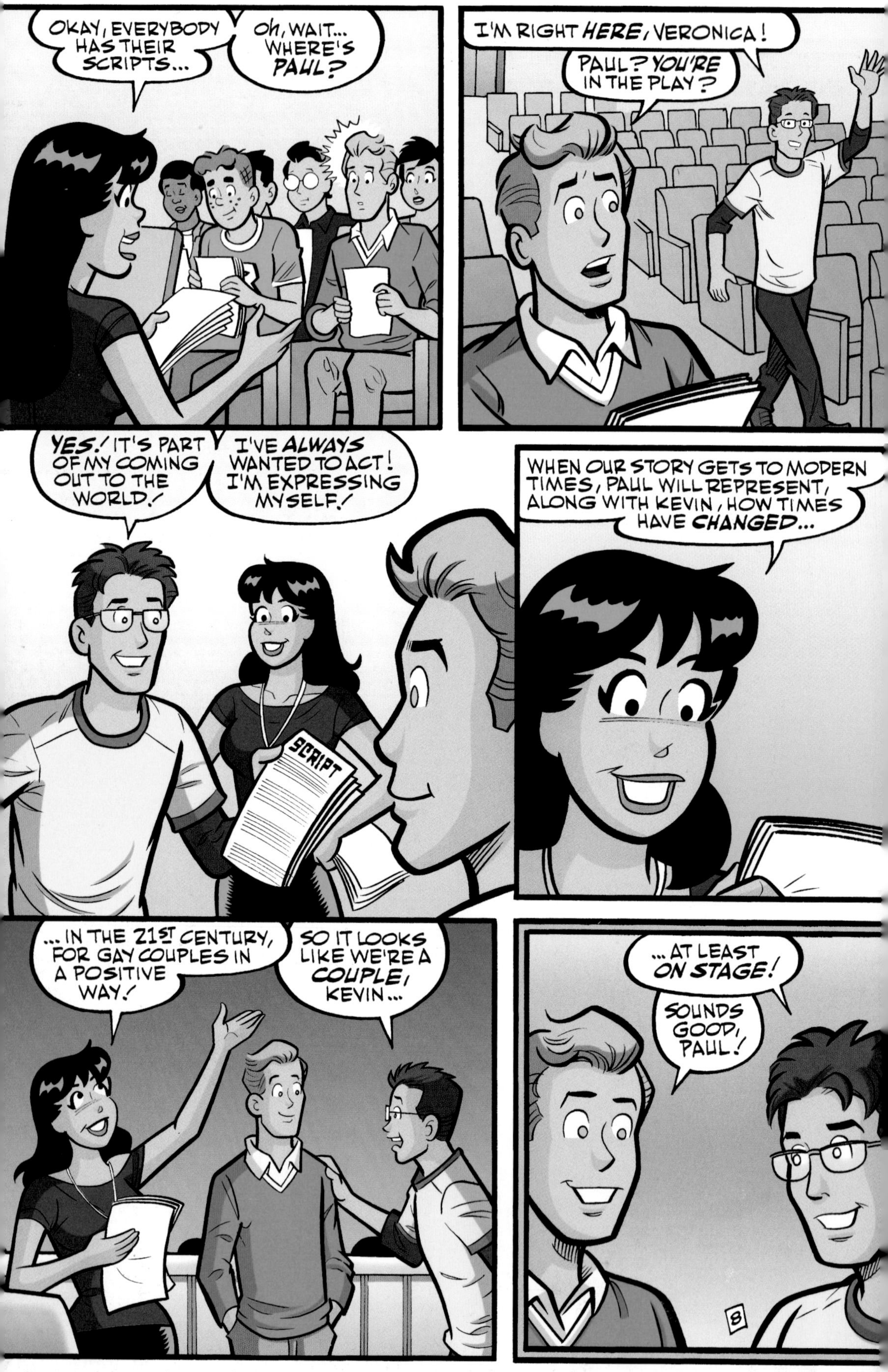

OKAY, EVERYBODY HAS THEIR SCRIPTS...
Oh, WAIT... WHERE'S PAUL?
I'M RIGHT HERE, VERONICA!
PAUL? YOU'RE IN THE PLAY?
YES! IT'S PART OF MY COMING OUT TO THE WORLD!
I'VE ALWAYS WANTED TO ACT! I'M EXPRESSING MYSELF!
SCRIPT
WHEN OUR STORY GETS TO MODERN TIMES, PAUL WILL REPRESENT, ALONG WITH KEVIN, HOW TIMES HAVE CHANGED...
...IN THE 21ST CENTURY, FOR GAY COUPLES IN A POSITIVE WAY!
SO IT LOOKS LIKE WE'RE A COUPLE, KEVIN...
...AT LEAST ON STAGE!
SOUNDS GOOD, PAUL!
8

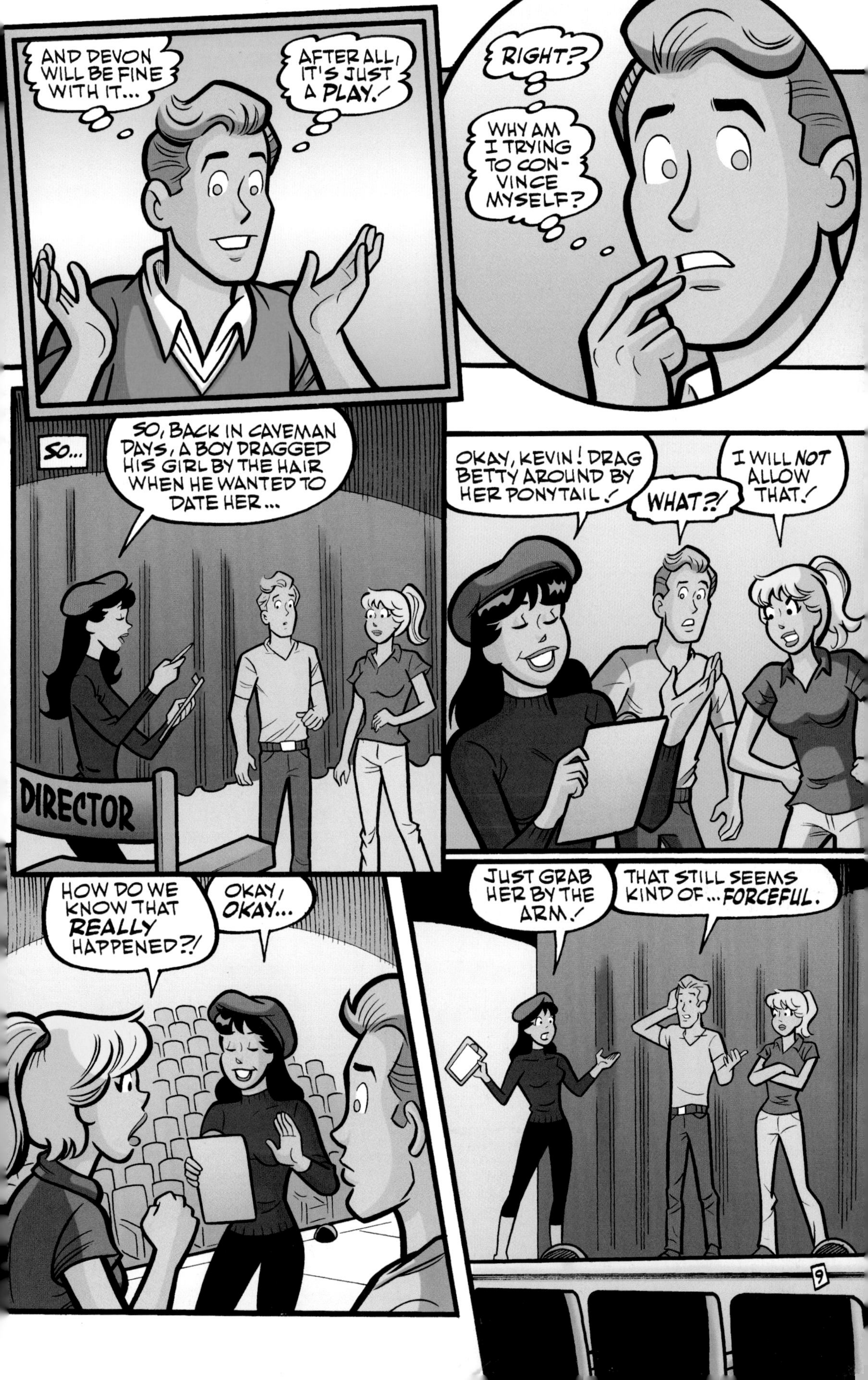

AND DEVON WILL BE FINE WITH IT...
AFTER ALL, IT'S JUST A PLAY!
RIGHT?
WHY AM I TRYING TO CON- VINCE MYSELF?
SO...
SO, BACK IN CAVEMAN DAYS, A BOY DRAGGED HIS GIRL BY THE HAIR WHEN HE WANTED TO DATE HER...
DIRECTOR
OKAY, KEVIN! DRAG BETTY AROUND BY HER PONYTAIL!
WHAT?!
I WILL NOT ALLOW THAT!
HOW DO WE KNOW THAT REALLY HAPPENED?!
OKAY, OKAY...
JUST GRAB HER BY THE ARM!
THAT STILL SEEMS KIND OF... FORCEFUL.

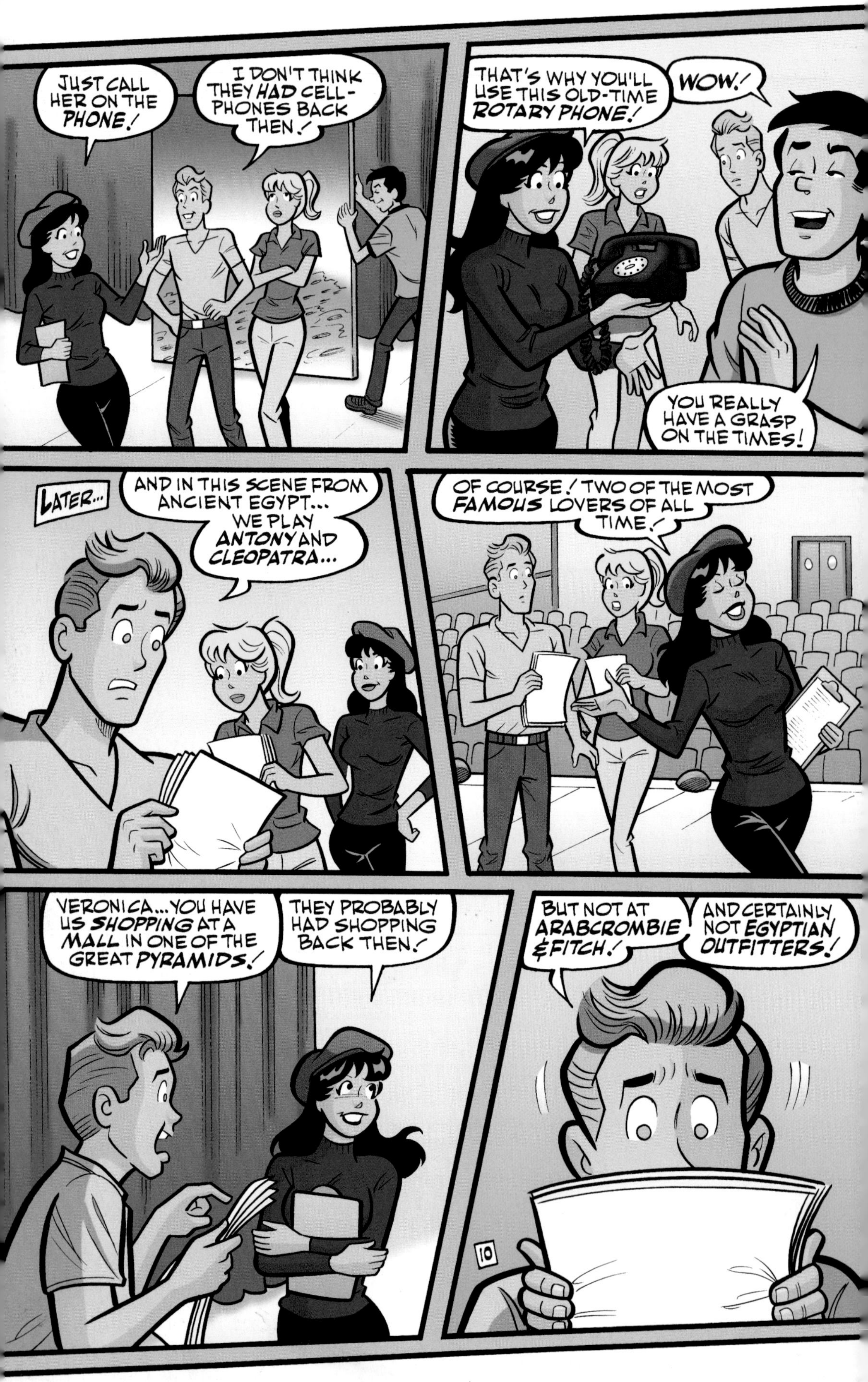
JUST CALL HER ON THE PHONE!
I DON'T THINK THEY HAD CELL-PHONES BACK THEN!
THAT'S WHY YOU'LL USE THIS OLD-TIME ROTARY PHONE!
WOW!
YOU REALLY HAVE A GRASP ON THE TIMES!
LATER...
AND IN THIS SCENE FROM ANCIENT EGYPT... WE PLAY ANTONY AND CLEOPATRA...
OF COURSE! TWO OF THE MOST FAMOUS LOVERS OF ALL TIME!
VERONICA...YOU HAVE US SHOPPING AT A MALL IN ONE OF THE GREAT PYRAMIDS!
THEY PROBABLY HAD SHOPPING BACK THEN!
BUT NOT AT ARABCROMBIE &FITCH!
AND CERTAINLY NOT EGYPTIAN OUTFITTERS!
10

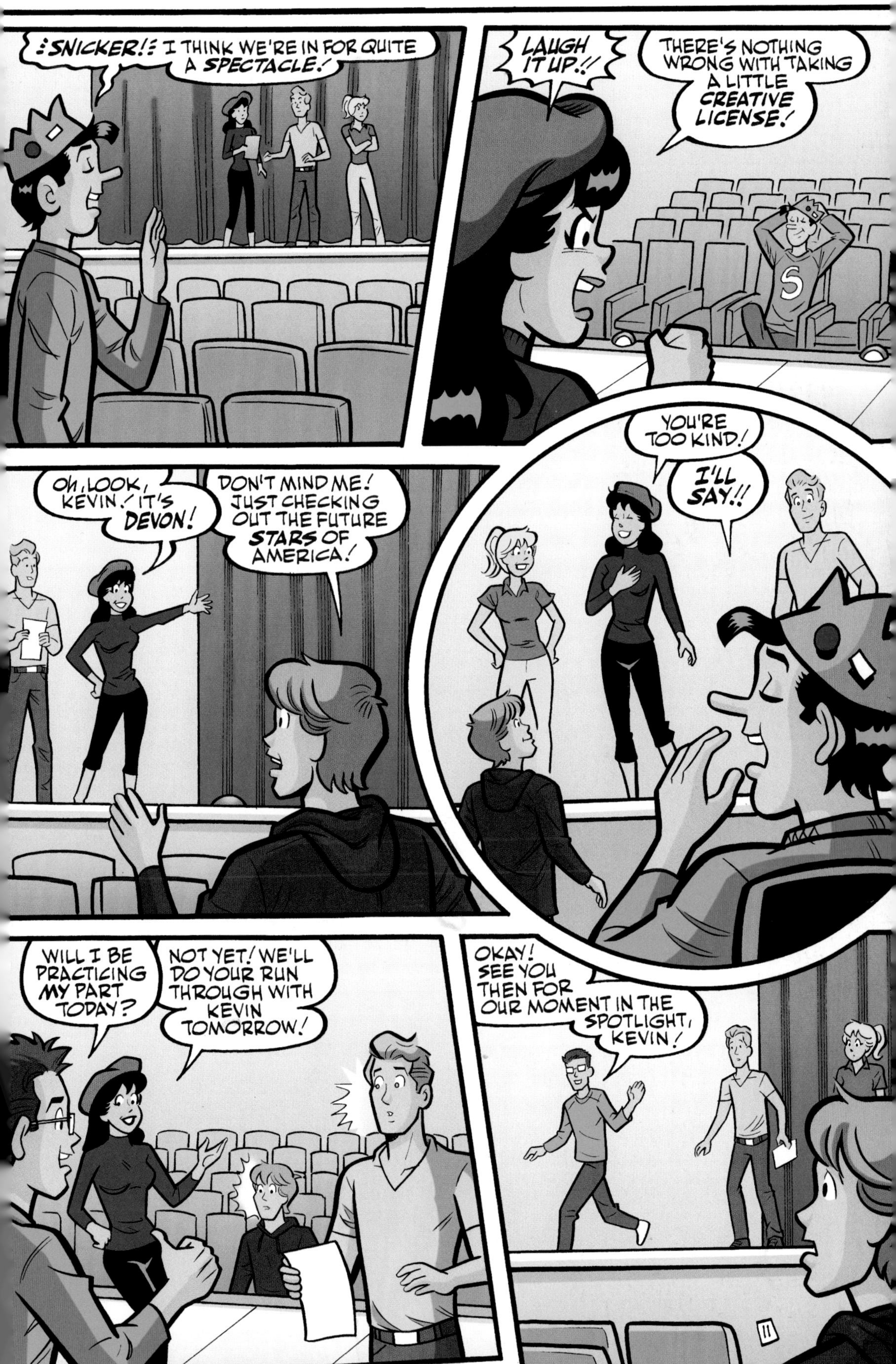

:SNICKER!: I THINK WE'RE IN FOR QUITE A SPECTACLE!
LAUGH IT UP!!
THERE'S NOTHING WRONG WITH TAKING A LITTLE CREATIVE LICENSE!
Oh, LOOK, KEVIN! IT'S DEVON!
DON'T MIND ME! JUST CHECKING OUT THE FUTURE STARS OF AMERICA!
YOU'RE TOO KIND!
I'LL SAY!!
WILL I BE PRACTICING MY PART TODAY?
NOT YET! WE'LL DO YOUR RUN THROUGH WITH KEVIN TOMORROW!
OKAY! SEE YOU THEN FOR OUR MOMENT IN THE SPOTLIGHT, KEVIN!

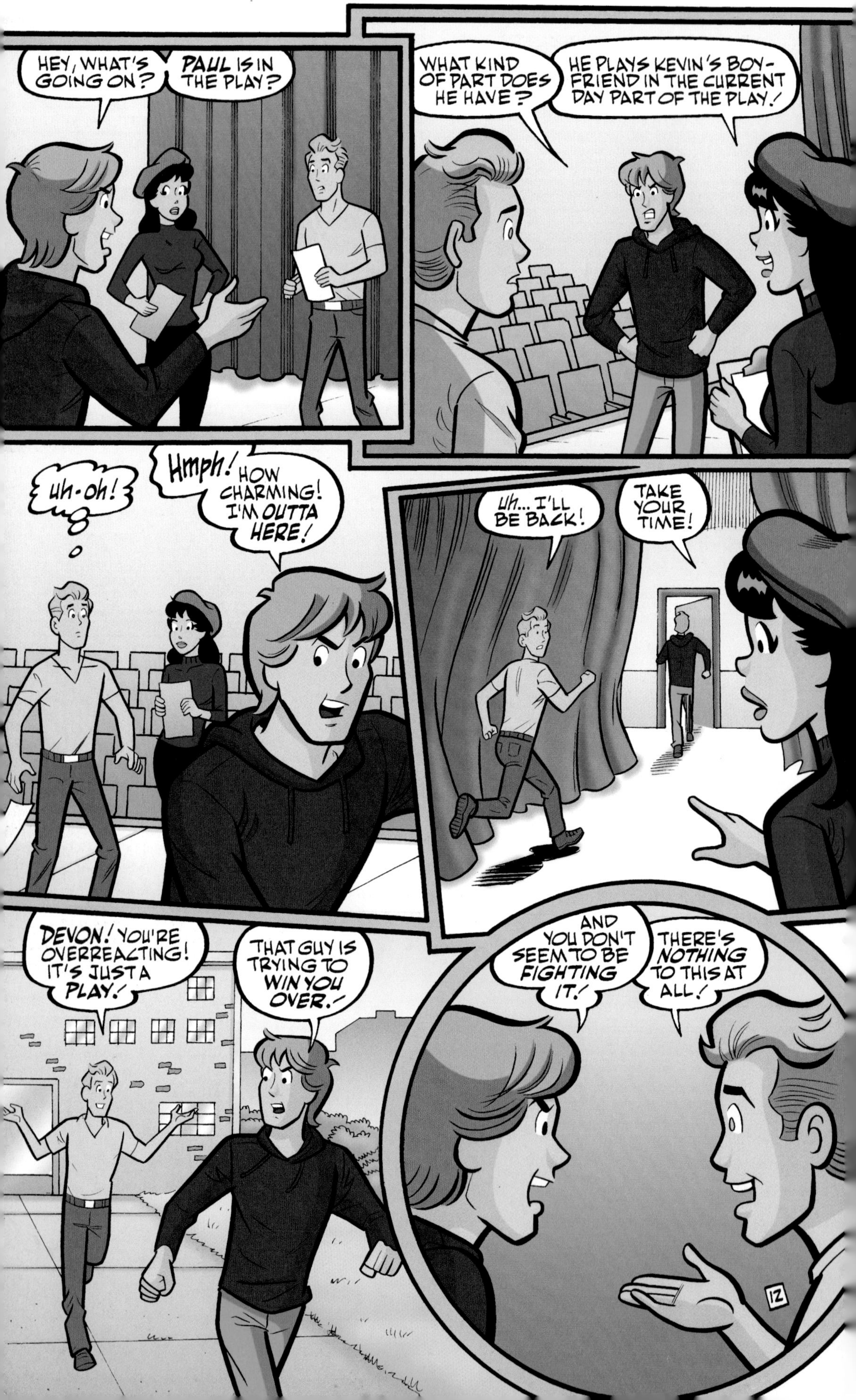

HEY, WHAT'S GOING ON?
PAUL IS IN THE PLAY?
WHAT KIND OF PART DOES HE HAVE?
HE PLAYS KEVIN'S BOY-FRIEND IN THE CURRENT DAY PART OF THE PLAY!
uh-oh!
Hmph! HOW CHARMING! I'M OUTTA HERE!
uh... I'LL BE BACK!
TAKE YOUR TIME!
DEVON! YOU'RE OVERREACTING! IT'S JUST A PLAY!
THAT GUY IS TRYING TO WIN YOU OVER.!
AND YOU DON'T SEEM TO BE FIGHTING IT!
THERE'S NOTHING TO THIS AT ALL!
12

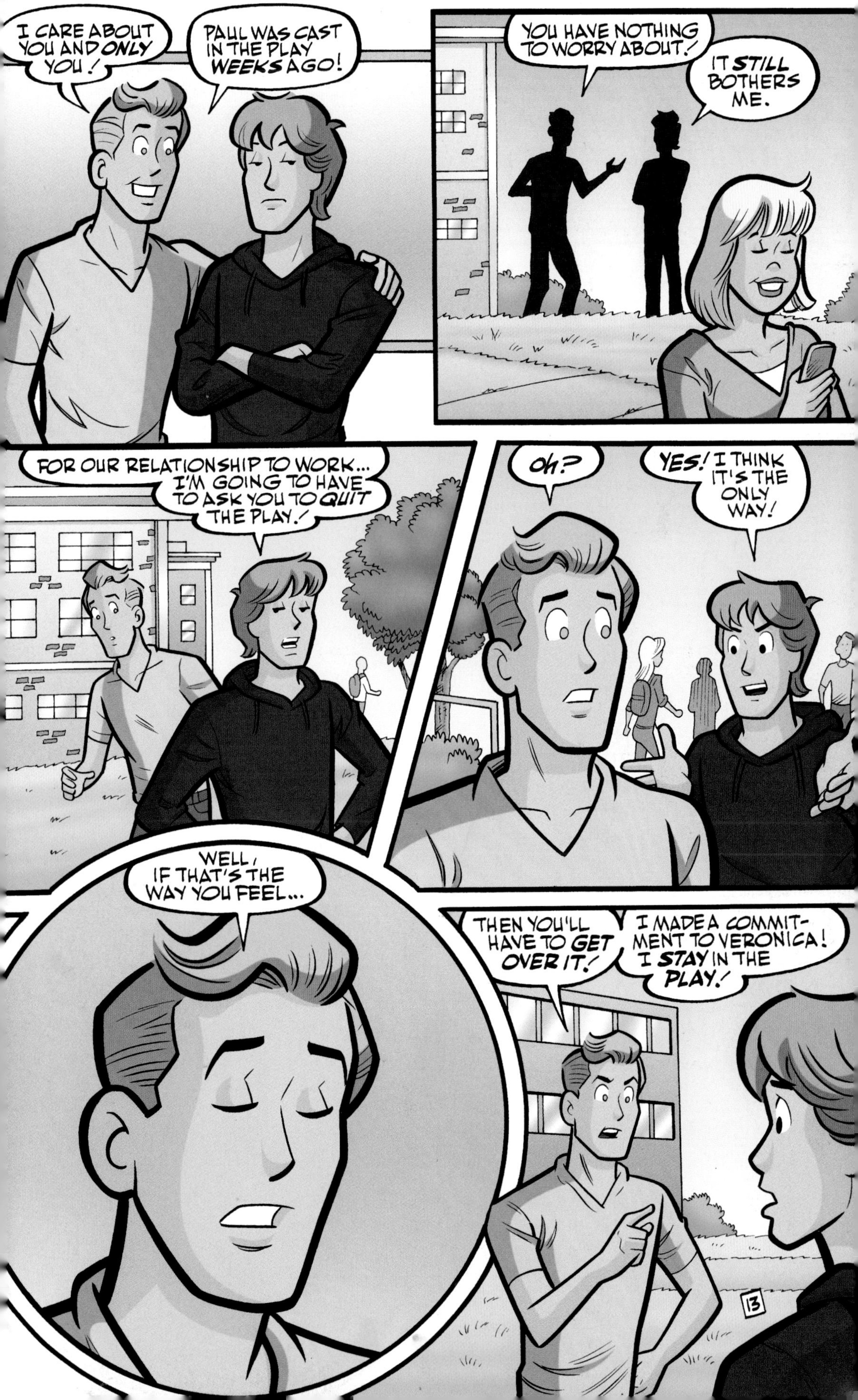
I CARE ABOUT YOU AND ONLY YOU!
PAUL WAS CAST IN THE PLAY WEEKS AGO!
YOU HAVE NOTHING TO WORRY ABOUT!
IT STILL BOTHERS ME.
FOR OUR RELATIONSHIP TO WORK... I'M GOING TO HAVE TO ASK YOU TO QUIT THE PLAY!
Oh?
YES! I THINK IT'S THE ONLY WAY!
WELL, IF THAT'S THE WAY YOU FEEL...
THEN YOU'LL HAVE TO GET OVER IT!
I MADE A COMMITMENT TO VERONICA! I STAY IN THE PLAY!
13

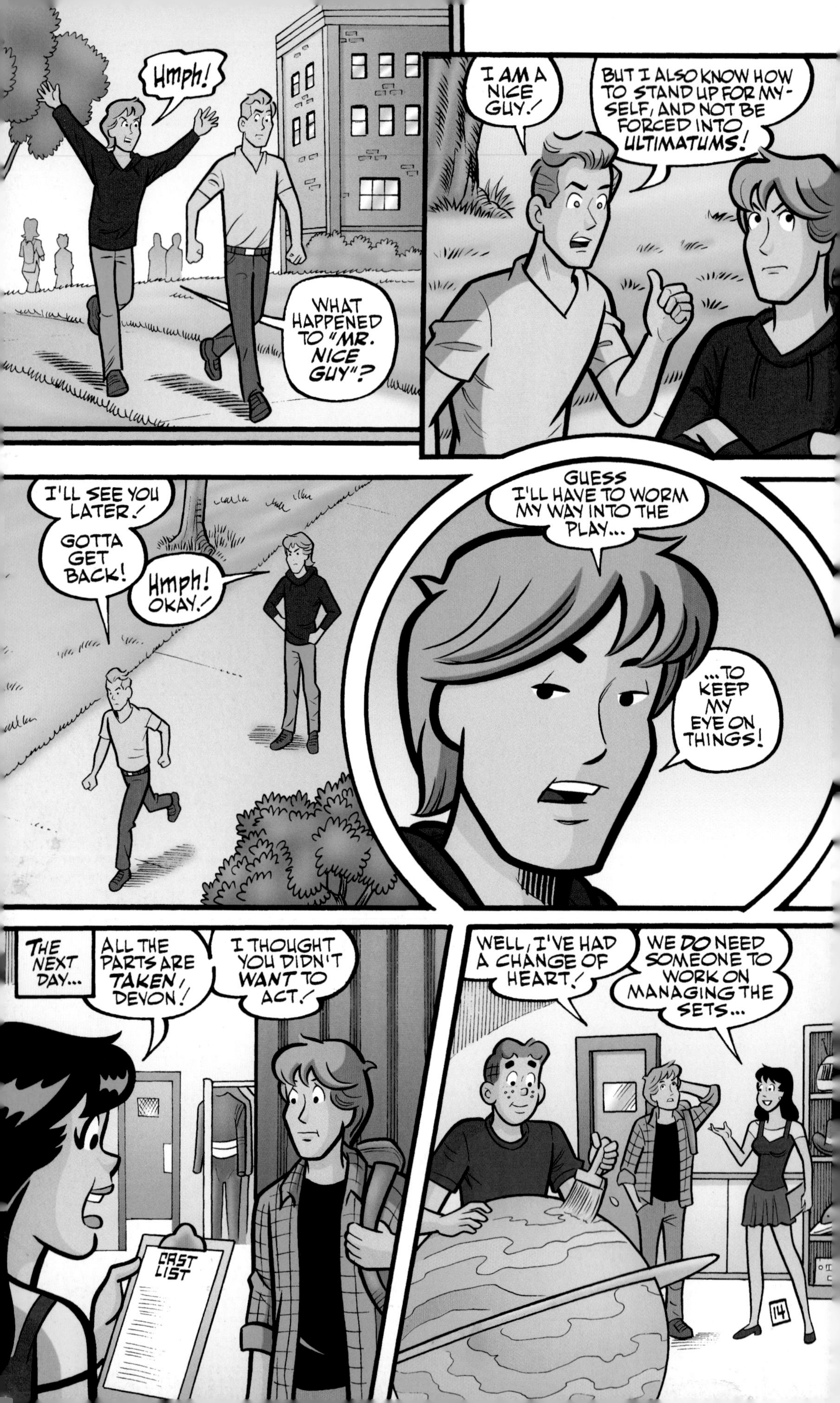
Hmph!
WHAT HAPPENED TO "MR. NICE GUY"?
I AM A NICE GUY!
BUT I ALSO KNOW HOW TO STAND UP FOR MY-SELF, AND NOT BE FORCED INTO ULTIMATUMS!
I'LL SEE YOU LATER!
GOTTA GET BACK!
Hmph! OKAY!
GUESS I'LL HAVE TO WORM MY WAY INTO THE PLAY...
...TO KEEP MY EYE ON THINGS!
THE NEXT DAY...
ALL THE PARTS ARE TAKEN, DEVON!
I THOUGHT YOU DIDN'T WANT TO ACT!
CAST LIST
WELL, I'VE HAD A CHANGE OF HEART!
WE DO NEED SOMEONE TO WORK ON MANAGING THE SETS...
14

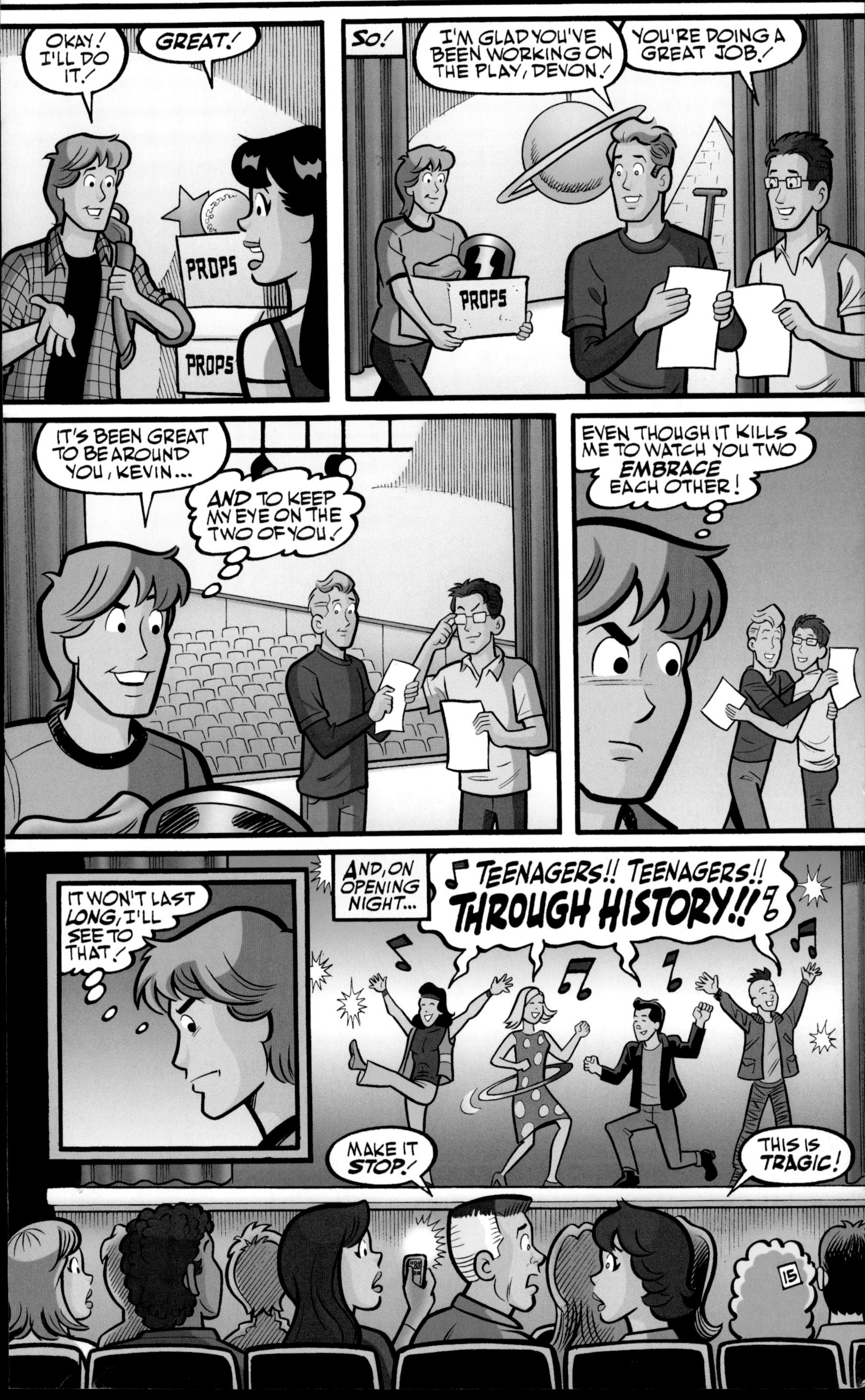
OKAY! I'LL DO IT!
GREAT!
PROPS
PROPS
SO!
I'M GLAD YOU'VE BEEN WORKING ON THE PLAY, DEVON!
YOU'RE DOING A GREAT JOB!
PROPS
IT'S BEEN GREAT TO BE AROUND YOU, KEVIN...
AND TO KEEP MY EYE ON THE TWO OF YOU!
EVEN THOUGH IT KILLS ME TO WATCH YOU TWO EMBRACE EACH OTHER!
IT WON'T LAST LONG, I'LL SEE TO THAT!
AND, ON OPENING NIGHT...
TEENAGERS!! TEENAGERS!! THROUGH HISTORY!!
MAKE IT STOP!
THIS IS TRAGIC!
15

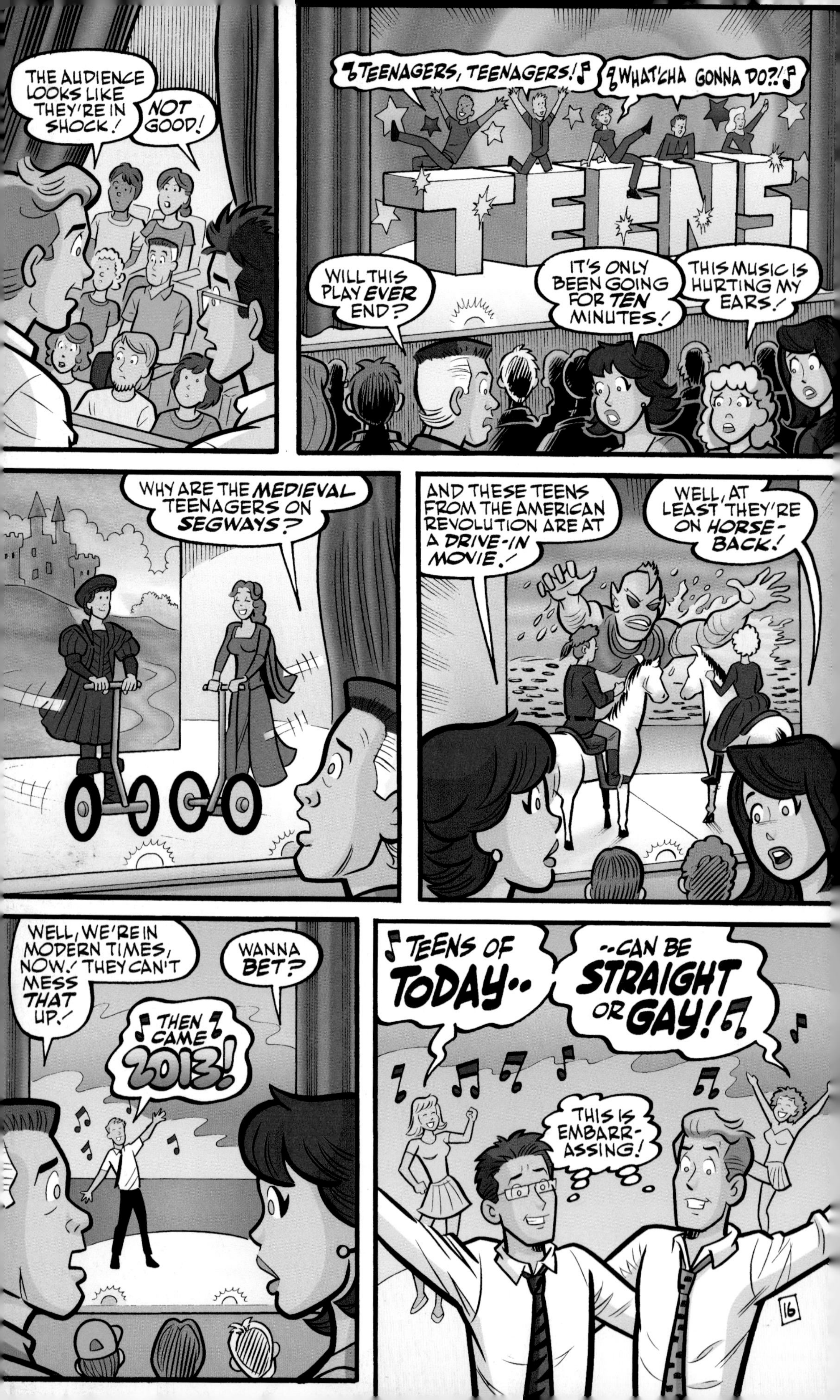
THE AUDIENCE LOOKS LIKE THEY'RE IN SHOCK!
NOT GOOD!
TEENAGERS, TEENAGERS!
WHAT'CHA GONNA DO?!
TEENS
WILL THIS PLAY EVER END?
IT'S ONLY BEEN GOING FOR TEN MINUTES!
THIS MUSIC IS HURTING MY EARS!
WHY ARE THE MEDIEVAL TEENAGERS ON SEGWAYS?
AND THESE TEENS FROM THE AMERICAN REVOLUTION ARE AT A DRIVE-IN MOVIE!
WELL, AT LEAST THEY'RE ON HORSE-BACK!
WELL, WE'RE IN MODERN TIMES, NOW! THEY CAN'T MESS THAT UP!
WANNA BET?
THEN CAME 2013!
TEENS OF TODAY..
..CAN BE STRAIGHT OR GAY!
THIS IS EMBARR-ASSING!
16

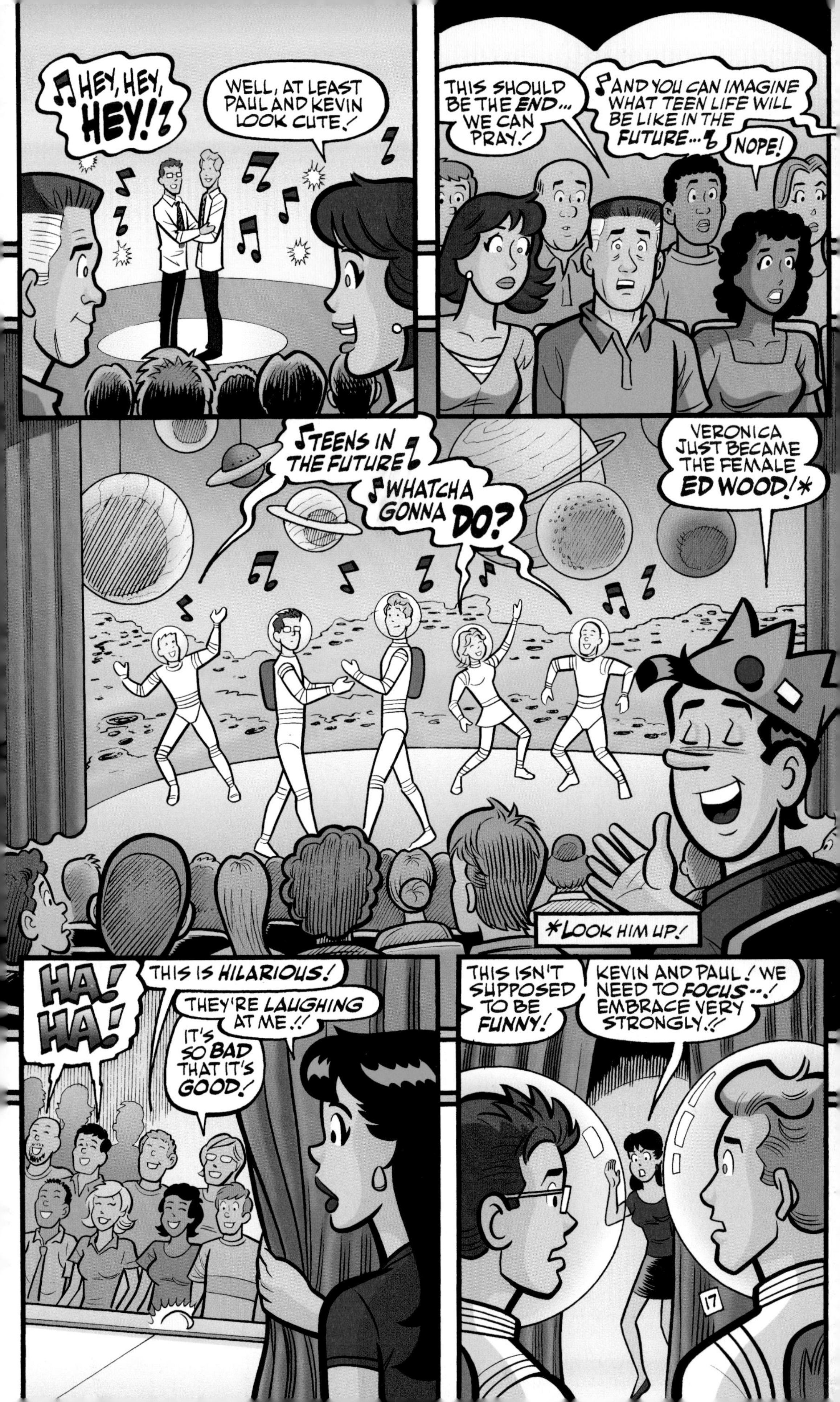
HEY, HEY, HEY!
WELL, AT LEAST PAUL AND KEVIN LOOK CUTE!
THIS SHOULD BE THE END... WE CAN PRAY!
AND YOU CAN IMAGINE WHAT TEEN LIFE WILL BE LIKE IN THE FUTURE...
NOPE!
TEENS IN THE FUTURE
WHATCHA GONNA DO?
VERONICA JUST BECAME THE FEMALE ED WOOD!*
*LOOK HIM UP!
HA! HA!
THIS IS HILARIOUS!
THEY'RE LAUGHING AT ME!!
IT'S SO BAD THAT IT'S GOOD!
THIS ISN'T SUPPOSED TO BE FUNNY!
KEVIN AND PAUL! WE NEED TO FOCUS..! EMBRACE VERY STRONGLY!!
17

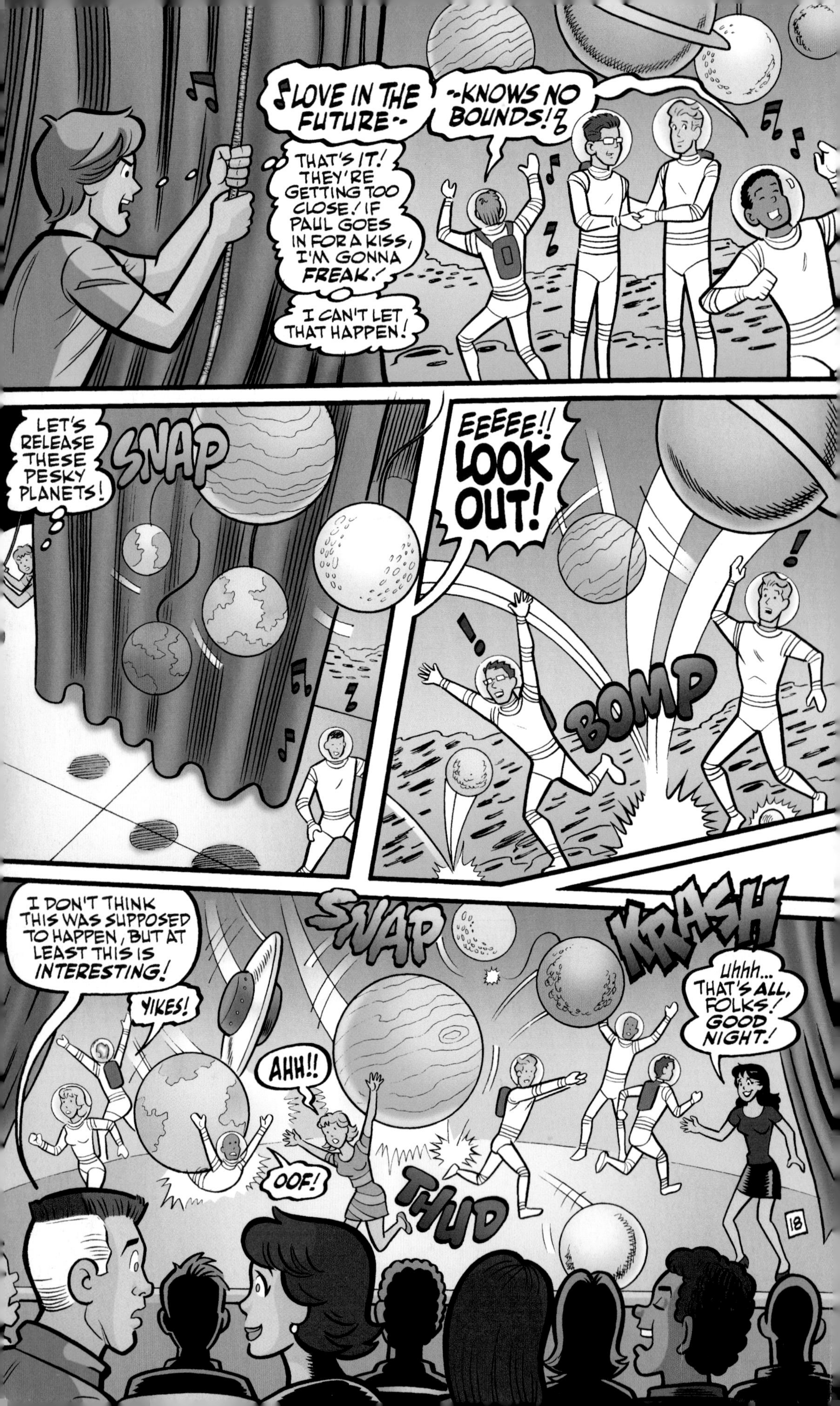
LOVE IN THE FUTURE--
--KNOWS NO BOUNDS!
THAT'S IT! THEY'RE GETTING TOO CLOSE! IF PAUL GOES IN FOR A KISS, I'M GONNA FREAK!
I CAN'T LET THAT HAPPEN!
LET'S RELEASE THESE PESKY PLANETS!
SNAP
EEEEE!! LOOK OUT!
BOMP
I DON'T THINK THIS WAS SUPPOSED TO HAPPEN, BUT AT LEAST THIS IS INTERESTING!
SNAP
KRASH
Uhhh... THAT'S ALL, FOLKS! GOOD NIGHT!
YIKES!
AHH!!
OOF!
THUD
18

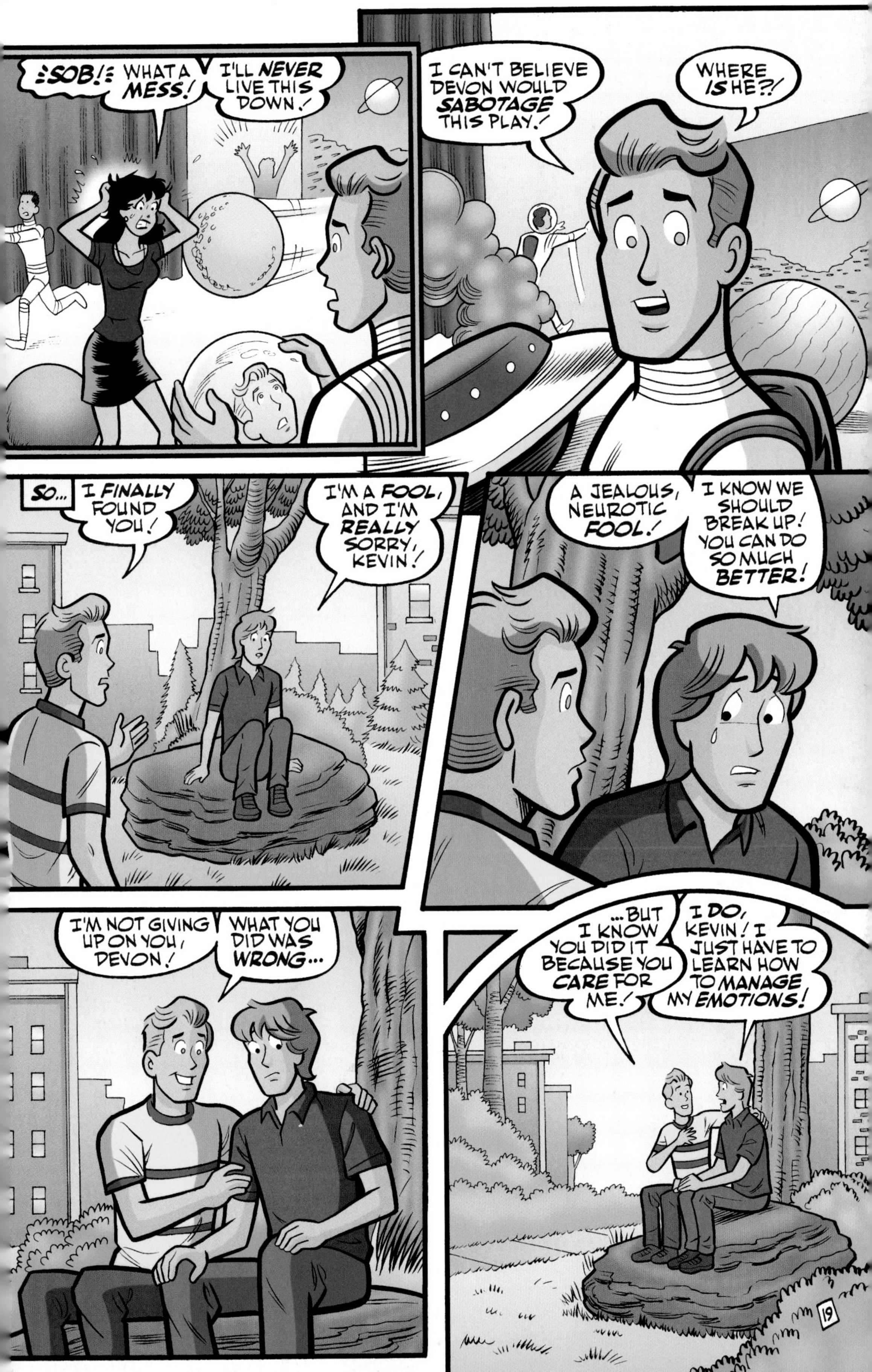

SOB!
WHAT A MESS!
I'LL NEVER LIVE THIS DOWN!
I CAN'T BELIEVE DEVON WOULD SABOTAGE THIS PLAY!
WHERE IS HE?!
SO...
I FINALLY FOUND YOU!
I'M A FOOL, AND I'M REALLY SORRY, KEVIN!
A JEALOUS, NEUROTIC FOOL!
I KNOW WE SHOULD BREAK UP! YOU CAN DO SO MUCH BETTER!
I'M NOT GIVING UP ON YOU, DEVON!
WHAT YOU DID WAS WRONG...
...BUT I KNOW YOU DID IT BECAUSE YOU CARE FOR ME!
I DO, KEVIN! I JUST HAVE TO LEARN HOW TO MANAGE MY EMOTIONS!
19

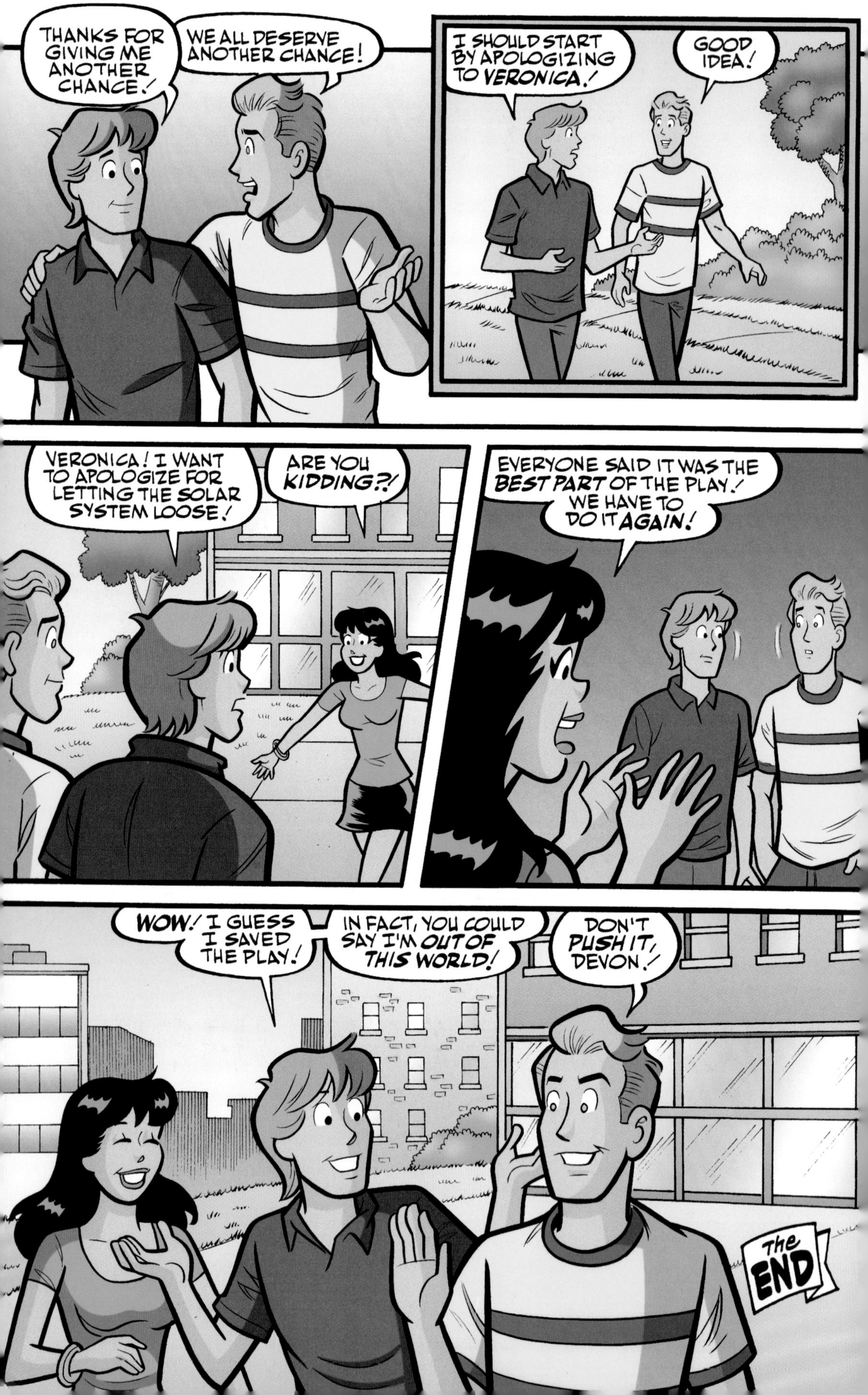
THANKS FOR GIVING ME ANOTHER CHANCE!
WE ALL DESERVE ANOTHER CHANCE!
I SHOULD START BY APOLOGIZING TO VERONICA!
GOOD IDEA!
VERONICA! I WANT TO APOLOGIZE FOR LETTING THE SOLAR SYSTEM LOOSE!
ARE YOU KIDDING?!
EVERYONE SAID IT WAS THE BEST PART OF THE PLAY! WE HAVE TO DO IT AGAIN!
WOW! I GUESS I SAVED THE PLAY!
IN FACT, YOU COULD SAY I'M OUT OF THIS WORLD!
DON'T PUSH IT, DEVON!
The END

OFFICIAL

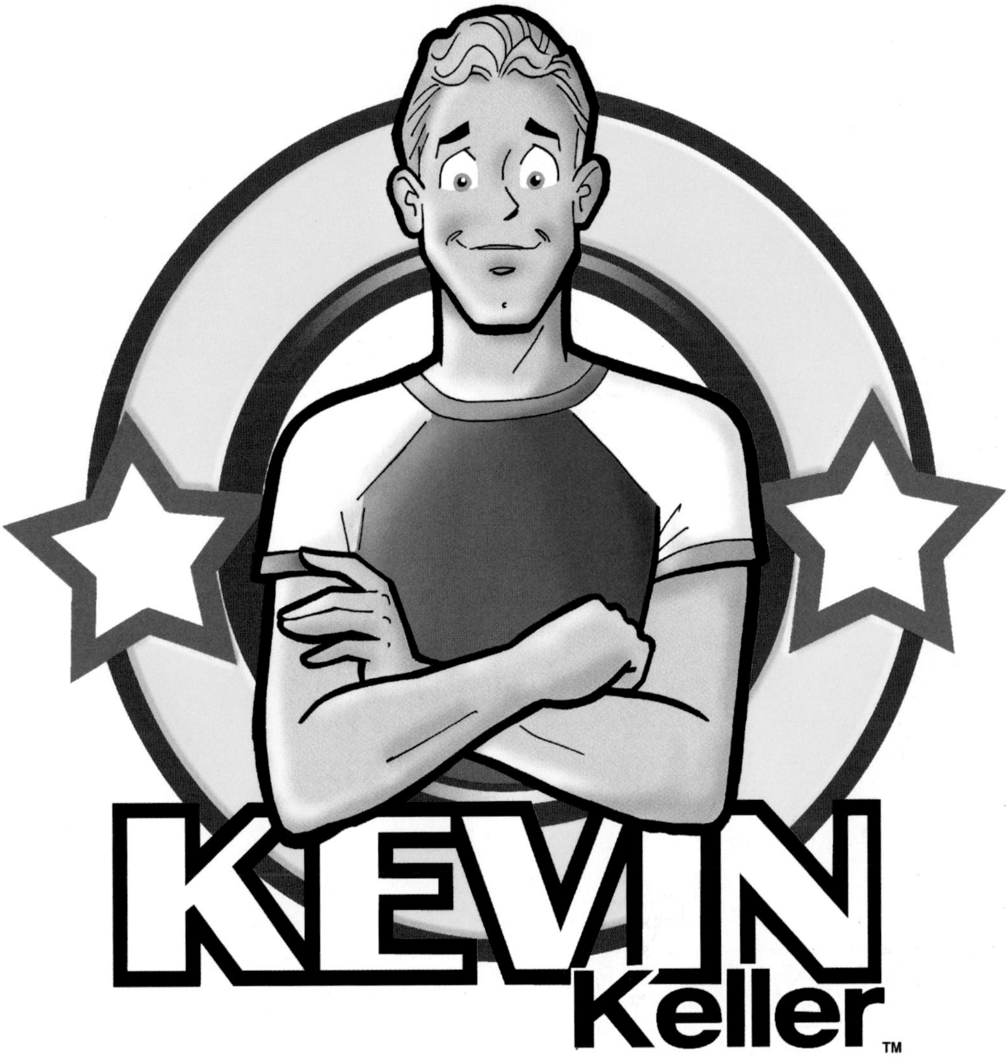

KEVIN Keller™

BONUS FEATURES

Including Kevin,
Betty & Veronica fashions!

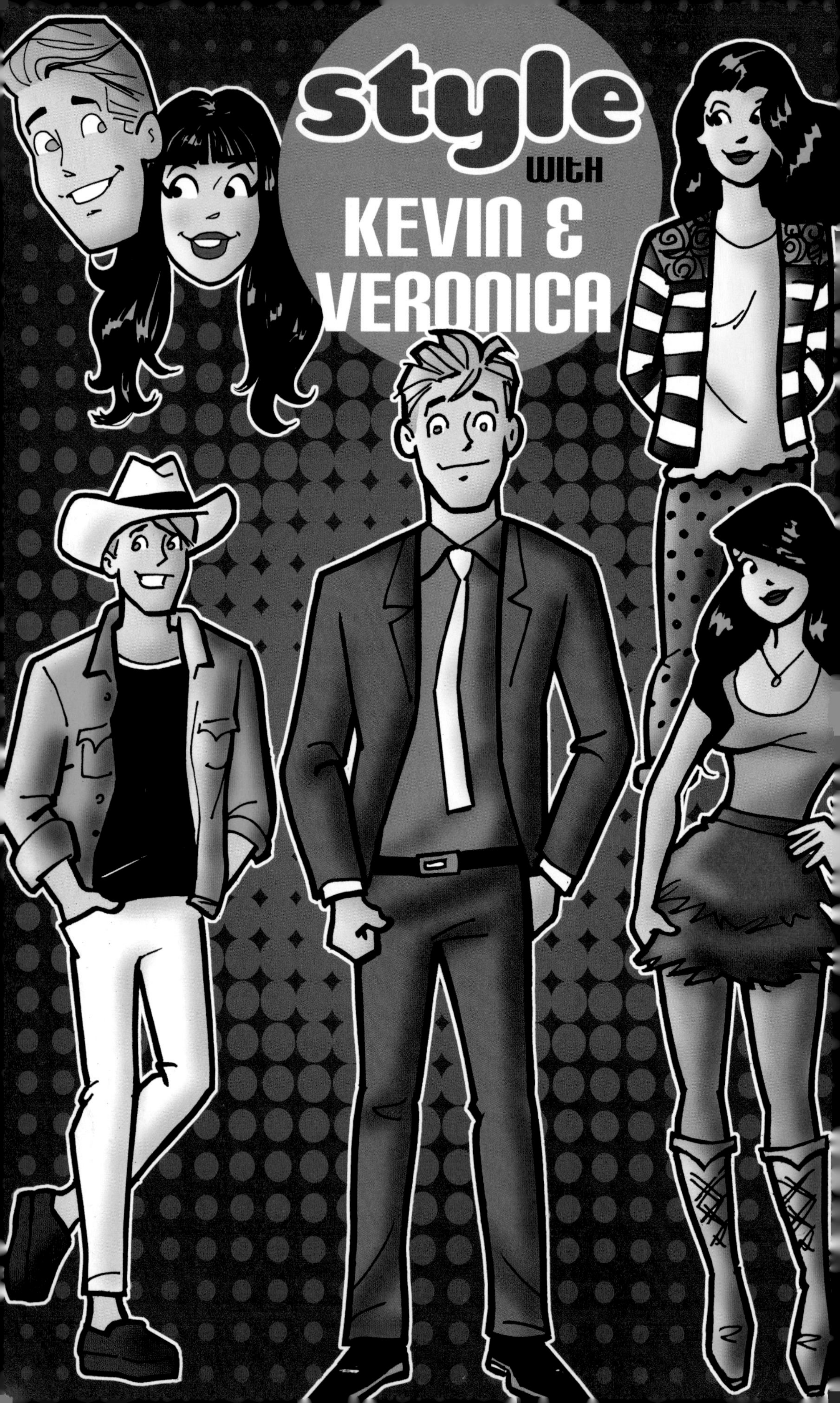
style
WITH
KEVIN &
VERONICA

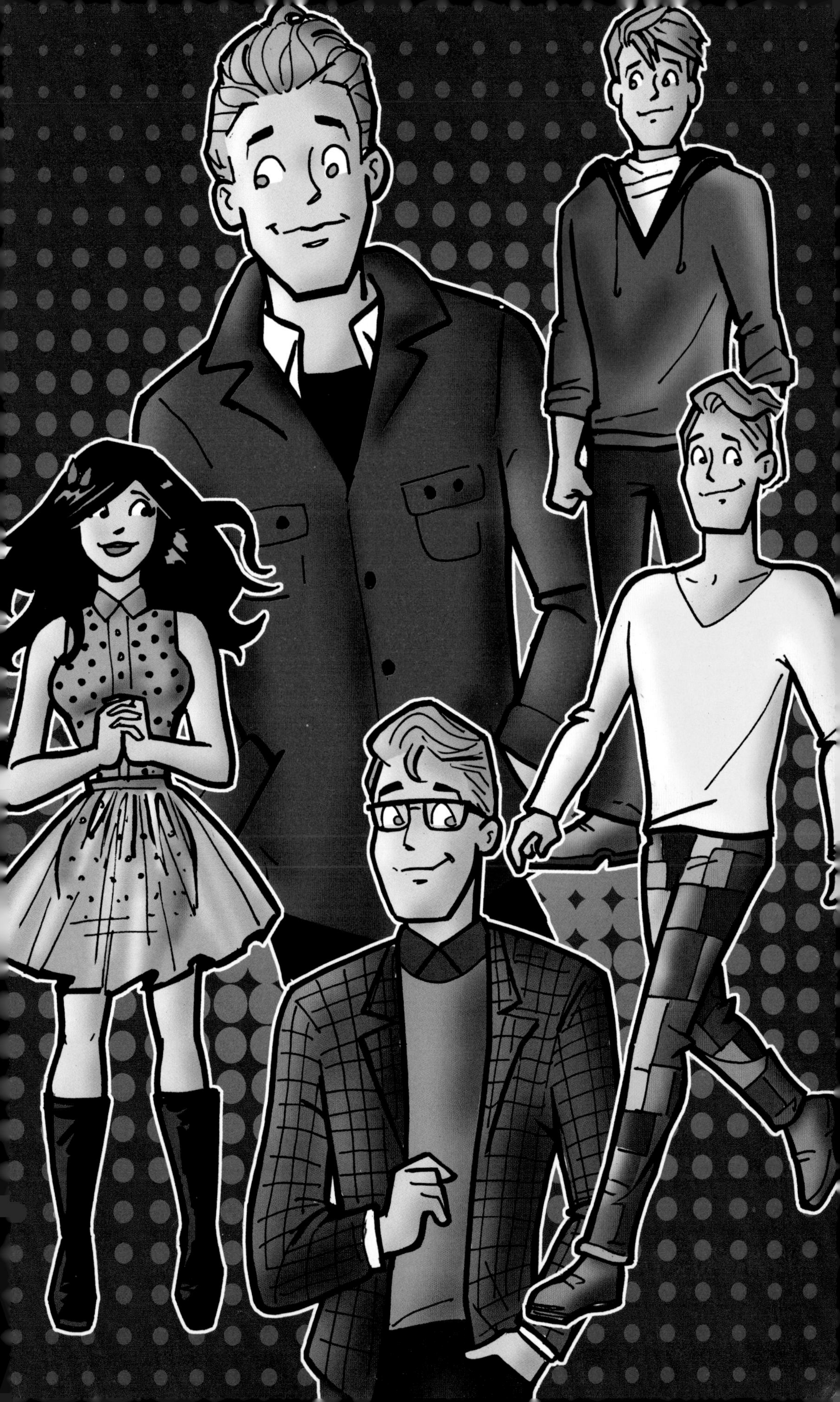

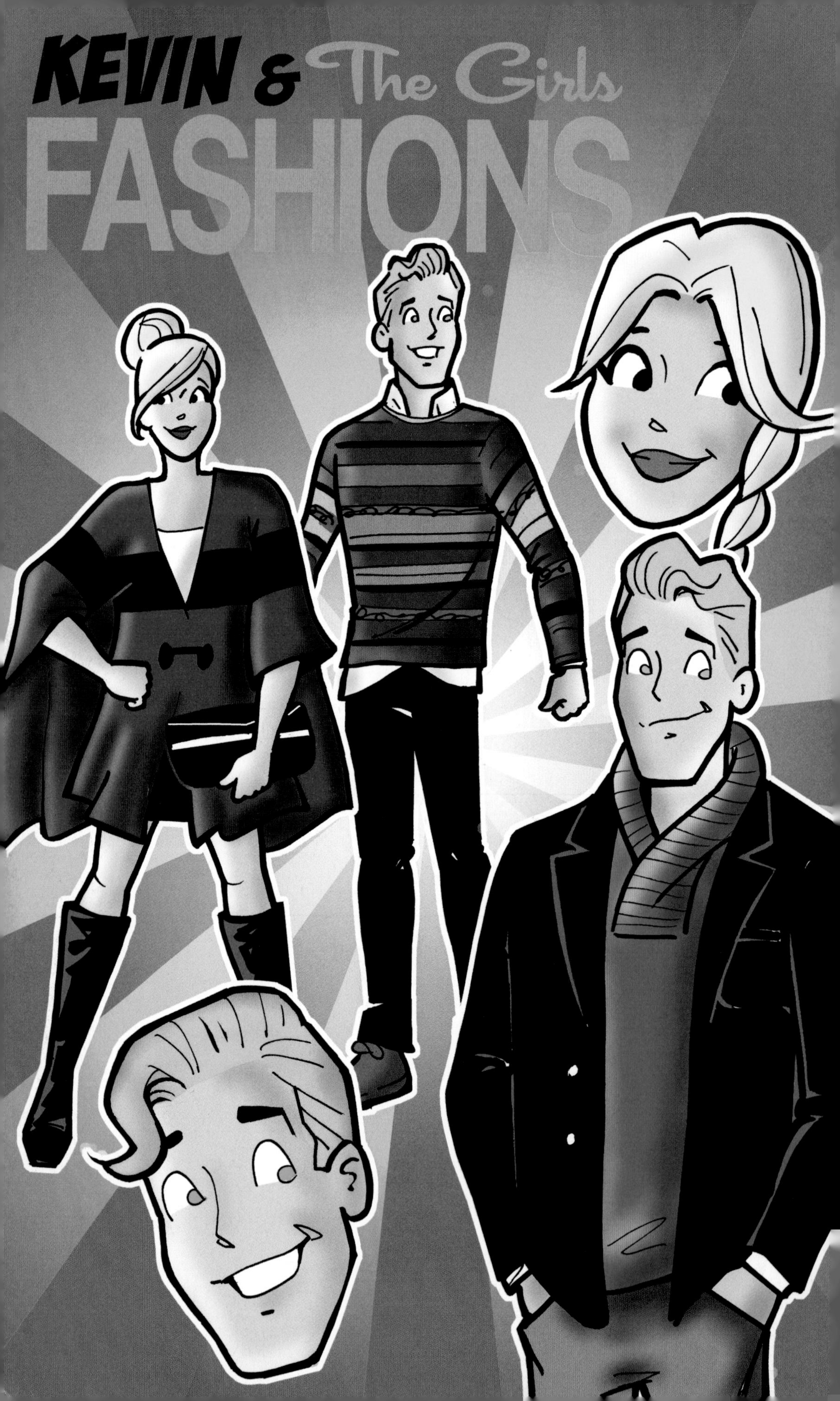
KEVIN & The Girls
FASHIONS

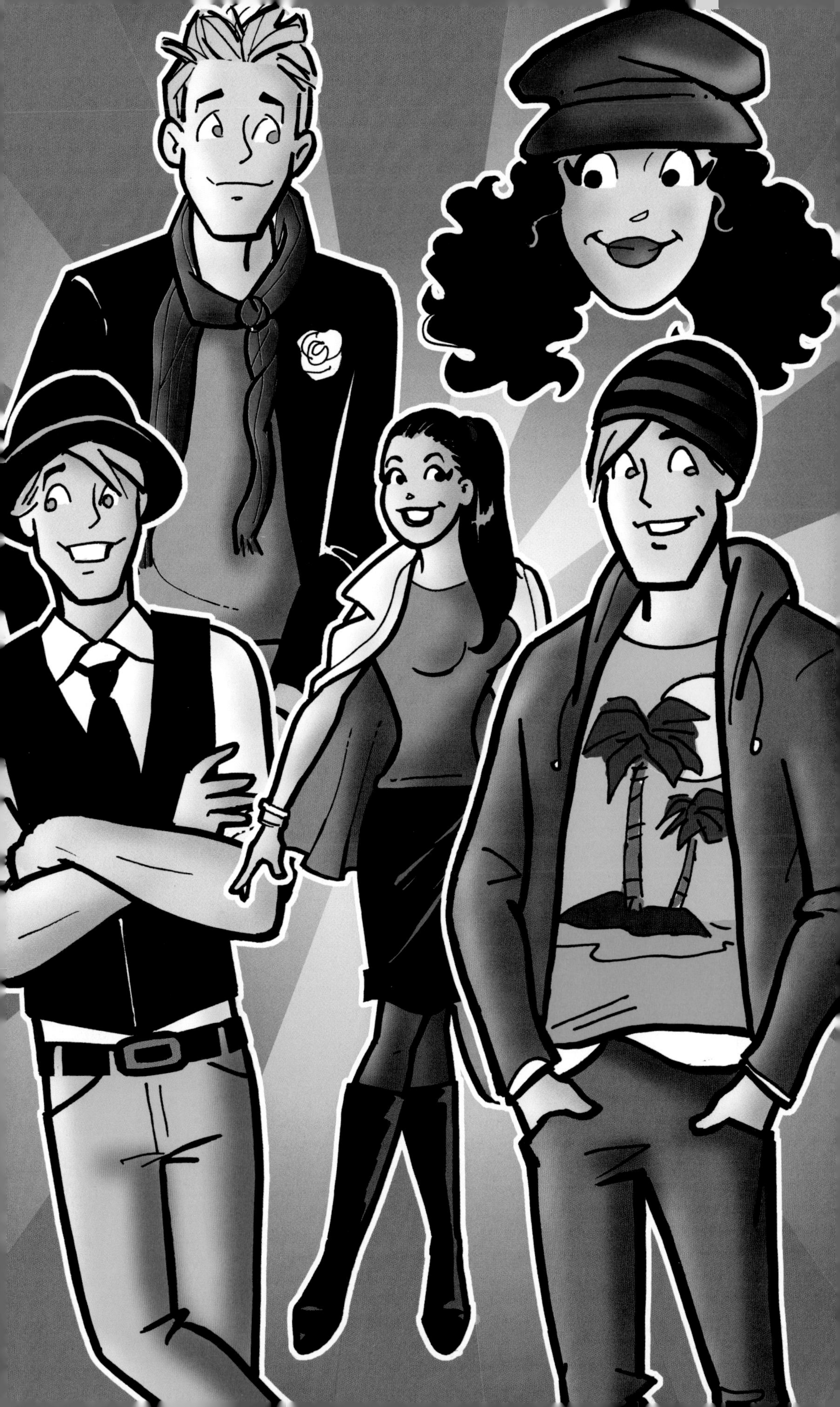

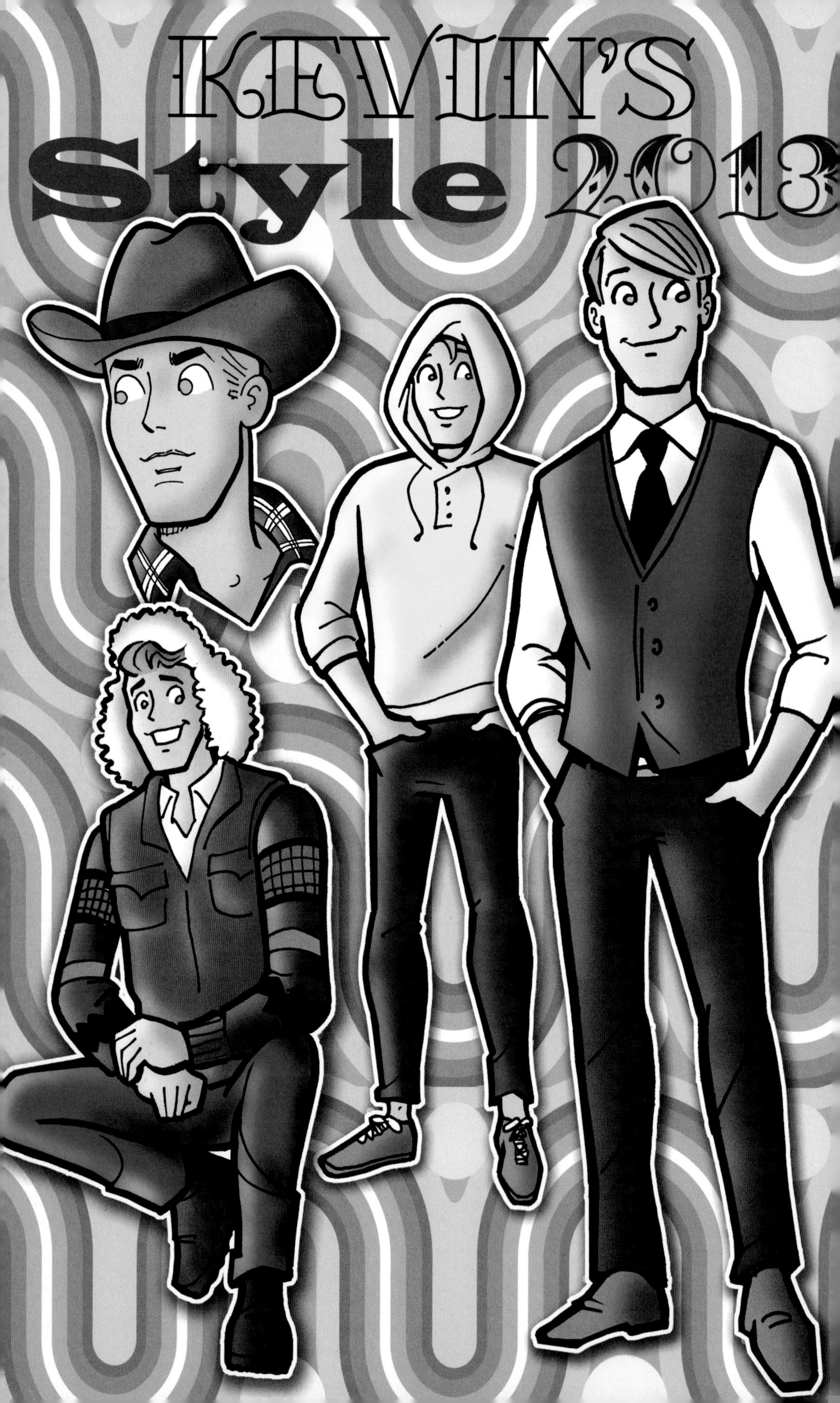
KEVIN'S
Style 2013

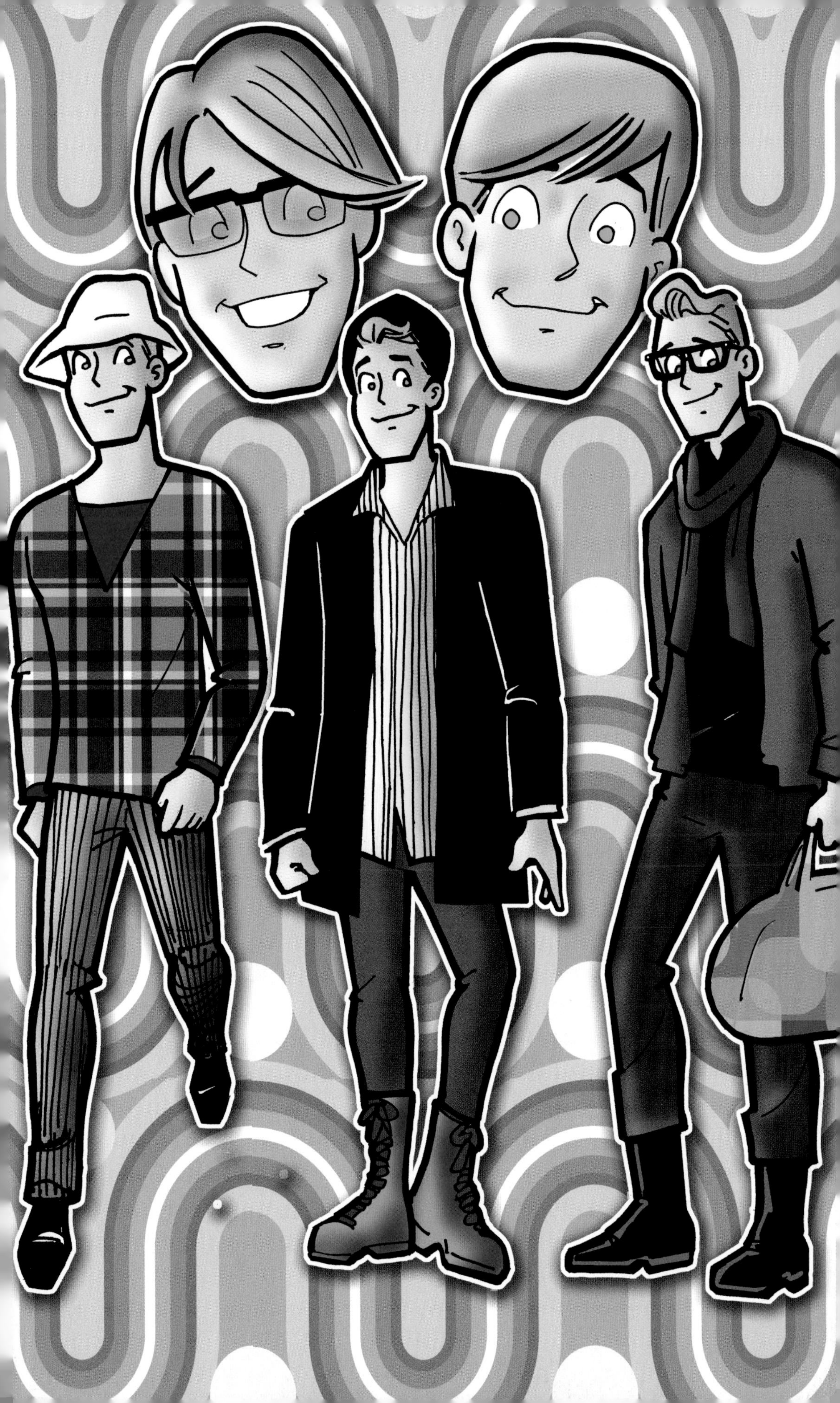

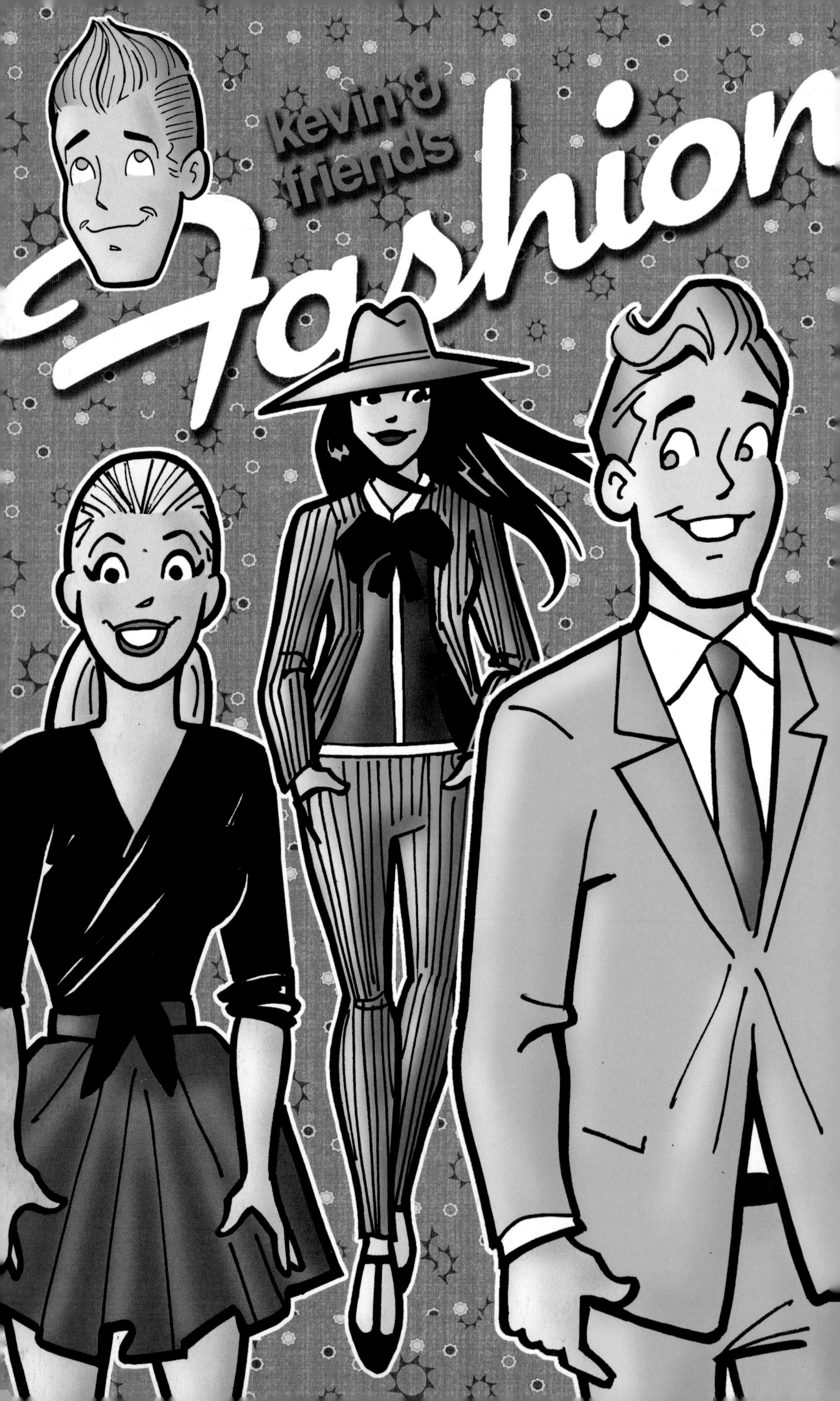
kevin & friends
Fashion

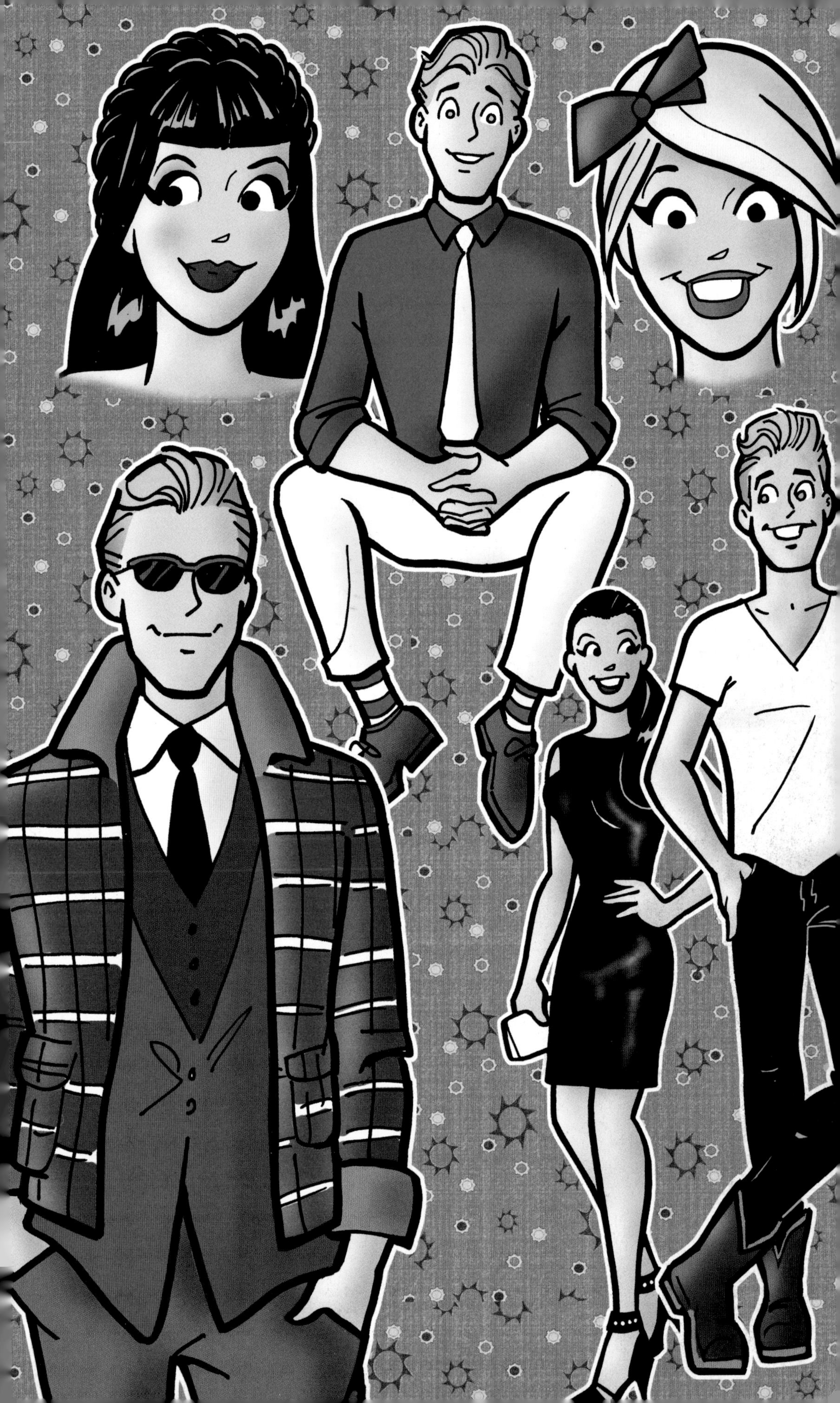

You can find these other  **KEVIN** Keller books from **Archie** COMICS at your local comic shop or bookstore and at ArchieComics.com!

Kevin is the new hardcover chapter book about Kevin's awkward early years by *The Married Life*'s Paul Kupperberg.

ISBN: 978-0-448458-52-6

You can see Kevin's future (including his wedding!) in *The Married Life Book 3*!

ISBN: 978-1-936975-35-8

Kevin Keller: Welcome to Riverdale features Kevin's first date, the prom and a trip to the London Olympics!

ISBN: 978-1-936975-23-5

This *Kevin Keller* hardcover collection includes his first comic appearance, moving to Riverdale and meeting Archie and the gang!

ISBN: 978-1-879794-93-1

Find even more Kevin online at ARCHIECOMICS.COM!